New Lease on Death

ELAINE ORR

ISBN-13: 978-1-948070-93-5
Library of Congress Control Number: 2023909274

New Lease on Death is a work of fiction.

New Lease on Death
ELAINE ORR

New Lease on Death is licensed for your personal enjoyment and may not be duplicated in any form.

Discover all books in the Jolie Gentil Series

Appraisal for Murder
Rekindling Motives
When the Carny Comes to Town
Any Port in a Storm
Trouble on the Doorstep
Behind the Walls
Vague Images
Ground to a Halt
Holidays in Ocean Alley
The Unexpected Resolution
Underground in Ocean Alley
Sticky Fingered Books
New Lease on Death
The Twain Does Meet (novella)
Jolie and Scoobie High School Misadventures (prequel)

Look for the **Family History Mystery Series**,
set in the Maryland mountains.

ome

elaineorr.com

elaineorr.blogspot.com

Dedication

To my husband and brothers and sister, who constantly
root for me. (Plus those great in-laws, too.)

And for all the real estate agents and appraisers
who have to go into vacant homes.
May you never find a dead body.

Acknowledgments

*Many thanks to beta readers
Karen Musser Nortman, J. Dave Webb
and Angela Parson Myers. Whenever they say, "What
do you mean?" I know something really doesn't make
sense.*

Prologue

HE'D LEFT OCEAN ALLEY SIX years ago, feeling oppressed by his terrible decisions. False accusations and a misplaced desire to protect a fragile friend could have ruined more lives than his own.

Back then, he couldn't have imagined the freedom he now experienced every day. No need to sign out of a building or tell someone when he would return.

On the first of October at the Jersey shore, life was nearly perfect.

He liked to walk enough that he hadn't yet bought a car. Maybe after he'd trudged a few miles in sleet or freezing rain later in the year. For now, the mile-long walk to the Second Round Cold Drinks and Tea Bar came easily, one long stride after another, always with the same rhythm.

One beat per step. Ba Ba Ba Ba Ba Ba BA BA BUM. Ba Ba Ba Ba Ba Ba BA BA BUM.

He entered Second Round's brightly lit dining area. Sal O'Grady, his Italian and Irish heritage on full display on the colors of his specially-made bar apron, greeted him. "Morning Josh!"

He smiled and returned the greeting. Sal had a hard time remembering names, so he was surprised at his accuracy. He remembered the few women who cut through the serving room to get to the meeting. Josh didn't think the bartender was flirting, more that he couldn't call them "bub" or "guy" or "buddy," or any other supplement to his fading memory.

And it had faded, even in the year since he had known Sal. How long could the alcohol-free bar, with its low-cost drinks, last without Sal? It wouldn't. It was his baby, and he probably paid himself just enough to meet basic expenses.

As friendly as the place was, Josh missed his long-ago friends and the Java Jolt Coffee Shop in Ocean Alley. Ownership had changed since he'd left the town. A couple months ago he'd heard someone say it had become the most welcoming place on the boardwalk.

He entered the meeting room behind the bar and surveyed the group. Michael H. wore his usual sleeveless tee-shirt; this one said, "Talk to Me at Your Own Risk." Cody M. had his head in the Big Book. Did he go anywhere without it? Jillian K., one of the few women who came regularly, spoke animatedly to Carson N, who at least pretended to listen attentively. She only stopped talking the minute the meeting began, and sometimes put her fingers on her lips to keep from offering unsolicited opinions.

Josh drowned her out.

Jillian's gaze went to him, and she grinned. "Hey, that beard's two inches longer than last week."

"And you talk twice as much," Michael said.

"Not possible," Cody threw in.

Josh smiled, but said nothing. He took his usual seat at the far end of the long table. Not at the corner on the left. He thought of that as the ass-hat chair. People who sat there tried to control the conversation until the second or third time someone reminded them to shut up when it wasn't their turn to speak.

Nearly time to start, and several other people had joined them, all men but one. Michael walked to the table-top podium at the other end of the table (opposite the ass hat seat) and opened the AA Big Book to the page he had chosen to read to start the meeting.

Jillian walked to the door to shut it. As she did, a new attendee arrived, panting slightly, and slid into the remaining chair, next to the podium.

Josh sat perfectly still. Why was the man here?

The newcomer was one of his favorite people from Ocean Alley. But Josh had decided not to visit the town where, even as a street person, he had felt more at home than anywhere since he came back from Iraq.

Why stir the pot for people he'd left behind? Then again, now that he could go anywhere, why remain so close to a place he had decided he no longer belonged?

Jillian returned to her seat and Michael cleared his throat to begin the meeting. The newcomer sat with his hands folded on the table in front of him, staring at them intently.

"I'm Michael and I'm an alcoholic. I'm leading today, and most of you know my favorite quote. *Alcoholics don't have relationships, they take hostages.* You're welcome to state yours when you introduce yourselves."

Laughter that sounded more like mutters came from a couple people, and several nodded quietly.

Michael turned to the newcomer, whom no one seemed to know, and nodded.

Josh wanted to leave the room unnoticed, so he quietly pushed back his chair and made for the door. He didn't care if people thought he needed the bathroom or was leaving the planet.

As he closed the door behind him, he heard the new man say, "I'm Scoobie. I'm an addict who's been in recovery for a while, and I need some help."

Chapter One

I LIVE AT THE JUNCTURE of Arrogant and Stubborn. On one side of the block is Buck Brock, a property developer who is pleased when real estate appraisals I do show a house's value is less than the contract he offered to a seller. He may get to pay less.

On the other side is Lester Argrow, whose aim in life is to sell houses for top dollar so he gets more commission — a common goal for realtors. However, since Lester entices buyers from larger cities with well-placed ads on social media, the hopeful homeowners may not be familiar with the Ocean Alley market. They offer larger sums than an appraisal will support.

Both men argue with me. I remind them the banks who will underwrite mortgages are my clients. Banks don't want to lend money and later learn a house isn't worth much more than the paper the mortgage is written on. The banks also pay for the work.

What is a woman to do?

Since she's a woman with a multifaceted life, this Friday afternoon she's going to take her four-year-old twins to Java Jolt Coffee House. She will sip brown goodness while she interprets the handwriting in the notes she wrote when she conducted a recent appraisal visit.

As I climbed the steps to the Ocean Alley boardwalk, I figured it wouldn't be long before I couldn't keep up with our twins. Today reinforced the point. Lance and Leia stopped abruptly at the top of the boardwalk steps and I almost rear-ended Leia's day-care backpack. "I thought you two were in a hurry."

Lance turned to his sister and frowned. "Don't you know you're supposed to look before you cross the street?"

"It's not a street." She moved past him and walked right, toward Java Jolt. "I want my apple juice."

Lance followed. "Me, too."

I glanced at the sand and ocean beyond the boardwalk. Calm in a busy world, but right now my focus was on busy.

"I need you two to drink your juice and talk quietly. I have to go over the notes from a house I just visited before I talk to Uncle Harry about the appraisal report I have to write up."

In tandem, they said, "Boooooring."

Every week or so they tested a new expression. At the moment, boring things included breakfast cereal, the stories Scoobie and I read at bedtime, and apparently quietly drinking juice after day care.

"I know you guys practiced saying that."

Lance glanced at Leia and his smirk gave them away. They began to trot and I picked up my pace.

We passed boardwalk shops that had the post-Labor Day fix-up time underway. The owner of the bright blue souvenir shop had bought pink shutters to place at each side of the door, and the cotton candy maker was changing the exterior color scheme from brilliant yellow to red and white.

As much as I would have liked a leisurely stroll, the appraisal I needed to finish was for a home Buck Brock had made a purchase offer for. As usual, it's an older bungalow. He'll make some basic repairs, paint the interior whatever the popular shade is in decorator magazines, and add furniture from a major online home goods store. Then he'll advertise largely to well-heeled adults who will pay outrageous prices for a week at the shore, even more for holidays.

Though I more often butted heads with Lester over a house's value, Buck's total lack of patience is a problem. Once he decides he wants a property, he thinks the seller, buyer, bank, and I should jump when called.

"Mom!" Leia spoke loudly. "You're walking past Java Jolt."

Lance stood holding the door for me. "Are you having a senior moment, Mom?"

"Senior moment! I'm thirty-four!"

Leia moved ahead of me, toward the counter. "Ancient."

Lance let the door bang me in the backside and ran ahead of his sister to the counter. "Megan. It's us!"

"Mom has money for apple juice," Leia added.

Megan smiled at them from her spot behind the counter. "Hello kids. Morning, Jolie."

I did a four-finger wave at Megan. She sells two-dollar boxes of juice but keeps a pitcher for regulars and charges only fifty cents. As she poured juice, I glanced around the cheery coffee shop. Sunshine streaming in through windows that faced the boardwalk danced on the light-colored wood of the tables spread throughout the shop.

My eyes went to a man I didn't think I knew. During tourist season, the boardwalk is packed with strangers. So much so that Scoobie and I pretty much only go to Java Jolt or stand in front of the saltwater taffy store so the kids can watch the huge machine wind the colorful confection in super-eight shapes.

The bearded man's examination of his coffee mug could be described as studious. People usually say hello, especially when Java Jolt is uncrowded. I felt as if he were deliberately not meeting my eyes. If I said that to Scoobie, he'd remind me that the center of the universe was somewhere west of me.

I thanked Megan for a cup of tea and turned my attention back to the twins to guide them to a table that overlooked the boardwalk. Watching people walk by would keep them occupied while I worked.

I sat at a nearby table to tidy the notes I took at a recent site visit for an appraisal. I needed to be able to read the room measurements when I entered them into the software at Steele Appraisals.

Now and then I took a surreptitious glance at the bearded man. He had turned slightly, apparently to read some of the notes on the white board.

"If you want a real jolt, stand on the beach during a thunderstorm."

"Uncle Sam won't want you if you can't swim like a seal."

The board, a recent addition, had been Scoobie's idea. When our friend Ramona worked at The Purple Cow, the town's office supply store, each day she posted a thoughtful saying on the white board in front of the store window. And when she was busy with a customer or in the back room, Scoobie would alter it or add a bawdy saying under it.

Scoobie had presented Megan with the idea for the board as a way to encourage conversation in the coffee shop. She told him as long as he placed it high enough that little kids couldn't write on it, he could buy it and hang it.

I didn't think the board was that interesting today, so I glanced again at the man. His hair hung to the collar of his lightweight denim jacket, and had a thorough dusting of white, more than his beard. That and the tinted eyeglasses made it hard to guess his age. Anywhere between thirty-five and fifty.

"Mom, can't you hear your phone buzzing?" Leia asked.

"You're getting a text," Lance said.

Ramona's text said, "Buck just passed the window of my gallery, headed your way."

I groaned, inwardly. "Thanks guys. Let me know if you see anyone you know on the boardwalk."

I hurriedly stuffed the notes and the listing for the house I'd visited into my canvas shoulder bag. Buck and his booming voice would bug me about the appraisal.

He would want the two-story duplex I'd visited to be appraised at less than the price he had negotiated with its buyer. The property was in decent shape, but the location — close to Ocean Alley's version of a strip mall — would be a disadvantage.

On the other side of the equation, Lester calls at least twice as I work on an appraisal report. "Did you notice the deck had been sealed?" or "The remodel of that second bath really adds to the value, don't you think?"

Lester's short stature, strong Jersey accent, and the constant unlit cigar at the corner of his mouth bring to mind a low-level mafia movie guy. The mole on his cheek adds character.

He never takes it personally when I hang up on him.

Buck likes to stand too close and use his height to intimidate people — with a broad smile of course. He does take it personally when I tell him to back up. Too bad.

I drank the last sip of the hot tea and turned toward the twins. "You guys ready to head home?"

"Home is boring," Lance said.

"Maybe we should get one of those Lego kits with 200 pieces," Leia said.

God give me strength. "I think Daddy is bringing stuff to make tacos."

"If he isn't late again," Leia said.

I stood as the door to Java Jolt opened and Buck strode in. He looked my way. "Jolie, I'd like a word."

Crud. "I've only got about two minutes before I have to get home with the kids."

"I thought you said," Lance began.

"Shh," Leia hissed. "It's the loud guy."

"Mom," Lance whispered. "Tell him not so many words."

I laughed. When he looked hurt, I said, "That's the perfect thing to say. Why don't you two take your cups back to Megan?"

I stayed on my feet while they did that, hoping to emphasize my limited time.

Buck headed my way with a steaming mug of black coffee. "Did you get a chance to check out the place on Conch?"

I nodded. "A couple hours ago. I should have the appraisal report done in two days."

He frowned, expecting, of course, immediate feedback. "Do you think they get some water in the east corner of that screened-in porch?"

"I didn't notice any indication, and the seller's disclosure statement said no water problems at all."

"That's good, because the lot's really too small for the house."

"Buck, Ocean Alley is only twelve blocks deep and two miles long. Every lot two blocks from the ocean is small. Unless you put a one-room cottage on it."

He frowned. "Too small. I need to be able to charge a lot when I rent the sucker."

"My job is to give the bank that requested the appraisal the most accurate information on a house's value."

"Yeah, well…"

I nodded toward the door. "My kiddos are anxious to get home."

Lance yelled, 'We might get more Legos."

I waved a quick goodbye to Megan. As I opened the glass door for the twins, I snuck a glance at the bearded man. He seemed to be smiling.

WE DID NOT STOP at the new toy store to buy Legos. I pulled into the driveway of our Cape Cod house, which sits across from my first Ocean Alley residence, Aunt Madge's Cozy Corner B & B. "You can ask Daddy if you can look at Legos on Saturday."

Leia whispered to Lance, "We need to tell him they're ejucational."

I smiled at her four-year-old pronunciation and shut the sliding door to the van. We walked toward the front steps, with Lance stopping to inspect a spot where he swears a frog hides. "Come on, you two, if you play quietly now, we can finger paint for a few minutes after dinner."

"Can we make something for Aunt Madge?" Lance asked.

"And Uncle Harry."

"Sure." I unlocked the door. "You could draw Mister Rogers and Miss Piggy." I can always distract them by mentioning Madge and Harry's two golden retrievers.

Our black cat Jazz, who had been dozing on a lamp table, lifted her head. When she saw the retrievers were not in the room, she returned to her snooze.

Leia used her school-teacher tone. "Mom, you don't draw with finger paints."

"Yep, no crayons or even pencils," Lance added.

"Good point, you two. Scoot to your room."

"Say please," Lance tossed over his shoulder.

SCOOBIE'S CAR PULLED into our driveway, but instead of turning off the engine he backed onto the street again. The twins, in the kitchen to supervise Jazz as she ate her nightly ration of canned food, did not see him.

I smiled to myself. He had worked an hour late and forgotten the ground beef and taco shells. I texted to remind him we had tomatoes, lettuce, and sour cream.

As I finished putting together a salad for us and plate of raw veggies for the kids, his headlights again appeared in the front window.

This time, Lance and Leia had been looking for him. They raced to the door amid the usual squeals of, "Daddy's home."

I've long since lost any sense of jealousy over which parent is the favorite. I tell myself it's mostly because Scoobie acts out nighttime stories more enthusiastically than I do.

Scoobie put the bag from Mr. Markle's In-Town Market on the floor and knelt on one knee to accept hugs and a flood of information on their time at daycare. I had heard some, but Lance had neglected to mention that daycare aide Marie Hall had scolded him for pounding his play dough so hard she had to peel it off his table with a plastic knife. I mentally gave Leia a gold star for not tattling.

"Okay, guys, We don't get tacos until I give this meat to Mommy."

"You didn't forget the shells this time, did you?" Leia asked.

Scoobie looked shocked. "Shells? Wouldn't they be really hard to eat?"

"Not that kind!" Lance shouted.

Leia gave me an eye roll.

I walked the few steps to Scoobie, pecked him on the lips and took the grocery sack. "Lance, Daddy's a kidder. Give him a minute to wash up and he can help me with dinner."

Lance said, "No way, Mom. You get him by yourself after we go to bed."

Leia said nothing, but took off for the bathroom.

Lance said, "Wait up," and went after her.

"Whew." Scoobie followed me the short distance to the kitchen. "Leia feel okay?" He began to wash his hands at the sink.

I took meat and taco shells from the bag. "Fine. They've learned to tell time on digital clocks, and now she keeps track of whether we're on time to pick them up or whatever."

"Jeez. Was I that late?"

"I told them you probably had to help someone."

I didn't know that he had, but I don't begrudge him a few minutes to himself. I controlled my schedule — as much as any parent of twins can. His work time was dictated by patient x-ray schedules, and he always had to be pleasant. I don't always want to be, especially to people with Buck's proclivities, but I don't need to smile all the time.

Scoobie dried his hands and turned the burner on under the frying pan. "I guess I dawdled."

AFTER DINNER CAME bath time. It took longer now that each twin wanted separate tub time. They had decided the tub in the first-floor bathroom was too small for both of them, and didn't like the upstairs shower.

Scoobie and I finally had alone time in the living room at eight-thirty. We've always sat next to each other on the couch, but we recently added a recliner so he can stretch his legs better than on the coffee table in front of the couch.

After a few attempts to get Jazz to use her cat bed, I put a towel on the couch cushion for her.

Before Scoobie dozed, I had a question. "I saw a man in Java Jolt today who looked familiar, but I couldn't place him."

"Somebody from high school, you think?"

"I don't think so. He had a mostly black beard that sort of crept onto his cheeks. Black hair that had a lot of salt in it."

"Hmmm. Tall?" Scoobie asked.

"He stayed seated. But thin, I think."

Scoobie pointed a finger at me in mock surprise. "And you were too timid to talk to him?"

I stuck out my tongue. "He had an aura that said, 'don't bother me,' so I stayed near the twins. And he had on sunglasses."

"Did you ask Megan? She knows everyone."

"Didn't get a chance. Buck came in so I wanted to get out of there before he bombarded me with suggestions about the house I'd just visited."

Scoobie snorted. "Remember when Lester was the most obnoxious realtor in town?"

I shrugged. "In the purest sense, he still is. I think of Buck as more of a property developer and landlord."

"True. Not really fair to take the title away from Lester."

Chapter Two

THE WEEKEND PASSED IN a flash, as they all do. Monday morning, I donned a lightweight jacket and walked across the street to Aunt Madge's Cozy Corner B&B at six AM. I'd been sleepy when I left our house, but the crisp air and light breeze had me wide awake when I entered her side door.

Mayor Madge, as everyone in town calls her, rarely has early morning meetings. Today, the Landlord Tenant Commission had an informal meeting with Buck Brock to discuss several complaints from people who had rented from him for weekend or one-week stays.

Aunt Madge pulled the first batch of her always-anticipated muffins from the oven of the large kitchen, which sat behind the guest breakfast room. Mister Rogers and Miss Piggy raised their heads from where they snoozed on dog beds by the sliding glass door. They always hoped for a sample. When Aunt Madge didn't call them, they put their heads back on their paws, dog tags tinkling.

"Do you have a long meeting agenda?"

Aunt Madge frowned. "That Buck Brock wants to make Ocean Alley into the year-round, short-term rental capital of the Jersey shore. He picked us because we're small and don't have all the rules spelled out. He knows the Commission isn't for short-term rentals, so we can't do much besides requiring a license."

"Some local businesses might see more income if he rents more."

"In the summer everything's booked already. Maybe a little restaurant business in the winter, but everybody else is closed after mid-October or Halloween." She effortlessly slid muffins onto a cooling rack. "I wonder how he attracts so many people after Labor Day."

"When Scoobie was at a continuing ed conference in Philly, he saw one of Buck's ads in the paper. It talked about how peaceful it is here, but then stressed it's a short ride to casinos in other Jersey shore towns."

"So that would take away from even extra restaurant business."

I took two small tubs of butter from the fridge and put them onto a tray with a pitcher of cream to carry to the breakfast room. "He's pretty quick to take advantage of any situation. What's got the Commission up in arms?"

"Mostly a couple complaints about off-street parking — or lack of what was promised. Some about cleanliness. Not big violations, but tourists don't differentiate between what the Commission regulates and what's under broader New Jersey code. We get the black eye."

I thought back to something Buck had complained about a couple weeks ago. "He said he's having a hard time keeping a cleaning service."

"Everyone does." Aunt Madge took off her apron and gestured at the cooling muffins. "You know the drill. I really appreciate you coming over this morning."

The door to the bedroom off the great room opened and Harry stepped into the conversation. "Not as much as I do."

I grinned at my nominal boss. "You mess up the muffins."

He walked to Aunt Madge, kissed her, and put on an apron. "You can't mess up perfection."

As Aunt Madge kissed him on the nose, I thought again how fortunate they were to have found each other late in life. And how lucky I was to have Harry as my boss at Steele Appraisals.

"Anything that has Scoobie as the sole dresser of twins is fine by me."

"What time does he have to be at the hospital?" Harry asked.

"Seven. We can drop the kids off early a couple times a month, no extra charge."

Aunt Madge picked up her purse from the large oak kitchen table. "I'll tell Buck you said hello."

AFTER AN UNEVENTFUL BREAKFAST time at the B&B, I headed to Steele Appraisals. Harry had left for the office earlier, under the pretense of responding to a backlog of emails. Or maybe to avoid doing the dishes.

I was anxious to see what new work had come in. Since I get half of the $500 fee when I do one, I always want more. And Harry is generous about giving me more of the workload — unless a twin is sick.

The small Victorian that housed the appraisal business once belonged to Harry's grandparents. I think he and Aunt Madge initially bonded over her advice on how to fix up the place, which he had purchased as a retirement project.

Now, the refinished hardwood floors and expensive paint made the house look almost elegant. At least the first floor.

I entered the center-hall foyer and turned right into our joint office. A fax sat on my desk. Harry sat behind his, smiling.

Lester, as usual, had a different opinion on a house I had appraised for a thousand less than the agreed-upon contract between buyer and seller. His comment was only slightly less impolite than usual. "I know you have a license to do your work, but where did you get it? I got a really peeved buyer." He had started to write another word that started with P, but crossed it out.

Harry grinned more broadly. "We should make him go look for comparable sales at the courthouse."

"I tried making him look for comps one time. He wanted to say that a four-bedroom house with two baths was worth the same as a three-bedroom with a bath-and-a-half."

"He must have had a good rationale," Harry deadpanned.

"Of course. They were on the same street."

"Sounds like his way of thinking. I saw Lester listed that five-plex on Seashore. You'll be pleased to know Buck made an almost immediate offer."

I groaned. "Have you seen it? It's the ugliest Victorian in town. I'll have to go to Lester's listing to see how he characterized it."

Harry pulled a listing document from his in-box. "He calls it a 'Charming turn-of-the century bargain with new siding and fresh paint in some rooms.'"

Probably painted over patches in the walls," I grumbled. "Did the bank request us for the appraisal?"

"Haven't heard anything yet. Maybe your buddy Jennifer Stenner will get it."

My former high school classmate took over the much larger appraisal firm from her father, who had been left it by his father. Their reception area had more expensive furniture than our entire first floor. "Only if we're really lucky."

I entered the data from the bungalow I'd been to Friday. It had been nicely remodeled except for the bathroom. The owner had liked the claw-feet tub, but no prospective buyer would be happy with a bathroom with no shower.

When I finished entering inside and outside measurements and outbuildings, I packed up to head to the courthouse to look for previous sales that could be used as comps. Fortunately, it wasn't one of Lester's sales, because the lack of a shower would lower the value.

The office phone gave the special ring we assigned to Buck's calls. "I have an errand." I quickly moved toward the front door. I almost made it.

From the office behind me, Harry said, "You called just in time, Buck, she was on her way out." He grinned as he handed me the receiver.

I covered the microphone on the handset. "I know you left this morning so you didn't have to do the dishes."

Harry grinned more broadly.

"Hello, Buck. What's up?"

"Your aunt jumped all over my case this morning."

I acted as if I had no idea what his early morning meeting had been about. "Did you double park outside of one of your properties again?" I held the receiver away from my ear so Harry could hear.

Buck is one of the few people whose bluster comes through the phone. "No! But I guess I put something in an ad about off-street parking."

"What's so bad about that?"

"Well…it's just there isn't much."

I laughed. "Did you get a fine? Or are you going to build driveways at all your places?"

"Are you kidding? I'd have to tear half the houses down to build driveways."

As Harry shook his head, I put the phone back to my ear. "So, a big fine?"

"I didn't want that on the damn record. I hafta give a free weekend to the whiners who complained about a dirty fridge. Do you know what that'll cost me?"

Harry interjected in a raised voice. "Jolie, did you finish that appraisal report?"

"Sorry, Buck, I have a pile of work."

"Is that my appraisal he's talking about?"

"Gotta run." I hung up and faced Harry. "Thanks."

"No problem."

AN HOUR LATER, Harry left for a Rotary Club meeting and I was back in the office looking online for recently sold houses that wouldn't be in courthouse records yet. The doorbell at Steele Appraisals began to ring incessantly. That could only mean Lester Argrow.

I stood on my side of the door and pretended to peer through the glass. "Could you identify yourself, sir?"

"Jolie. Lemme in!"

His tone was so urgent I didn't continue to tease him, but opened the door. "Are you okay?"

He moved past me, shoulders stiff, hands almost clenched, and walked right into Harry's and my office.

I followed him and bowed slightly. "Do come in."

Lester completed his march to my desk and sat in the client chair next to it. He turned so he faced me as I returned to my computer. "Do you know what the son-of-a-biscuit did to me?"

In deference to our edict that he not swear around the twins, I appreciate his creative alternatives. "I'm sure you'll tell me."

He transferred his unlit cigar from the right to the left side of his mouth. "I signed a flippin' contract to buy that great bungalow on D Street."

I sat with one leg curled under the other, facing him and almost squeaked. "You mean the one three doors down from us?"

"Yeah. And you know what he did? He swooped in and offered five thousand more and the seller took his money!"

I didn't know the owners of the small yellow house well. "That's weird. When does the seller have to return your deposit? What's the penalty?"

Lester took his cigar out of his mouth to point it toward me. "Well, there's the rub. See, uh..."

"They took it as a zero-down contract? Who does that?"

"They were in a hurry to sell. And I wanted them to take the offer, so I put in a no-penalty clause."

I gaped at him. "You aren't planning on getting into the rental business, are you?"

He put the cigar back in his mouth and chomped on it so hard I expected to see bits of tobacco on his lips. "I been thinkin' about it, but I wanted that place for myself."

I arched my eyebrows. "Really? You're in those sandstone-colored apartments two blocks back from the courthouse, right?"

"Yeah." He offered no further explanation.

"Are there bells in the air I don't know about?"

He snorted. "Not for me, but I been kinda hopin', you know... Ramona and what's-his-face."

"Um. You mean like all of you live together?" I thought Scoobie's best friend, George, would have a heart attack if anyone mentioned the idea.

"Not hardly, but her parents retired to Vermont, for some God-awful reason. I think George had to be hatched. So, maybe, if there's more little kids..."

"Why Lester, you old softie."

He waved a hand. "I didn't come to talk about that. What can we do about Buck Brickface Brock? We gotta stop him..."

I laughed too hard to hear the rest. He was right. Buck has a rectangularly-shaped face, and it's often red because he's usually mad about something.

Lester scowled. "Not funny."

I wiped my eyes with the back of one hand. "What he does isn't funny. But his face is shaped like a brick." I adopted a serious expression. "What can we do other than have you include a penalty clause and make enough of a down payment with your offer that you don't get outbid after the fact?"

"He can always outbid me, but I've heard sometimes he's hard-up for actual cash."

"Yes, but after a contract is signed, the seller has to return your deposit and maybe pay a penalty. They can't just back out scot-free."

"I'm thinkin' of spreading a rumor about his places having sand fleas."

I shook my head. "That'll come back to bite you in the bum." I thought about Aunt Madge's and the Landlord Tenant Commission's meeting with Buck. "Besides, he may dig his own grave. Give him time."

"Yeah." Lester paused, then seemed to decide to continue. "There's nobody in the business he hasn't ticked off. He trash-talks everybody, and don't get it that we all talk to each other. Whatever he says gets back to people."

"He's been here what, fifteen months? Who are his friends."

Lester snorted. "Nobody, far as I know. The Board of Realtors tried not inviting him to the monthly lunches, but he got wind of them and barged in."

"Hmm. Wonder why he even cared to be there?"

Lester stood. "I really wanted that house."

I stood to walk him to the door. "I'm sorry you didn't get it. I bet Aunt Madge and Harry would love to have you as a neighbor."

"Heh, heh. You didn't mention Scoobie."

I smiled.

"Hey, that old house is a lot for her and Harry to keep up. Is your aunt thinkin' of sellin' anytime soon?"

He had opened the storm door and I patted his shoulder. Perhaps more like a shove. "Go away, Lester."

He went down the porch steps, raising a hand in goodbye without looking back.

I shut the door. So, Uncle Lester was hoping Ramona and George would get married and have kids. He and George butt heads even in Java Jolt.

The big question was, should I tell Ramona he planned to be an active great uncle? Maybe when the four of us were together. Then Scoobie could see the look on George's face, too.

Chapter Three

RAMONA AND I MET AT Java Jolt Tuesday morning to talk about ways to get more tourists to come to her art gallery in the winter months. Or so she said.

In keeping with her semi-hippie style of dress, she had made a poncho-type coat. On it was the imprint of a few of her beach still-lifes and one of the front of her gallery. Tastefully placed, of course.

She placed the coat on a chair between us, and I touched the fabric that depicted her gallery. "How do you do this? It's beautiful."

"Thanks. I either scan a painting or take a photo of it. I give the fabric store a digital copy of the image, and they put it on fabric I buy there or take to them."

I grinned. "That coat makes you a walking advertisement. I bet you can deduct it on your income taxes."

Megan came over with a coffee carafe to warm our cups. "I know my accountant would say I could."

Ramona shrugged. "I never thought of that. Hey, Megan, have you ever thought of putting up a bulletin board so local businesses could put their cards on it?"

Megan shook her head. "It seems every one of those type of boards ends up with signs about bars or rental properties. I don't want to be in the position of taking down tacky-looking ads."

"What about one with a glass cover that locks?" I asked. "I could see what one would cost."

"And people would give me their cards?" she asked.

Ramona sat up straighter. "You say it's only for business cards, not to promote events. And not to sell a specific thing. If you do retail, it's just to advertise the business itself."

I thought about it. "You'd have to decide if you didn't want one someone's card, but if it's a local business they'd probably all be okay."

A bell above the door to the boardwalk dinged and George came in. "Hey Megan. I'm just stopping by to say hi to my gals."

The three of us exchanged glances.

"Oh, jeez. You know what I mean." He pulled up a chair and sat next to Ramona.

Megan grinned and walked toward the counter. "So, you pay double next time."

Ramona smiled at him and explained the idea for a locked wall cabinet to display business cards. "Jolie's going to look into costs."

George grinned. "Tattoo parlors, too?"

Ramona nodded. "It's a thing. Remember when that couple asked me to design a tattoo for their wedding?"

"And I remember where the bride was going to place hers." George adopted an expression of innocence. "She obviously hasn't thought how much longer it'll be in twenty years."

I tossed a balled-up napkin at him as my phone buzzed with a text. "Aunt Madge." I read it and laughed. "The Landlord Tenant Commission really did get Buck to agree to give a free weekend to a couple who complained about the place they rented from him. I wasn't sure whether to believe him."

"Imagine that," Ramona said, dryly.

"He was in the diner this morning," George said. "He said it was because there wasn't off-street parking."

I regarded the text again and smiled. "Aunt Madge says if he says it's because of parking, I can tell him I heard it was because the kitchen wasn't spotless and there was food from the last tenant in the fridge."

"When did your aunt learn to type that fast?" Ramona asked.

"She dictates." A second text came in. "Huh. She thinks the wife, Eleanor, is a friend of Reneé's, from Lakewood. I haven't seen her in years." I typed a response saying I'd call her in a few minutes.

"Your sister's what, six years older? You wouldn't know her well, would you?" Ramona asked.

George said, "Maybe you could suggest other places for them to stay."

"I doubt Buck would mind. One less thing for him to complain about."

"He likes to complain," Ramona said.

George stood. "I have to go do a background check on a potential hire for the bank." He bent to kiss Ramona on the cheek. "Tell Jolie if she throws more napkins at me I'll teach the twins to do it."

As he went out the door, I looked at Ramona. "Did he think this was the type of work he'd be doing when he got his private investigator license?"

"He calls it his bread and butter work. Better than tailing wandering husbands."

A thought crossed my mind. "The more time I have to deal with Buck, the more I wonder how he got to be so nasty. Do you think I could ask George to do a background check on him?"

Ramona shrugged. "What would you do with the results if they really worried you?"

Chapter Four

JOSH FELT ODD TO be at an AA meeting in Ocean Alley, but at the same time it felt familiar. As expected Scoobie attended the evening meeting in the basement of First Presbyterian Church. Scoobie grinned and they exchanged polite nods.

Josh usually didn't stay for coffee after a meeting, but intuition said Scoobie wanted to talk. They walked with a group that went to Java Jolt. Josh took half a cup, drank it in three minutes, and headed for the door. Then he stayed on the boardwalk to lean on the rail and stare at the ocean.

He felt Scoobie's approach, but didn't turn.

Scoobie stood next to him, elbows on the boardwalk railing. "It's good to see you."

"You, too." He paused, feeling guilty. "I should have answered your letters, especially after you wrote to say to say the twins were born."

"I get that. Ocean Alley would be a hard place to have to leave."

"Yep." The surf seemed quieter than usual, even for a calm night. A gull landed on the railing a few feet away and squawked.

Scoobie turned to it. "My kids feed you, not me. Shoo."

"Friend of yours?"

"Even when all the boardwalk stores close for winter, a few of them hang out to pester anyone who stands still. I knew you left the halfway house, because the last letter came back."

He turned to Scoobie. "Did Jolie know you wrote to me?"

"Never really came up. We're…a good team." He shrugged. "When you marry in your thirties you sometimes have a few more private things than if you marry your high school sweetheart right out of school."

He smiled. "I recall hearing you liked her a lot when she lived in Ocean Alley for your junior year."

Scoobie smiled as he stared at the ocean. "Yeah. Took her a while to catch up."

"How can I help you, Scoobie?"

"What makes you think I need help?"

"I was in the meeting when you walked in, at Second Round."

"What? I didn't see you."

"I walked out as you introduced yourself. I thought you might feel freer to talk if you didn't see me."

Scoobie resumed his stare at the ocean. "Huh. Not so much that. I would have been really surprised. Glad. Is that why you came to the meeting at First Prez tonight?"

"Yep. Want me to go away?"

Scoobie shook his head, firmly. "Thanks for reaching out."

"Okay then." He waited a moment to see if Scoobie would say anything else. When nothing else was forthcoming, he asked, "How's Max?"

Scoobie turned fully and grinned broadly. "You wouldn't believe how good he is. Jolie and George, and Lester. You remember Lester?"

"Who could forget him?"

Scoobie laughed. "Lotta days I'd like to. They helped Max get a VA loan to buy a small house a few blocks back from the ocean. Every morning he goes by Java Jolt to help Megan during the morning rush."

"You're kidding."

"Nope. He hardly ever drops the tub of dirty mugs anymore. Megan has to remind him not to jump into conversations the customers are having."

He was glad he hadn't gone to Java Jolt in the morning. "Does he still repeat everything."

"Does the Pope visit the woods every morning?"

Josh laughed. "That's the one thing I don't miss."

Scoobie faced the ocean again. "We got one of those smaller VA clinics on the edge of town a couple years ago, near St. Anthony's Catholic Church. They have a weekly…sort of informal session for guys who have PTSD or other brain injuries."

"What's a sort of informal session?"

"Man and woman who run it are volunteers. They get guidance from the psychologist out there, but that guy's so busy he wouldn't have time to do everything the people in that group need. Gives Max and a few others, mostly guys, a place to relax and just talk. Not a lot of probing."

"You didn't answer my question."

Scoobie looked genuinely surprised. "Something else about Max?"

"Can I do something to help you?"

Scoobie's shoulders sagged slightly. "I don't…I'm missing something. But that's ridiculous. Super wife, best kids ever, my job at Ocean Alley's hospital is more than okay. It's like…"

He let the silence hang before asking Scoobie, "Are you waiting for the other shoe to drop?"

"Maybe. George thinks I'm kind of an idiot."

He frowned. Scoobie's friend could be callous sometimes. "Same old George."

Then the $64,000 question, one he would never ask in a meeting. "You been drinking or using?"

Scoobie shrugged.

"So, that's a yes?"

"I bought some gummies one time. This new stuff…"

"I hear it's a lot stronger than our parents' marijuana."

Scoobie smiled, tightly. "Yeah. I didn't even like the way it made me feel. I just wanted…something. Maybe I am an idiot."

"You aren't."

He broke the silence that followed by asking, "Do you and Jolie still run the Harvest for All Food Pantry?"

"Mostly Jolie, and we have more volunteers." Scoobie chuckled. "When she got pregnant, Reverend Jamison and Father Teahan were afraid she'd quit. They're always looking for more people to help and…

From behind them, a man's voice called. "Hey, Scoob. Jolie's looking for you."

Scoobie turned, fast. "Damn, it's late."

George Winters loped toward them. He had on the same kind of Hawaiian shirt he'd worn years ago, but with cargo pants instead of shorts.

George grinned. "Jolie was just worried. I told her you were probably helping someone."

Josh said, "I should have figured I was keeping a dad out too late."

George turned his head. "Hey, don't I…Josh!" He stuck out his hand. "Man, I didn't recognize you in the beard." He touched his own head. "And that little bit of snow on the mountain."

Josh smiled and shook his hand.

"Been what, six years?" George asked.

"About that. Thought I'd stop by." He nodded toward Scoobie. "Ran into this old man at the meeting."

"Yeah, I had to…hey, Scoob, call Jolie." George made a clucking noise.

Scoobie pulled out his phone. "Shut up, George."

Josh laughed. "Now I know I'm back."

Chapter Five

THE TWINS SOMETIMES SENSE when something is off, and they play quietly. Or they sense I'm preoccupied and ask for a cookie. This evening, they sprawled on the living room floor, intent on their coloring books.

I reminded myself that just because Scoobie hadn't let me know he'd be late after the meeting it didn't mean anything was wrong. But he always said if he'd be late.

I didn't want to start the kids' baths without Scoobie. It's hectic. Instead, I rearranged the food in the refrigerator.

My mobile phone rang and caller ID announced Buck Brock. "Nuts." I pushed accept and said, "Hi, Buck. A bit late for a home with toddlers."

"Sorry, Jolie. You probably heard I made an offer on that Victorian on Seashore. How fast can you do an appraisal?"

I pictured Seashore Avenue, which ran perpendicular to G Street, one of the twelve long Ocean Alley blocks that paralleled the ocean. The shabby Victorian Harry had mentioned earlier sat in the so-called Popsicle District, with its varied-color houses. However, its owner hadn't stuck to any apparent color scheme as he added vinyl siding.

"Buck, you know very well that a bank has to request that Harry and I do the appraisal. They'll call us or Jennifer's firm after they do an initial loan application evaluation."

"Yeah, but you could sort of go by, couldn't you? Get the lay of the land."

"Have you ever heard Mayor Madge use the phrase 'trying my patience'? She doesn't use it a lot. Mostly after long-winded city council meetings."

"Uh, maybe."

"Okay, you're trying mine. If we get a referral from a bank I'll do my best to get on it fast." I hung up.

My phone buzzed again and I saw it was Scoobie. "Hello, stranger."

Both twins looked up.

"Sorry. George just reminded me I'm late. Be home soon."

"Okay. Buck just called to annoy me. I'd almost forgotten about you."

He laughed. "Don't do that."

AT EIGHT O'CLOCK, HEADLIGHTS beamed in the front window and the twins raced to the door, knocking over a bucket of crayons on the way. I shut the fridge and followed them.

Scoobie jogged up the porch steps and pretended to have trouble opening the storm door.

"Pull harder," Lance shouted.

"He's fooling us," Leia said.

Scoobie pulled the door open. "I am." He picked up both of them and carried them, squealing to the sofa. As he dumped them, he turned to me. "I'm sorry I didn't text, Jolie. Someone we used to know surprised me at the meeting."

"Can't wait to hear." I put my hands on my hips and adopted a serious tone. "Someone needs to have the first bath. A short one."

Leia frowned. "Mom, you know we have to have Daddy play time first."

Scoobie lay on the floor and spread his arms wide. "Two minutes of tussling. Then we have a contest to see who can pick up crayons the fastest."

ONCE THE TWINS WERE in their beds pretending to be asleep, Scoobie and I flopped on the couch, feet on the coffee table. "Don't keep me in suspense."

Scoobie hesitated. "You remember Max's friend, Josh?"

I sat up straight and faced him. "As in Josh, the man who tried to imply I might be in possession of a murder weapon six or so years ago?"

"The same. You remember he was briefly incarcerated, then in a VA treatment program for PTSD, and then a halfway house for a while."

I shook my head. "I accept that he wasn't trying to frame me, but I honestly don't think about him unless Max is rambling for more than two minutes. Then I wonder how Josh put up with it by himself when they were homeless." I paused. "So, not too often anymore."

"He's been on his own again for…I guess I didn't ask. A year, maybe? He's been on the shore, but not in Ocean Alley."

"Homeless?"

"I don't think so. I feel like a dope, but I didn't ask a lot of questions. He looks…at peace."

I wasn't comfortable with the idea that Josh might be nearby, but he wasn't dangerous, as far as I knew. In fact, he'd been kind to Max for a long time. I now see acquaintances in terms of who I want the twins to be around. As in not too much of the loud talker, as they termed Buck. Josh? I didn't know how I felt.

Scoobie had watched me ponder. "I know it's…complicated. I think maybe he stayed away so he wouldn't upset us."

"Does Max know he's around? If not, maybe you should tell him. I mean, we don't know anything about Josh now."

Scoobie hesitated. "I didn't have a long conversation with him. Oh, George saw him. He was looking for me, and Josh and I were talking on the boardwalk."

I flushed. "I shouldn't have called."

"No problem." He grinned. "I usually tell you if I'm doing a meeting after the meeting or something." He sobered. "I'll find out if Josh plans to be around."

"Where will you find him?"

Scoobie hesitated. "He mentioned that he sometimes goes to meetings at Sal's place, Second Round, a couple miles from town."

"Oh, right. You and George have gone there, too, right?"

"George has gone to meetings there. He and I have stopped by for Sal's famous iced tea."

I relaxed back into the couch. "I won't worry until I have to."

WEDNESDAY MORNING, I headed to Steele Appraisals. I dumped folders on my desk and then made a cup of coffee in the kitchen at the rear of the house. Back at my desk, I noted the message light blinking as I sat down.

Buck Brock was more rude than usual. "Jolie, the mayor and stupid Landlord Tenant people said I have to do a better job cleaning my units after guests leave. Who do you know can do that?"

My first thought was why me? The second was at least he didn't call Aunt Madge stupid.

I checked the fax machine for new work and then called Buck back. He kind of snarled hello, so I skipped a polite greeting. "Buck, what happened to the people you used before? They probably aren't full time. Can't you give them more hours?"

He said nothing for several seconds, then, "The thing is, they quit me. Stupid reason."

"Were you rude to them?"

"Not until they quit."

I had a hard time not laughing. "Before I think about people I might recommend, why did they quit?"

"They wanted me to pay for the cleaning stuff. I never did that."

"That's the only reason?"

"Maybe a little bit the pay. People try to screw me over all the time."

I chose my words carefully. "Bosses have to be a lot more flexible these days. There aren't enough workers. Someone else will pay them another dollar or two an hour and provide the Lysol or whatever. What will you pay?"

He quoted a price and I snorted. "I can't recommend anyone for that pittance."

"I tried paying them a flat rate based on number of bedrooms, but that didn't work, either."

There was no point asking about the rate. "Your guests sometimes leave a place in reasonable condition and sometimes it's a mess and takes more work. Pay hourly and have a short form where they can check off what they did or say if the kitchen was especially filthy."

Silence.

I repeated my question about the hourly rate he'd pay and he gave a better answer. "Now people might be willing to work for you." *Only if they don't know you.*

"Okay, okay. Who do you know?"

"I think I know a guy who might..."

"Not that Max weirdo, is it?"

I hung up and ignored the phone the two times he called back. The idea that he would call a brain-injured veteran a weirdo infuriated me.

I fumed as I turned back to the computer. What would make a person so needlessly rude? In my experience, it's usually an acquired habit. He said everyone screwed him over. Had he been cheated by an unscrupulous partner? Badgered during a divorce settlement? The man probably needed a friend, but it couldn't be me.

I had just finished entering measurements for a house I'd visited yesterday when someone knocked on the office door. I walked to the door, surprised to see Buck. I opened it but didn't gesture that he should come in.

Buck shifted from one foot to the other. "I shouldn't ought to have called the guy a weirdo. I'm sorry."

I stood aside and let him in, surprised at his contrition. "I appreciate that you came by to say that." He started for the living room on the left, but I pointed to the office. "Have a seat."

He lowered his six-foot-two frame into the chair next to my desk. "I been stressed. You heard people complained about some of my places, and now I have to give a free weekend to one of the loudmouths."

I frowned at him. "I heard it was a legitimate complaint."

He shrugged. "What's dust to me is muck to somebody who's picky."

I said nothing. According to Aunt Madge, the complaint wasn't about dust.

"What's with this Max guy, anyway? Do you think he could do cleaning work?"

"No to the second question, he'd need more structure. He got a brain injury in the first Iraq war."

"Oh. That's no good. You guys all knew him when you were kids?"

I shook my head. "He and another vet initially came here homeless. People helped them get veteran benefits, and even helped Max buy his house." I didn't add that Josh had just returned after a crime-related hiatus.

"Think he wants to sell?"

I pointed toward the door.

"Okay, okay." He shrugged, more in frustration than uncertainty. "Before here, I mostly worked in bigger towns. I thought there'd be less stress here, but it's just different kinds."

I regarded him thoughtfully. "It's possible you create some of your own stress by pushing hard and sometimes overlooking… let's just say dirt."

"Maybe. I like to keep moving. So, who do you know who can clean?"

"A guy who used to be here and just came back." I thought that was a neutral way to characterize Josh. "Scoobie knows his phone number, I don't. I'll text Scoobie now and get back to you."

"When?"

I stood and forced a smile. "When Scoobie gets back to me. He'll have to let the guy know you'll call."

Buck stood. "What's his name?"

"I'll let Scoobie tell you." He started to say something else. "I'm trying to work on an appraisal, and the bank contacted us about doing one for the Victorian on Seashore."

He turned quickly toward the front door. "I'll call you later."

I wanted to say I'd call him, but I didn't want to keep talking to him.

After Buck left, I thought about whether to ask Scoobie to talk to Josh.

I shook my head and took out my phone to text Scoobie. I felt as if Josh and I could resolve any hard feelings, but wasn't sure

I wanted a link to his life. Maybe Scoobie should be the one to decide that.

AUNT MADGE CALLED JUST after lunch. "I'm letting you know your name may have been used in vain."

"Wouldn't be the first time. By whom?"

"Buck, who else?" she said. "He called me early this afternoon."

I laughed. "I told him Scoobie and I might be able to help him find someone to clean. I sent Scoobie a text to see if he wanted to talk to Josh about it."

She paused before responding. "Scoobie texted me that he'd be around. I always admired how he helped Max."

"Me, too." I changed the subject. "Buck talked about how it came out with the Landlord Tenant Commission."

"Probably as well as it could. He knows we can't tell him how to compensate a disgruntled guest, but he said he'd listen because he didn't want people picking on him later."

"So tactful. He said he had to give someone a free weekend."

Aunt Madge chuckled. "I think I texted you that it's Renée's friend Eleanor, used to be Covington. She married Kevin Fielding."

"I remember her being at the house with Renée when I was in middle school, but they were enough older I didn't really know her. Renée showed me Eleanor's wedding pictures a couple years ago."

"The place they previously rented is one of the few properties Buck has with a view of the water. His ad didn't say you had to go onto the porch and look to the left to see it."

"Even Lester wouldn't write an ad like that. I'm glad he has to give them a free weekend."

Aunt Madge laughed. "We suggested he do it at the one place he has that's actually on the water. I figured it wouldn't be rented now."

"Lucky Eleanor. You need more morning help this week?"

"We're good. You can bring the kids over one day after school if you want."

I said I'd try and hung up. Then I stared at the phone for a moment before I got back to work. Something about Eleanor tickled my brain, but I couldn't think of what it was."

THE CALL FROM Renée that evening refreshed my memory. She started by asking if I'd heard Eleanor and her husband would be in Ocean Alley for another weekend. When I said I had, she added, "Eleanor wasn't too put out about the place they had before, but Kevin had a fit. He has a...strong personality."

"So does Aunt Madge," I teased, "but in her we call it gutsy."

"Kevin can be...temperamental. I think he's pretty good to her, especially now. She's been worried about some balance issues. Hopefully just an inner ear infection or something."

That's what Renée had said a few weeks ago, but I'd forgotten the book club member she mentioned was Eleanor. "That's no fun. Maybe it'll be over before their weekend."

Headlights came in the front window, but it was only someone turning around in our driveway. "Scoobie's helping an old acquaintance after the meeting tonight. I'm getting adept at overseeing baths on my own."

"Does Terry help?" She asked.

I smiled at the thought of Scoobie's high school junior brother. "He does when he's here. Supposedly he studies at the library every night."

Her tone conveyed worry. "You don't think he does?"

"He probably gets some done. But our librarian friend Daphne assures us there is a lovely sophomore who keeps him company a lot of times when he studies."

"Who would have thought you'd be dealing with teenagers at the same time I am? If you see Eleanor and Kevin, tell them I said hello."

I smiled to myself. When we'd found out we'd become the guardians for Scoobie's much-younger brother, I was pregnant with the twins and had felt pretty panicked. What a blessing then eleven-year old Terry had been.

Right now, I felt out of sorts by myself, which was funny given that I often longed for silence in the middle of dinner or when I was helping at the co-op nursery school. *Is Scoobie trying to carve out some distance between us by helping Josh get reacclimated to Ocean Alley?*

I chided myself. That was ridiculous. Or was it?

My gaze fell on one of Lance's sneakers mixed in with a pile of Legos. Aloud I said, "That would make him laugh."

I smiled to myself. Scoobie had talked to Josh about working for Buck, and he liked the idea. It would be good for Josh and would keep Buck from asking me for advice on a cleaning crew or complaining about the city holding him to account for messy rental units.

Scoobie loved our lives. This was probably another one of those times when Scoobie would remind me the center of the universe was somewhere west of me.

I emptied the dishwasher and was about to resort to doing a load of laundry when lights again came through the front window. Scoobie shut off his car and almost bounded toward the front steps.

I opened the front door, blew a kiss as he got to the bottom step, and put a finger on my lips as he got to the door. "They're already asleep."

He shut the door, pulled me to him, and grinned. "Super. There's something I think we should do before we go to bed. Or go to sleep, anyway."

Chapter Six

THURSDAY MORNING, WITH Scoobie's encouragement, I planned to meet Josh at Java Jolt at nine-thirty. George got there at eight-thirty and he and Megan prepped Max to see Josh again.

George called me when he got to his office at nine. "Megan was pretty busy. I talked to Max for a few minutes and told him I'd seen Josh at a meeting. Then Megan said he'd been in Java Jolt once, and told Max that Josh seemed fine."

"Was Max worried about seeing him?"

"I wish. He was actually mad at me for not bringing Josh with me. He wants to invite him to stay at his house."

"Oh, boy. Don't you think that would drive Josh crazy?"

George grunted. "Max drives me nuts in five minutes. I don't know how Scoobie can stand taking him shopping sometimes."

I smiled to myself. "That's our Scoobie. Will Max still be there when Josh and I meet?"

"Yep. But Megan told him it would be like other Java Jolt customers. He can greet you but not sit with you or interrupt your conversation."

"Okay. I'll let you and Scoobie know how it goes."

"Tell Scoobie." George hung up.

I ARRIVED AT JAVA JOLT at nine-fifteen so Max could tell me his big news.

He was so excited when I came in that he left the dirty dish tub on a table and almost ran to me. "Jolie! Did you hear Josh is back? Josh is back?"

I headed for the self-serve coffee thermos on the counter. "Scoobie told me. That's why I'm meeting Josh here in a few minutes." I grabbed a mug and began filling it.

Megan spoke quietly from the other side of the counter. "Max, you need to get your tub and bring it to the sink in the back room."

His eyes strayed to the gray plastic tub and back to me. "I need to get busy. Busy." He turned toward the dirty dishes.

Megan grinned at me, her brown eyes almost sparkling. "Scoobie texted me that you might have some work for Josh. That was fast."

I added cream to my coffee and shrugged. "It's cleaning for Buck."

Her smile faded. "Isn't that some form of corporal punishment?"

I laughed. "Buck's people quit, and we talked about how to treat people better and pay them more."

I took my coffee to a two-person table near the window and glanced up and down the boardwalk. The day was overcast, so even the bright colors of boardwalk businesses didn't lighten my nervousness.

There was no reason to feel that way. Josh and I had been friendly before he tried to falsely implicate me in a crime. I know his reasons, and that he believed no one would take his anonymous tip seriously. It still ticked me off.

I momentarily closed my eyes and took a breath. *Don't dwell in the past.* But if I did, I also needed to remember he had helped with a food pantry fundraiser and taken good care of Max.

The door opened and the same bearded man I'd seen a few days ago came in. From Scoobie's description, I knew this was Josh. He glanced around, saw me, smiled, and pointed to the counter.

While he and Max had lived on the streets, with occasional nights in a motel, they had both had a soft appearance. Josh had been beardless and rarely smiled. In addition to the beard and salt-and-pepper hair, he now looked fit and relaxed.

He went to the decaf thermos on the counter, apparently already familiar with Megan's winter rules. Take what you need and put money in the huge sugar bowl.

Max came from the doorway to the back room. "Josh!" He moved quickly to the friend who had almost been his caregiver, but stopped a few feet from him.

I could tell Max's instinct had been to hug him. Instead, he stuck out a hand. "You look good. Good."

Josh grinned and gave his hand a quick shake. "You, too. I heard you help Megan keep Java Jolt ship-shape." He stayed half-facing Max, but went back to getting coffee.

"I do, I do. Megan gives me donuts and a luncheon sandwich. Sandwich."

I smiled at the formality of his words.

Josh finished getting his coffee and nodded toward me. "I need to talk to Jolie for a few minutes. Then maybe you and I can head to the boardwalk for a walk for a few minutes. For old time's sake."

"Old times." Max turned abruptly and headed for the dishwashing area behind the counter.

Josh followed him with his eyes and turned to me. As he got to the table, I stood and we shook hands. I smiled. "That went better than I thought it would. I thought he might cry, and then he'd be embarrassed later."

"It did." We both sat. "Thanks for talking to me."

I smiled slightly. "You apologized years ago, and I'm glad things worked out for you."

He nodded. "Thanks to Reverend Jamison and Father Teehan, the county prosecuting attorney was willing to let me plead to manslaughter in self-defense. I went to a low-level facility for a year and then a VA center for PTSD treatment."

I nodded. "Scoobie let me know. And I guess he kept Max in the loop."

"What you guys have done for Max. Helping him buy that house, Megan having him in here every day."

"Java Jolt gives him some structure to his days. And he doesn't break too many mugs anymore. Scoobie and George spend more time with him than I do."

"George," he said. "I remember him as a kind of impatient reporter for the *Ocean Alley Press*. Wouldn't have thought he'd step up."

"He's been a lot calmer since he got fired from the paper. Though he still does some articles now and then. And," I debated mentioning Ramona, "he's been subjected to a calming influence."

"Huh. You're friend with the kind of hippie clothes?"

I laughed. "You remember Ramona, yes. She doesn't work in the office supply store anymore. She has a small art gallery on the boardwalk."

His eyebrows arched. "Is there enough business to do that?"

"She gives watercolor lessons, too, and sells some of her own work. She's getting a pretty good reputation. Speaking of making a living…"

"I have a VA disability pension. Not huge, but you won't hear me complaining. And I get health care. I'd like to supplement that, but not with anything too…complicated."

I didn't know specifics of Josh's Iraq War experiences, but figured he had PTSD for a reason. "You'd be cleaning Buck Brock's rental units when vacationers leave. Buck can be overbearing, but he swore to me that he'd pay a decent wage and you could charge for the actual hours you work."

He laughed lightly. "George said he's an ass-hat but he's afraid to tick you off."

"George said ass-hat?"

"No, but I wouldn't use his language in front of you."

"The twins occasionally test a word they've heard and know they shouldn't be saying. And I've used a few on occasion myself."

He took a sip of coffee. "You have twins, Aunt Madge is the mayor."

"And did Scoobie tell you about his brother, Terry?"

He grew somber. "That was terrific good fortune."

"Yep. He's really more of a big brother to the twins. They're getting close to the point where we can explain he's really their uncle. And I still have my black cat, Jazz, who moved to Ocean Alley with me more than eight years ago." I heard myself prattling and stopped.

He drained his coffee cup. "Do you have any idea how many hours this Buck will need me? Or if I have to negotiate my pay?"

"No to the first question, but he doesn't own a huge number of properties and they don't all rent in the off-season. And I'd say tell him what you want, maybe five dollars or more above the state's minimum wage."

"If I decide to stick with it, maybe I'll take some of my pay in a room with a kitchenette."

Scoobie had told me Josh lived near Sal's Second Round place. Before I could ask about it, Buck's bellow came in from the boardwalk. He seemed to be trying to talk the souvenir shop owner into letting him put up ads in the store's front window.

I tilted my head toward the boardwalk. "That's Buck."

Josh grinned. "I guess you could say his reputation precedes him."

I LEFT JAVA JOLT almost as soon as I introduced Buck and Josh and headed for Steele Appraisals. After I checked for new business, I'd head to a house Lester had written a contract on. I hadn't appraised a house in the Popsicle District for a few weeks, and missed the sometimes jarring mix of colors.

Then I would stop by Harvest for All to check for empty shelves. I felt fortunate not to have to work too many of our two-mornings-a-week food distributions; mostly if someone was sick. I smiled as I thought of our late friend, who had left us money for the large refrigerators and after whom we named our boy.

I checked email and the fax machine and headed for a two-unit bungalow, this one painted bright royal blue. I studied it from my car. The owner had added some large flowerpots — with silk flowers this time of year — and replaced some boards on the front porch and then painted it.

The house had an air of neglect, but the decision on the value Harry and I would give to the bank was more on structure, size, and condition. Smart appearances were more important to real estate agents.

I took outside photos before going inside, and prepared myself for at least an hour of work to measure the two units and make sure the heating and plumbing worked. If I were the buyer, I'd definitely hire a home inspector and give the seller a list of repairs.

TWO HOURS LATER MY slacks had dirt spots from kneeling on dusty floors to take measurements and I probably needed a shower. Since I was heading to the not-open pantry and then stopping at Markle's Market for milk, I skipped cleaning up.

At the pantry, I compiled the list of items we were out of and decided to postpone doing the monthly order for the regional food pantry until the next day. I'd have to ask Mr. Markle to order some things we couldn't get from the food bank.

Mr. Markle greeted me with the dour expression that hides his generosity to the food pantry. "Morning Jolie. Don't have the little scamps with you?"

He's called the twins that ever since Lance, who was pretending to be a bull, charged into an end cap display of soup. Mr. Markle had turned beet purple and was about to yell, but Lance started crying, something he rarely does.

The twins and I scurried around collecting cans. I volunteered to pay for the dented ones, which Mr. Markle had grumbled he could not sell.

After more grumbling, mostly for show after Lance's obvious contrition, Mr Markle agreed to a $5 reimbursement, and suggested Lance could do extra chores for Mommy and Daddy. Then he had Lance put the dented ones in a box for Harvest for All.

Scoobie went by with our checkbook when he got off work, but Mr. Markle said he'd make the dented cans a charity tax donation.

I replied to the grocer's greeting today with a breezy, "Just getting milk today."

He met me at the cash register. "When did your buddy Max learn to text?"

"Scoobie taught him. But, uh, I don't think he gave him your mobile number."

Markle half snorted. "He asked for it. Said he was putting in all his friends' numbers. I told him he could text me twice a week."

My shoulders relaxed. "Always good to put some limits with Max."

Markle gave a rare smile. "He's excited about Josh being back."

I took the milk jug by its handle and headed for the door. "It's been a long time."

I was getting into my car in the market lot when Josh's text arrived. "Buck and I figured out a wage and how to account for my time. He seemed to be on good behavior. I start tomorrow. Thanks again!"

WHEN I GOT UP ON Friday, I knew it would be extra busy because my day would start with morning parent duty at the twins' co-op day care. Scoobie had traded a morning with me, and promised to do major yard cleanup without my help. Fine by me, and lately he liked to do projects by himself.

I arrived at Sand and Sea Daycare with the kids but minus my morning cup of coffee. It would be a long three hours.

Since the parent volunteers handle hanging up coats and getting kids to the coloring table, the first half-hour always passes quickly. Then the child care staff splits the kids into smaller groups by age and interests. I always seem to end up with the boys who like to play with trucks.

At ten-thirty I took refuge in the kitchen to prepare the snack. I snuck a peak at my phone and saw a thank-you text from Josh. He'd finished cleaning one of Buck's bungalows and was about to meet Max at Java Jolt. Good to know, but I hoped not to get regular updates.

I left the daycare to do a commercial building appraisal at a swimwear shop across from the courthouse. Those were always harder, and not just because I mostly do residential appraisals.

With Ocean Alley being two miles along the shore and twelve blocks deep, there isn't a lot of commercial property compared to larger towns. I had few prior sales to compare to the current property, which sometimes made it harder to be decisive about a property's value. Harry and I really had to put our heads together for stores or restaurants.

By two o'clock, I was calling board members of the Harvest for All Food Pantry to try to organize a meeting so we could plan a fundraiser. Aunt Madge watched me do it while I sat in her kitchen before getting the kids from daycare.

She handed me a cup of tea. "The phrase herding cats comes to mind."

Mister Rogers rose from a spot by my feet and nudged my fingers for a pat. That brought Miss Piggy from her spot to remind me she needed a scratch.

I patted and scratched and glanced at Aunt Madge as she read a draft of last night's city council minutes. She looked up and grinned. "No one ever said small-town life was less busy. Just less traffic."

Chapter Seven

JOSH NEGOTIATED A MODEST weekly rate at Beachcomber's Alley Motel, a place he and Max had stayed many times. The manager remembered Josh and gushed his pleasure about Max owning a house.

With the motel only half a block from the ocean, on Friday Josh was up early and took a brisk walk along the boardwalk. The lack of a breeze made the forty-five-degree weather almost pleasant.

He had almost reached the shuttered ice cream shop when a man climbed up the steps from the street and began walking toward Josh at a fast clip. As he grew closer, Josh thought the middle-aged Black man looked familiar.

The man noticed him, slowed to a stop, and stuck out a hand. "Josh. Heard you were back in town. Stuart Cambridge. I was running for City Council a few years ago, when you and Max helped Jolie and crew with the Talk Like a Pirate Day fundraiser."

"Oh, sure. You walked around wearing a pirate hat and handing out flyers or something."

Cambridge laughed. "You have a good memory. Listen," his expression grew somber. "Buck Brock ran into me at Markle's Market last night."

"Is that a good thing," Josh asked, smiling slightly.

"Uh…"

"If you're still on City Council, I won't quote you."

"Didn't win. But I am on the Landlord Tenant Commission, and we met with him a couple of days ago."

Josh shifted his weight from one foot to the other. "I think that's the reason Buck hired me. According to Jolie."

Cambridge seemed surprised. "Buck didn't mention the meeting?"

"He did, but you might not want to hear what he said."

Cambridge's deep laugh went on for several seconds. "You could run for office. What I wanted to say was, well, I hope Buck Brock treats you well. My sister-in-law's cousin worked for him for a time, and he was…I think she called him a demanding complainer."

"He is rough around the edges, but so far, so good. He's not anxious to get on Jolie's bad side."

When Cambridge didn't say more, Josh asked, "Anything else I should know?"

"You don't usually see a man his age, a businessman, getting into fights. But he's thrown punches a couple times at the Sandpiper Bar and Grill."

"Huh. Hadn't heard that. I'll remember what you've said. Thanks."

Josh continued another half block and turned back. He thought about what Stuart Cambridge had said. Good to know, he supposed, but it wouldn't deter him from sticking with the job.

He expected his second day working for Buck to get off to a better start than the first. Yesterday, Buck had come to both bungalows to "see how it was going," as he put it. Josh finally figured out that he not only wanted to check the work but make sure Josh hadn't hot-fingered any of the smaller items in the fashionably furnished rentals.

He'd also had to listen to Buck explain his theory that if he used fashionable — but still "kinda cheap" — furniture, artwork, and what he called kitchen doo-dads, he could charge higher daily rates than other short-term landlords at the Jersey shore. Josh had to admit that the bungalows he'd cleaned the day before had been attractive. Although some of the furniture probably wouldn't hold someone who weighed more than about 200 pounds.

He showered, dressed, and made his way to the two-unit home he would do today. The bungalow he did yesterday sat several blocks from the shore. Buck had proudly explained that the larger duplex Josh would do today was his pride and joy. It sat closer to the southern end of Ocean Alley, where the sandy beach was wider than the area closer to downtown.

Sitting in the car he had rented until he could buy one, Josh peered at the house, which had beige siding and dark blue shutters. The top and bottom floors had large porches. Buck could probably rent each floor for a lot more than his bungalows.

Josh let himself in from the door that faced the street and walked through to what was technically the front of the house, facing the ocean. The water was perhaps 150 yards from the house, but the wind had picked up, so the sound of the surf was intense.

He reentered and walked through to the car to get his cleaning supplies. He decided to tackle the kitchen first. The last guests had taken out their trash and wiped down the counters.

They'd also stripped the beds and put a neat pile of sheets on the bedroom floor. He bet not many guests did that. Josh smiled to himself. Buck had tried to get him to take sheets to the laundromat, wash them, and then bring them back.

They'd finally agreed that he'd drop them at a laundry, which would wash and fold them. Josh would pick them up the next day, and Buck would buy more sheets so there would be three sets for each unit instead of two. That way, there would always be a spare set, even after Josh changed the sheets. He'd have to remember to keep track of the extra sets.

Josh checked the refrigerator, where Buck said he had placed a small tray of cheese and crackers. Very clean. All he'd have to do would be wipe it down.

He smiled to himself. Buck had complained that the upcoming weekend's renters were getting a "free ride because they were complainers." Josh hadn't asked what the history was, but doubted there were snacks in the fridge on the last visit.

He only had to clean the bottom unit today. It took a little more than an hour to carefully scrub the kitchen and bathroom and dry mop the laminate floors in the two bedrooms. He dusted end tables, dressers, and the coffee table before deciding the place should pass muster.

When he juggled the mops and dirty sheets through the street entrance just after ten AM, he noticed a gift box sitting near the door. The rectangular, wrapped box looked to be chocolates, and bore a card that said it had been purchased at the In-Town Grocery.

Josh smiled to himself. Mr. Markle had been patient with Max years ago. Max would occasionally pick up something and put it down on a different shelf. Once, after paying for a soda, he had absently picked up a candy bar as he walked out. Markle could have charged him with shoplifting, but just grumbled that Josh needed to better explain paying for things.

He loaded his paraphernalia into the rental car, went back to the porch, retrieved the wrapped package, and placed it on the coffee table. Then, since he didn't know the time the guests would arrive, he put it in the fridge.

As he locked the house, he felt a keen sense of satisfaction. He'd come back to Ocean Alley, his friends had been gracious, and Scoobie had said maybe this weekend or next he and Jolie would have him over for dinner. What could be better?

Chapter Eight

I HAVE A BAD HABIT of putting off ordering food for Harvest for All from the Lakewood Regional Food Bank. Since it was a monthly chore, it took a while. To treat myself as I did it, I had come to Java Jolt late Friday morning to work on the order.

As I seated myself at a table by the window overlooking the boardwalk, I waved to Megan. She supervised Max as he transferred dirty coffee mugs from a tub to the sink behind the counter. He'd be over to talk to me when he was done.

I studied the order form. I didn't want to pass it to another volunteer. Partly because I didn't want to discourage volunteers and partly because I don't let go of things easily.

The regional food bank had a lot to offer, but we needed some items they didn't stock. Especially things that would appeal to elderly people who might not want spicy or hard-to-chew food. And baby formula.

What we needed was a date board members could agree to meet so we could schedule a fundraiser. What I *really* needed was an extra two hours every day.

Max stopped at my table. "When you finish your coffee, Jolie, I'll take your mug. Your mug."

I smiled. "I know you will. I'm doing an order to the Lakewood Regional Food Bank. You'll help at the Harvest for All counter next week, won't you?"

"Of course, I will, of course."

Megan called from behind the counter. "Would you check the napkin holders for me, Max?"

He nodded to her and turned back to me for a moment. "I'm busy, Jolie, busy."

"Yes. And we all appreciate it." As he walked toward the napkin holders near the coffee thermoses, I smiled at Megan.

The door to Java Jolt opened and a man and woman entered. It took a moment, but I recognized them as Renée's friend Eleanor and her husband; I thought his name was Kevin. Buck had griped about the free weekend stay only yesterday.

Kevin kept a hand under Eleanor's right elbow in a gesture that could be considered thoughtful, but also looked necessary. As she placed her left hand on the counter, it was clear she did it for balance.

Megan greeted them and asked Eleanor if she would like to try the pumpkin-spiced coffee, a fall special.

"I think I'll pass and have a latte. Some chocolate I ate not long ago disagreed with me."

Kevin added, "Not a brand we'd had before."

While Megan took their order, I texted my sister. "Renée, your friends are in JJ. Does Eleanor still have a problem with balance?"

I went back to my food order form for a minute, then saw Renée's reply.

"It may be more than an inner ear thing," Renée texted. "At book club this week, she said they're doing some neurological tests. Could be multiple sclerosis, hopefully less serious."

Eleanor and Kevin had their coffee and were getting close to my table. I texted back, "Ugh."

As they settled into their chairs, Kevin placed Eleanor's mug close to her and helped her take off her coat. Eleanor, a tall woman, sat somewhat hunched over, as if keeping her spine straight was an effort. Quite a contrast to Kevin, who could be in an ad for tennis racquets or skis.

The marriage vow says, "in sickness and in health," and almost every day I'm happy the twins keep Scoobie and me in in good shape.

I left my notebook and food bank order form on my table and moved to theirs, smiling. "Don't get up. I don't know if you remember me, Eleanor. I'm Jolie Gentil, Renée's sister. Welcome back to Ocean Alley."

Eleanor's smile erased her weary expression. "Renée gave me your phone number in case we needed anything." She nodded to her husband. "Though Mr. Thoughtful here thinks of everything."

Her husband was closest to me, so I shook his hand. "I've seen your wedding pictures, but I don't think you and I have met."

"Kevin Fielding."

He held my hand for a couple seconds longer than most people do, and gazed at me directly. If I hadn't known better (did I?), I'd think he was flirting.

He added, "Eleanor mentioned you. She said you have four-year old twins. You look so relaxed. You must have a nanny."

Eleanor smiled. "Renée says Jolie is the Energizer Bunny. Are you still leading the food pantry in town?"

"Harvest for All. Yes, but with a lot of help." I gestured to my table, "I'm doing an order to send to the Lakewood Food Bank. I'll leave you to enjoy your coffee. I just wanted to say I hope this visit is a good one for you."

"Great," Kevin said. "You must have heard we had a less-than-perfect stay a couple weeks ago. This one is off to a great start."

Eleanor nodded. "Mr. Brock had a cheese and cracker plate from the local market and a box of chocolates in the fridge for us."

"I'm glad to hear it. Enjoy the brisk fall weather." I went back to my table. A glance at the order form told me I was less than half done. Since my coffee was cool, I headed back to the counter.

Megan, who is my favorite Harvest for All volunteer, grinned. More of a smirk, actually. "Having fun with the order?"

"If I wouldn't complain, it would go a lot faster." I added hot coffee to my mug from the self-service thermos on the counter. "When will Alicia be home from college again? She's the twins' favorite babysitter."

"Homecoming is this weekend, so not until at least..." Her eyes had traveled behind me.

I turned to see Eleanor half standing, shaking slightly. For a few seconds I stayed still. If this was normal for her, I didn't want to embarrass her and Kevin by rushing over.

In a few seconds, she began to sink to her knees. I moved quickly, and took one arm while Kevin steadied her other one and tried to lower her into her chair.

"Sweetheart, this will pass. Try sitting." He glanced at me. "Thanks."

Sweat had broken out on Eleanor's forehead, and she began to shake even more.

Megan raised her voice, "Should I call an ambulance?"

Kevin frowned and looked at Megan. "This usually passes, so…"

In the second he looked away, Eleanor lost consciousness and her head thumped onto the table.

"Eleanor!" Alarm overtook his forced calm. "Please call! She's never done this before."

HALF-AN-HOUR LATER, Eleanor, who had regained consciousness, was strapped to a gurney. The EMT — I thought his name was Ronnie — spoke in a reassuring tone, "Could be just dehydration, but it's a doc's opinion that counts. You might be back at your hotel in a couple hours."

I thought his cheerfulness sounded forced.

Kevin, a frown on his handsome face, put his hand on her shoulder. "I know you don't like hospitals, but I bet this'll be quick."

Eleanor nodded and closed her eyes. "I'm sure you're right, Sweetheart." She opened them and glanced at me. "Don't tell Renée."

I must have looked puzzled, because as he picked up her purse from the table, Kevin added, "She doesn't want people to worry."

"Good attitude," Ronnie said. "Let's roll." He and his partner guided the gurney onto the boardwalk.

As the door shut behind them, Kevin's words drifted to us. "You have two handsome drivers, Sweetie."

I stayed at the counter. The few other patrons had quietly left, Megan having poured their drinks into to-go cups.

Megan stared at the door and then at me. "That didn't look good."

Because it was the ever-discreet Megan, I said, "Renée said she's been having balance issues. Doctors in Lakewood are conducting tests. But maybe don't mention it."

Megan shook her head. "Of course not."

I glanced behind her. "Where's Max?"

"He slipped out when the EMTs came in. You know how hard it is for him when he doesn't know what to do."

"Right. I better tell Scoobie and George he might be upset."

"Speaking of Scoobie, did you text him to say she's coming?"

"I didn't want to text about it in front of them. I'll do it now and he can call when he gets a minute." He could get her for x-rays or a scan of some sort of her head.

I texted, "Renée's friend Eleanor had a balance problem in JJ. Letting you know she's en route. Her husband, Kevin, is with her." As an afterthought, I wrote, "You might be able to get more information if you let Eleanor's husband know you're Renée's brother-in-law."

When I placed my phone next to my now-cold coffee cup, I remembered Scoobie would know Max came to Java Jolt in the morning, so I texted again. "Max was here and left. I'll let George know to keep an eye out for him."

Sometimes it's annoying to have to constantly consider what's going on with the chattering Max, but I reminded myself it was more than annoying for him to have had his brain badly injured.

SCOOBIE DIDN'T GET back to me for two hours. Then he called rather than texted.

"Hey, Jolie. I'm on lunch break. I asked her husband if I could update you. He said fine as long as you keep it to just you and Renée for now. He was really definite about that."

Scoobie never talks about patient status without checking. He might say he'd x-rayed someone's broken arm, but only if we both knew them and everyone would see the cast anyway. The fact that he specifically checked meant something could be really wrong with Eleanor.

"Is she okay?"

"Well, she's getting good care here, but it may take the docs a while to figure this out. Her head scan is fine."

"Did she feel better after she got there?"

He said nothing for a moment. "They gave her fluids, which may have helped. She certainly knew what was going on."

"Guess you can't talk more now."

"Yep. I'll stop by the house before I get the kids."

I frowned. "Sounds serious."

"Maybe, maybe not. See you after 3:15."

I pushed the end call button. I hadn't called Renée yet, and I debated waiting until Scoobie told me more. But I'd want to know if something was going on with Ramona. I dialed Renée.

Her cheerful voice asked, "Hey sis. Did you see Eleanor and Kevin?"

"They were in Java Jolt this morning." I hesitated.

Renée's tone sharpened. "Is everything okay?

I told her about Eleanor's situation and that Scoobie had called after he'd seen her. "He said she was alert."

"Is he really allowed to tell you more?"

"He asked her husband, who said it was okay if you and I didn't spread the word."

In a clipped tone, she said, "Kevin."

"What does that mean?"

"He acts friendly, but it seems he thinks of reasons to cut her off from old friends. They used to hang with a bunch of the people we went to high school with. You know, movies and stuff. Now I only see her at book club, and she doesn't come a lot."

"More than the usual merging two groups of friends after you get married?"

"Seems like it was all part of subtly controlling her. Oh, and the antiques. She had several beautiful oak pieces of furniture and a maple-encased barometer. He wanted everything modern, so she gave them all away."

Furniture wasn't at the front of my mind. "When did you first notice the balance issues?"

Renée thought for a moment. "About six months ago, but it seemed to calm down. She joked about being a klutz. When I walked to the car with her after book club not long ago, she would have fallen if I hadn't grabbed her by the upper arm."

"Hmm. I don't know a lot about MS, but she seemed to be, I don't know, kind of woozy, too. Like somebody who fainted is when they come around."

"The mom of a girl in Michelle's class has it. I know it's a neurological illness, but you can mostly only see the physical part. I hope Eleanor's okay."

"I'll call you after I talk to Scoobie."

Max had not responded to my text, so after I hung up with Renée, I texted him again. I didn't want to stop by his house unannounced, but if he didn't get back to me, I'd have to. Or get George to do it.

This time Max replied. "I am home, I had grilled cheese for lunch."

For Max, the response was equivalent to two paragraphs. Scoobie and I have talked about Max's lack of repetition in texts. I think he may not want to type much, but Scoobie is probably right when he says if Max can see the words he is less likely to want to repeat them.

I smiled as I texted back. "Sounds good. The woman who had a problem in Java Jolt is OK. Scoobie saw her at the hospital."

He answered, "Scoobie is good."

I HAD A POT OF chili cooking when Scoobie came in the door at 3:15. He kissed my cheek. "Smells good."

"Thanks. How is she?"

He leaned against the kitchen counter. "She has a bump on one side of her forehead. Her husband said she'd had some recent balance issues. Did you know about that?"

"Her head hit the table at Java Jolt." I relayed what Renée had told me about helping Eleanor after book club, and added, "Renée isn't fond of Kevin. She thinks he's pulled her away from her old friends."

Scoobie plucked an apple from the fruit bowl on the kitchen table. "Huh. He's attentive, that's for sure. Maybe he's seen her symptoms for a while and is being protective."

"Could be. Has there been any talk of a diagnosis?"

"No. I think the bump on the head is getting more attention than any balance issues. Since the head scans look good, I suppose they'll address other symptoms now."

I almost snorted. "Maybe she wouldn't have had the bump if it weren't for the other issues. How do they diagnose MS now? I thought an MRI would do it."

"She had one in Lakewood. They sent the results, but I didn't see them."

I remembered something. "Probably nothing, but she told Megan she wanted a latte instead of pumpkin-spiced coffee because some chocolate she ate made her queasy. Or something like that."

"Huh. Surely she or her husband would have mentioned that." He glanced at his watch. "Gotta get the kids." He bowed. "I'm always at their service."

Chapter Nine

WE HAD TO LET the twins stay up to spend a few minutes with Ramona and George on Friday evening. The plan was for them to camp out in Terry's room on the second floor. They used to sleep in the same play tent, but recently decided they should have separate ones. Which they will outgrow in six months.

Terry beat Scoobie to the front door to greet Ramona and George. I figured Terry had an ulterior motive, so I watched the fracas from the kitchen doorway.

"Jeez, Terry, you grew another inch." George clapped Terry on the shoulder and slipped something into his hand.

George was right about one thing. The scared almost eleven-year-old who joined our family about five years ago had grown to be a handsome young man with an infectious grin. If his hair were not brown, as opposed to Scoobie's dirty blonde, you'd almost think they were the twins in the household.

As we moved toward the living room, George spoke to Lance and Leia. "What's that handshake and fist bump routine you showed me a couple weeks ago?"

They obliged, with some disagreement on how to end it. The routine reminded me of rock-paper-scissors, which I've never mastered.

"Now Scoobie and Terry," George said.

Ramona and I exchanged glances. George seemed wound up about something.

Scoobie appeared a trifle irritated, but smiled at Terry. "You start, Bro."

Terry pounded one fist on the other and held out his hand for Scoobie to shake. I didn't remember that part of the routine.

Scoobie frowned lightly, but took it. There was a buzzing sound and Scoobie yelled, "Yow. What the…?"

Jazz sped toward the twins' room for a spot under one of their beds.

George and Terry nearly collapsed in laughter. The twins, initially uncertain, decided this must be funny and joined in.

"Scoobie?" I asked.

He opened his palm. In it sat a round device about one-and-a-half inches wide. He turned it over and revealed a tiny button that must have popped up when Terry released it into his hand — thus the buzzing.

I put my hand on my hips. "George Winters!"

He sobered slightly and glanced at Ramona, who was shaking her head. "Remember that bit about acting your age?"

Together, Terry and Scoobie said, "He doesn't."

I pointed a finger at Terry and tried not to smile. "You know you're going to have to calm them down, right?"

"I'm always calm!" Lance shouted.

Terry grinned. "Oh, sure you are."

Leia used her day-care teacher voice. "I don't think so."

I kept my voice quiet. "Calm or not, you have snacks upstairs and Terry is going to put on *Frozen* for you to watch.

As they scampered up the steps, Lance's voice carried to us. "You know what they need in *Frozen*? Some trucks. Really big trucks."

"Maybe," Terry said, "but then they'd have to buy a lot of snowplows."

Scoobie and I exchanged smiles, and he said, "Taught that boy everything he knows."

"At least the smart-aleck part," George said.

For a moment I thought Ramona was going to tear up. She looked from Scoobie to me. "Do you guys ever stop to think how lucky you are? Great kids…"

George interrupted her. "And Terry's a built-in babysitter." He plopped into one of the beanbag chairs we store under the dining room table and take out when we have extra people.

I looked at Ramona, thinking she would continue what she'd been saying, but she moved toward the kitchen. "I'll put the guacamole dip I brought into one of your blue pottery bowls."

"Sure thing." I wondered if George had deliberately interrupted her. I know he really loves Ramona, but he doesn't like conversations about kids. At least when Ramona brings them up.

We worked silently for a minute, then I spoke in a low voice. "Scoobie was going to tell you two something your uncle said, about buying a house three doors down from us."

She smiled as she arranged crackers on a plate. "Because George is so fond of my Uncle Lester?"

"Uh, no. Because Scoobie wanted to see the look on George's face."

"There's no way George could be more annoyed at Uncle Lester than he usually is."

"You might be surprised. Lester wanted to buy a house with several bedrooms so you and George could drop by with…any kids you might have."

Two crackers tumbled into the sink. She turned her head and her eyes looked moist. "You know what? Scoobie *should* tell us. I want to see the look on George's face."

When Ramona and I took in the snacks, I reminded him of Lester's thwarted home purchase. George stopped chewing the cracker he had smothered with guacamole.

"The thing is, George," Scoobie finished, "him not buying on our street means we don't have to see much of him. But you'll have to visit Lester wherever he lives."

Ramona almost purred. "And that would be so much fun, wouldn't it George?"

TWO HOURS LATER, Terry carried the twins downstairs and put them in their beds. Then he left to study with friends at the diner, since the library would be closed.

When the door shut behind him, Scoobie grinned at George. "He actually thinks we'd believe that story on a Friday night."

"Do you worry about him?" Ramona asked.

I answered before Scoobie did. "We trust him. Plus, if he were into something he shouldn't be, Ocean Alley is such a small town we'd hear about it."

Scoobie agreed. "I decided not to worry about it. I would like to meet the girl, though."

Ramona and I were in the process of trouncing Scoobie and George in Scrabble, generally an impossibility. However, Ramona had formed the seven-letter word 'paradox' and managed to place it on a triple-word score.

Ramona didn't gloat. I did.

Scoobie's phone pinged and he glanced at a text and smiled. "Max wants to know if I saw Josh today. I'll tell him Josh was working so I didn't." He typed his response.

"That reminds me," George said, "when I stopped at the gas station for a Coke, this guy was complaining about your buddy, Buck Brock. That's who Josh is cleaning for, right?"

I frowned. "He's not my buddy."

Scoobie snorted. "He's certainly not Aunt Madge's."

"Was it another disgruntled renter?" I asked.

"I don't think he has any other kind," Ramona said.

"Apparently, the guy and his wife had a bad experience with one of Buck's properties, and the city made him give them a free weekend at another property."

"What's not to like about a free weekend?" Ramona asked.

George shrugged. "The guy figured this weekend's place will be sub-par, too. I know Buck irritates most people he does business with, but why not make nice with the people who pay him rent?"

Scoobie and I exchanged a look.

"Aunt Madge told me he agreed to a free weekend. They can't make him do it, but he didn't want to get on the bad side of the Landlord Tenant Commission."

"Jolie's sister knows the guest," Scoobie said. "Says he's a real charmer."

"Why does she know him?" Ramona asked.

"They live in Lakewood and his wife, Eleanor, went to high school with Renée."

Scoobie again looked my way. Clearly, George had not heard that someone fainted and fell in Java Jolt earlier today.

"What?" George asked.

"I heard an ambulance went to Java Jolt today." Ramona said. "Was it for him?"

I shook my head. "His wife. She's been having some…balance issues, for lack of a better term."

"That's too bad." George looked at Scoobie. "Did they keep her?"

"Yep. Her husband, Kevin, said I could talk to Jolie and Renée about it. Since you don't know her, you won't discuss it with anyone." He said it calmly, but it was a clear warning to George not to look for a story for the *Ocean Alley Press*.

Ramona asked me, "Have you been over to see her?"

"I'll go tomorrow morning. My live-in paramour can be with the kids."

"Does Scoobie know about that guy?" George asked.

Even Scoobie rolled his eyes.

I added, "How do you know it's a guy?" and was pleased to see George blush.

We had finished putting away the Scrabble board when the house phone rang at ten PM. I started. It's not usually good news when it rings that late.

Scoobie hopped up. "Hope they aren't asking me to work tomorrow. The new x-ray tech thought she was getting a cold."

He looked at caller ID. "Blocked. Sometimes hospital calls come in that way." He answered. "O'Brien and Gentil residence."

George smirked. "Your last name comes first in the alphabet."

"He alternates. I just say hello."

Scoobie's expression went from serious to almost pained. "I'm so sorry. What can we do?" He listened. "Sure. I can do that. I'll be there in twenty minutes." He hung up.

"What is it?" I asked.

Scoobie squared his shoulders. "I'm sorry to tell you that Renée's friend Eleanor doesn't look as if she's going to make it through the night. Kevin asked if I'd come to the hospital to sit with him."

I REALLY NEEDED TO give myself permission to sleep, but I wanted to know what was going on with Eleanor. Should I call Reneé? Would Scoobie wake me up to tell me if I dozed off before he came home?

Normally I would text him, but this was not a time to put my need to know ahead of what would be someone else's grief.

When Terry came home at eleven, he offered to stay downstairs near the twins so I could go to the hospital.

"I've been telling myself Kevin, Eleanor's husband, met me at Java Jolt and Scoobie at the hospital today. He asked Scoobie to sit with him. I need to respect that."

Terry gave me a quizzical look.

"What?"

He shrugged. "The old Jolie would have jumped at the chance to get over there."

I sighed. "The new Jolie wants to. But if something happened to Scoobie — or you — and I called Ramona, I might not want George there right away."

"Good call. I could stay up while you sleep some. I'll make Scoobie wake you to tell you anything."

After a moment, I nodded. "One of us has to be alert tomorrow. The twins have to go to a birthday party for a friend. We usually stick around so Lance isn't too rambunctious after he gets a sugar high."

MY EYES FLEW OPEN at the sound of voices in the living room. The clock told me it was three AM Saturday morning. One voice was Scoobie's. The second male voice was not Terry's.

That voice sounded congested. Was it Kevin Fielding? Why was he in our house?

I sat up in the bed. Eleanor must have died and Scoobie brought him home. My heart went out to Kevin. He was in a town where he knew few people. Thank goodness he'd had the good sense to call Scoobie.

The men were talking quietly, probably to let me sleep. Where was Terry? Maybe he'd fallen asleep in the recliner in the twins' room.

I gently moved Jazz off my chest, got up, put on my blue cotton bathrobe, and combed my hair. I wanted to brush my teeth, but the bathroom was in the hall. I needed to check on Scoobie and Kevin first.

Almost gingerly I opened the bedroom door and walked the short distance to the living room. The men had turned on only one lamp, and they sat side-by-side on the couch, with a foot or so between them. Kevin sat bent over, his face in his hands, sobbing quietly. Scoobie had one hand on his shoulder.

Scoobie looked up and nodded to me. "Hey, Jolie, could you bring us some water?" To Kevin's bent head, Scoobie asked, "Would you like some coffee or decaf? Or something else?"

Kevin nodded without looking up, and spoke like a man who had cried a lot. "Decaf, please. Cream if you have it."

"Sure thing." I moved into the kitchen, turned on the light over the stove, and plugged in the coffee maker.

Within five minutes, I placed a steaming mug of coffee in front of Kevin and returned to the kitchen to pour three glasses of water. When I came back to the living room, Kevin had drunk some coffee and now leaned into the back of the couch, eyes closed but no longer crying.

I sat in the recliner and spoke quietly. "I'm so sorry, Kevin. What a shock for you."

He opened swollen eyes, bleary from lack of sleep. "I can't believe it. We were just sitting in that coffee shop…" His voice trembled, but he steadied it.

"The hospital's running a lot of tests on her blood." Tears rolled down his cheeks. "They're talking about a damn autopsy. Cutting up my wife!" His head went back to his hands.

Scoobie and I looked at each other. He shrugged, almost imperceptibly.

I spoke gently. "Kevin, you're welcome to stay here tonight. We have a guest room upstairs, and you'll probably have a lot to do later today. Even a little sleep would help."

He lifted his head, and the practical suggestion seemed to have calmed him a little. "That would be great. I don't want to go back to a place with…with Eleanor's things."

I stood. "I'll go put some towels in the guest room upstairs."

Scoobie nodded to Kevin as I left the room. I heard him say, "I'll get you some sweatpants and a tee-shirt to sleep in. Do you want a bowl of cereal first? Or anything else?"

I peeked in the twins' room and saw Terry sleeping in the recliner. Then I climbed to the second floor and made quick work of checking the guest room for errant toys and brought some towels into the room from the linen closet.

As I finished, I heard Scoobie's footfalls on the stairs. He came into the room and we hugged.

"I'm so glad you could help him."

We pulled apart. He shook his head. "The thing is, all I could do was watch with him. They never figured out what was going on, just that her organs were failing. It was so fast."

I spoke in a hushed tone. "Really fast, given that she looked pretty normal in Java Jolt. I'm so sorry if they have to do an autopsy. Maybe more bloodwork will show something and they can avoid it."

"I'll give him some duds to sleep in. He's in the downstairs bathroom now."

"I'll put a new toothbrush in this bathroom."

When we went downstairs two minutes later, Kevin had apparently washed his face and appeared calmer. Not that he needed to. If Scoobie died, I'd be submerged in grief.

I realized I knew little of Eleanor's family. "Is there someone you'd like us to call?"

Kevin shook his head. "Her father passed a few years ago. Her mom's in a retirement community in Lakewood. I'll tell her myself in a few hours. Thankfully, she has a lot of friends there to support her, but it'll still be really hard for her."

He paused to think for a moment. "The hospital said they wouldn't release any information about her, so I don't think her mother would hear from anyone else."

Kevin turned to Scoobie, then faced me again. "Can you hold off on calling Renée for a few hours?"

"Absolutely.

The hospital would respect the couple's privacy, but word had likely spread about an ambulance being called to Java Jolt yesterday. It could be hard to contain the information in Ocean Alley.

65

Chapter Ten

TERRY TOOK THE TWINS to breakfast at Arnie's Diner, which left us free to talk when Kevin got up just after eight. To avoid going upstairs and waking Kevin, Terry had put on a pair of Scoobie's jeans and a dark red hoodie. The twins thought him wearing Scoobie's clothes was hilarious, but they muffled their laughter.

We had told them to be very quiet when they got up, but didn't tell them the wife of the man sleeping upstairs had just died. Only that he was a friend who couldn't get a hotel room in town. There would be plenty of time later in the day to talk about it. After the birthday party, if we could get away with waiting that long.

I made some scrambled eggs, toast, and turkey bacon, Scoobie's favorite weekend breakfast, and the three of us took plates and cups of coffee to the dining room table instead of eating in our smallish kitchen. Even Scoobie had coffee, though it was more milk than coffee.

A perpetual list-maker when I'm busy, I had brought a couple of five-by-eight yellow pads and two pens to the table. "Random things you need to do will pop into your head. You'll want to write them down so you don't forget."

Kevin smiled. "I don't know your sister too well, but I've seen her pull a spiral notebook from her purse and add to a list. When their book club met at our place." His smile faded.

"You can tell Scoobie and me what you want us to do." I smiled. "That's why I brought two pads."

"Good idea. I really need to get to Lakewood to tell her mother."

I nodded. "I remember her last name was Covington before you two married."

"Her mom is Helen." He sighed. "Would you be willing to go to that house and pack up Eleanor's things? I can do mine later, but I don't really want to see her stuff around when I do it."

We both said, "Sure." I added, "We can bring it all here for you to get later, if you like."

Kevin said he'd get his clothes himself, probably this afternoon, and stop by our house to get Eleanor's. As he finished, we heard steps on the front porch. I glanced at Scoobie as he stood. "You expecting anyone?"

"Nope." He walked toward the front door.

I smiled at Kevin. "Kind of early in the day for Girl Scout cookies."

His eyes were unfocused for a moment then he looked at me. "Eleanor still had a sash with all her badges." He frowned. "But I'm not sure where it is."

"You don't need to worry about that now."

The sound of Sergeant Morehouse's voice caught me by surprise.

"Scoobie, sorry to barge in so early."

Scoobie let him in. "You wouldn't be here if you didn't have a good reason."

I turned to Kevin. "That's Sergeant Morehouse, from Ocean Alley Police. He's a good guy. Maybe just needs some routine information."

Kevin had almost finished his breakfast. He frowned slightly as he stood. "Let's see what's going on."

Morehouse had seated himself in the recliner and Scoobie offered coffee, which he declined. When Kevin entered the living room, Morehouse stood and offered his hand. "I'm so sorry about your wife, Mr. Fielding."

"Kevin. Call me Kevin." He sat on the couch, and I grabbed a dining room chair to sit on. Beanbag chairs didn't seem appropriate.

Morehouse sat again, and his words were only for Kevin. "I know you had a terrible night. I wouldn't barge in, but I think you can provide some information that may help the hospital figure out why your wife died."

Kevin regarded him with a frown. "Of course. Anything. But why you? Why not a doctor or somebody?"

"And you will talk to some medical personnel later."

Somehow, I had a feeling it would be the town medical examiner, who was an MD.

"I'm sorry to tell you that when they examined additional vials of blood, it appeared that your wife had a high level of mercury in her system. It's never good for anyone, but her amount would almost always be toxic."

Kevin's mouth opened slightly, then shut while he held Morehouse's gaze. "You mean, like from shellfish or something?" One hand went to his mouth. "She never ate much fish. I love mussels and crab. She started eating a lot after she met me. Could that be…?"

Morehouse shook his head. "There are traces of mercury in some fish caught off the Jersey coast, but she'd actually get more from eating a dozen sushi appetizers a week. Did she eat a lot of sushi?"

Scoobie moved from where he had been standing near the dining room and sat next to Kevin.

"No. I mean, occasionally. No more than I…Hey, should you test my blood?"

"People from the hospital will probably talk to you about how it might have entered her system. Definitely more than from eating seafood occasionally. I'm not going to ask you for a blood sample," he smiled briefly, "but I bet the hospital would be willing to test you for it. Or ask your own doc."

Kevin nodded quickly. "Good idea."

I sensed he felt that he would be able to do something constructive to find out more about Eleanor's cause of death.

Morehouse paused. "We don't have too many deaths by poison other than opioids. There's no forensic toxicologist in this county, but the state people will likely investigate. Now," he took a notebook from the pocket of his polyester sports jacket, which I think of as his uniform.

Morehouse tried a sympathetic expression. "They tell me the symptoms she had the last few months could indicate a longer-term exposure. Then it seems she recently ingested enough more that it almost had to be drunk or eaten."

Kevin put his head in his hands, but lifted it quickly. "I can't believe this."

Morehouse nodded. "It is hard to understand. She didn't work in the kind of industry where she'd have had exposure."

Kevin shook his head. "She used to be a financial planner in a firm where they helped people create trusts and other financial instruments. They offered her a big promotion, and it made her realize she didn't want to help make some people rich while others…weren't."

Morehouse nodded. "So did she quit or just turn down the promotion?"

"She went to work for a nonprofit that helps prepare disadvantaged parents to get jobs. Men and women, mostly women."

Morehouse's smile was perfunctory. "So, she liked her most recent work, but probably made a lot less. Not, uh, that it matters at this point, but could you two afford the pay cut?"

"Oh, sure. I make good money for a firm that deals with medical devices, some pharmaceutical development, but not much. I'm a chemist by training, but I'm in management."

His pen scratched his small notebook for a moment, and Morehouse asked, "You didn't have an old-fashioned thermometer at home, did you?"

"You mean not digital? Those glass ones from when we were kids?" Kevin asked.

Morehouse nodded. "Not all of those had mercury, but if the stuff in them was silver, that'd be mercury."

Kevin shook his head slowly. "We didn't. Do they even make those now?"

Morehouse shrugged. "If anyone makes them, they wouldn't be readily available. Not for home use." His tone became softer. "I know this is a terrible time, and I wouldn't bother you now except you may be able to help us figure this out."

Kevin nodded firmly. He seemed almost energized. "Absolutely. How can I help?"

"Walk me through the last couple days and this morning. We'll think about any places where she might have had an accidental exposure."

"Sure." He stared ahead for a moment, thinking. "Night before last, we ate at home. We always eat out when we go away for the weekend, so we ate in Thursday night. Lasagna. It had been in the freezer from when we had it a week or so ago."

"And you both felt fine afterwards?" Morehouse asked.

"We both felt the same as always. For Eleanor lately, that's been tired sometimes, especially in the evening."

He went through their Friday morning routine — cereal for breakfast so they could get on the road by eight-thirty. "She did say her stomach was feeling queasy, so she didn't eat much. We talked about waiting until she felt better, but we wanted a walk on the beach when the October sun was high."

"So, you got to Ocean Alley about what, ten-thirty?" Morehouse asked.

"A little before that, yes, but when we went to the house, there was a mop on the porch and the door was open. We figured someone was still cleaning."

"You talk to the cleaning crew?"

"No, we went for gas, then drove to the part of the boardwalk that's level with a parking lot and sat there, just looking at the ocean." He took a tissue from a box on the coffee table and blew his nose.

"Then you went back to the cottage?" Morehouse asked.

"Yes. We were going to drop our things and head out, but we found cheese and crackers and chocolates. I thought the crackers might calm Eleanor's stomach."

"Eleanor got to feeling better?" I asked.

"Morehouse frowned at me.

"Enough that I picked out two of Eleanor's favorite chocolates for her. Then she suggested Java Jolt." He nodded at me. "Jolie's sister said she and her friends like to go there. So, we planned on coffee there, a walk, and then a late lunch."

"But by then her stomach was more upset?" I asked.

Sergeant Morehouse glowered at me, which Kevin didn't see because he had turned his attention to me.

"Yes, I guess. She didn't say she felt nauseous, just a little queasy. Until...you know." He grabbed another tissue and blew his nose.

Morehouse finished writing something. "We'll check the cheese and chocolates, but you ate them, so I'm thinkin' they couldn't have had mercury."

Kevin sighed deeply. "It's all so puzzling."

"Of course. Now, another way you can help is to think about where she might have been exposed, even if you think you don't know."

Kevin nodded.

Morehouse continued, "The next few days, you'll see a lot of people you know, perhaps remember places you've been. Normal stuff after a death. You don't want to think about it 24/7, but I'd like you to keep mercury exposure in mind. Someone may say something...I'm not sure what. Someplace she might have gone to with friends, without you."

Scoobie spoke. "If she was exposed at an event or something, wouldn't other people be sick?"

Morehouse shrugged again. "Hard to say. We have to start somewhere. Now," he turned toward Kevin again, "I need to get just some basic information. Where you live, all of your phone numbers, that kind of thing."

I barely listened as Kevin gave Morehouse what he needed. Scoobie, fortunately, was more alert. He jotted down phone numbers.

During the brief conversation with Sergeant Morehouse, Kevin said he was a chemist. That didn't exactly floor me, but it seemed like an incredible coincidence. Chemists can work with a lot of materials. Could his company have produced something...? No, that was dumb. Any firm involved in medical activities would be incredibly careful. And they wouldn't have mercury lying around. And Kevin wouldn't have brought some home.

I came out of my thoughts as Morehouse stood. Scoobie stayed seated next to Kevin, so I walked the sergeant to the door.

He put on what I thought was a forced tone and jerked his head toward the police car in front of our house. "I got some information for Terry in the car. Walk out with me."

"Sure. Soccer stuff from the league he and your nephew play in?"

"Soccer schedule." He walked down the steps ahead of me.

Across the street, I saw Aunt Madge on her large front porch. I waved and did a thumbs up sign. Morehouse followed my gaze and waved briefly. Aunt Madge went back into the B&B.

Morehouse opened his passenger side door, reached into the glove compartment, and pulled out the soccer game schedule that I recognized as last summer's.

"But this isn't…" I began.

"I know what it is. Mr. Fielding don't. But it's your reason for walking out with me." He looked directly into my eyes. "Do not get involved in this."

My eyebrows went up. "I don't even know what *this* is."

He eyed me, a shrewd expression on his face. "You're smart. Usually. That woman did not die of natural causes. Do not put your nose where it don't belong. Or anywhere it could smell mercury vapor."

Chapter Eleven

I HOPED SCOOBIE WOULDN'T notice I looked like I'd been swatted with a box of saltwater taffy. Fortunately, when I reentered the house, he and Kevin were in our bedroom. Kevin was close to Scoobie's size, so I supposed he was borrowing clothes so he didn't have to go back to the house by the ocean before he went to talk to Eleanor's mother.

I had a ridiculous urge to giggle about Scoobie lending clothes to a high school kid and a chemist in the same day. I suppressed the impulse by biting my lip, and carried the breakfast dishes to the kitchen.

As I dumped them in the sink, my phone vibrated with a text from George. He wanted to know the "status" of the woman who had become ill in Java Jolt. He wouldn't text me unless Scoobie had already ignored him.

I texted back, "Text in a half-hour or so. Don't call."

I ran water in the sink but turned it off when Scoobie and Kevin reentered the living room. I joined them, noting that Kevin now wore a cotton knit sweater of Scoobie's.

Scoobie nodded toward me. "Hey, Jolie. Kevin's about to leave for Lakewood to talk to Eleanor's mom."

Kevin turned. "I don't want her to hear it from anyone else. If you talk to Renée, please ask her not to call anyone else right away." He hesitated for a second and crossed the room to give me a quick hug. "I can't thank you guys enough."

The hug surprised me. I said, "Happy to help, sorry for the reason."

"No problem," Scoobie added.

Kevin straightened his shoulders and picked up car keys and an expensive looking pair of sunglasses from the table next to the front door. "I'm glad I have the shades. I wouldn't want her mom to see my red eyes before we can talk for a minute."

Scoobie walked him the short distance to his car and raised his hand as Kevin pulled away. I was surprised to see him driving a baby blue Lexus. If I'd thought about it, I would have expected a sports car or Jeep.

When he got to the stop sign at the corner, our house phone rang. I glanced at caller ID and picked up the receiver. "Morning, Aunt Madge."

"We didn't want to intrude, but I heard about Eleanor's death because it's what Captain Tortino called 'suspicious.' Is her husband okay?"

It made sense the police would call the mayor in a situation such as this, but it hadn't occurred to me. "I suppose it's the standard as well as can be expected. Thankfully, he called Scoobie and asked him to sit with him at the hospital last night."

She rarely sounded alarmed, but just now she did. "What? Why Scoobie?"

Scoobie heard the last part of what I said as he came into the house. I mouthed "Aunt Madge." He nodded and did a gimme gesture.

"Aunt Madge, Scoobie wants to talk to you." I handed him the receiver and listened as he gave a quick summary of the last twelve hours. She then apparently relayed what she'd been told. His eyebrows went up.

I fished the old soccer schedule from a pocket and held it up. "I'll tell you what Morehouse said."

Scoobie put Aunt Madge, now with Harry, on speaker, and he and I sat on the couch. I explained what little Morehouse had told me, ending with, "It sounds as if they think she ate it in something. I…darn it!"

The three of them said, "What!?"

"I should have told Morehouse that Eleanor said some chocolate she ate yesterday tasted funny. I need to call him."

"Didn't Kevin tell him that?" Scoobie asked.

"He said they ate the candy, but I don't think he said Eleanor mentioned the chocolate made her feel queasy."

"Do you remember what Sergeant Morehouse told you about where to put your nose?" Aunt Madge asked.

"I believe it was where not put it," Harry added.

"Funny. Kevin went to Lakewood to tell Eleanor's mother." I looked at Scoobie. "You heard him ask me to wait a bit before I talk to Renée."

Scoobie nodded. "Death is part of life, though horrible surprises about it aren't. When I walked him to his car, he said now is okay to call as long as Renée promises not to tell anyone for at least a couple hours."

Aunt Madge asked if she needed to look after the twins, something she and Harry are more at ease doing now that the twins are older. I told her we probably wouldn't have to ask.

We ended the call and Scoobie shook his head. "I can't imagine what I'd do if it were you."

I tried to put a light spin on it. "With all the pot you smoked when you were younger, you'll probably go years before me."

He grunted. "I'm serious." Then he smiled. "You're so intense…" He stopped when my mobile rang.

To the universe, I said, "That's the ring I have for Renée."

Scoobie stood. "I'm going to grab a quick shower."

Renée's worry came through the phone. "Jolie, I called the hospital. They said they weren't giving out information about Mrs. Fielding."

"I'm sorry, Renée, she died very early this morning."

"What? What happened?" Her voice caught. "You said her stomach was queasy. Did she have a heart attack or something?"

For what could be the first of several times today, I went over what we knew about Eleanor's death. "Kevin's driving to Lakewood now to tell her mom."

"Good heavens. I know her pretty well. I should probably head to her place."

A sense of almost panic went through me. "Kevin was pretty specific about wanting to tell her himself."

"I'll meet him in the lobby and tell him if he wants me to, I can stay with her when he leaves. He'll probably have a lot to do."

Slowly, I agreed. "That's probably a good idea. If you're going to do it, leave now. He could be there in twenty or thirty minutes."

I showered as soon as Scoobie was finished, so I'd be dressed when Terry brought the twins home. I thought about responding to George's text, but decided to leave it to Scoobie.

When I called Sergeant Morehouse, he was not happy that neither Kevin or I had relayed Eleanor's comment about needing a latte because the chocolates may have made her stomach queasy.

He swore softly. "If her husband left your place thirty minutes ago, he could have cleaned up…whatever at their rental place."

I found myself feeling great sympathy for Kevin. It was hard to think of him as a murderer. "He said he would go straight to Lakewood. He was really broken up about her death."

"Yeah, yeah. I need to get a warrant for the cottage they stayed in."

"It's one of Buck Brock's. Can't he let you in?"

"If she had been staying there alone, or if they had checked out, yes. But legally, her husband's still a tenant. I need a warrant." He hung up, as usual without saying goodbye.

WE FINISHED WRAPPING a birthday present for a nursery school pal Lance liked. Leia thought Toby was bossy. I smiled at the idea that she thought anyone bossy.

"Mom," Lance said. "You told us only one present, but who gets to carry it?"

Leia looked up from her A B C book. "It's a dumb present. You can carry it."

"It is not! He wants a toy jet ski."

"He's too young to ride one," Leia began.

I raised my voice slightly. "What's important is that Lance knew Toby would like a toy jet ski."

"Right," Leia said, sarcasm evident.

We have got to work with her on her condescending comments.

Lance bristled and started to say something. I overrode him.

"We have to leave for the party in ten minutes. Is your room tidy? Did you leave anything in Terry's room?"

Saying nothing, they hurried to their room. They wanted the points toward their allowances they get when they do their chores. I cleaned wrapping paper scraps from the table and put the scotch tape and scissors back in the kitchen junk drawer.

From above, a couple of minutes later, Scoobie urged the twins to look under Terry's bed for any toys left in his room from last night.

Scoobie left them to it and ran quickly down the steps. "Listen, can you take the kids to the party by yourself? I really need a meeting."

My eyebrows went up. "Oh, sure, of course."

"If not, I can," he began.

"It's all good. I'm so glad there's an AA meeting late Saturday morning."

"Yeah. More daytime ones on a weekend."

The twins started down the stairs.

He picked up his car keys from the bowl on the table by the front door. "I'll split before they're down here."

I stared after him for a moment.

Scoobie has often told me that twelve-step meetings helped him reach sanity after a home life of, at best, verbal abuse and neglect. He saw his father as someone who never loved him until he learned that the man left to save himself. But why leave a little kid with a monster mother?

He took kindness where he found it, mostly at school. When Scoobie was older, he visited all the local churches, which is how he and Aunt Madge developed a wary sort of friendship.

Then I came to Ocean Alley for junior year of high school — furious that my parents had left me with Aunt Madge for a year and mad at the world. And in the world of Ocean Alley, I met Scoobie and that drew him closer to Aunt Madge.

We joke that he fell in love with her first, but I was more age-appropriate. Harry agrees.

But after junior year, I went back to my cosseted life in Lakewood and gave Scoobie little thought until I returned to

Ocean Alley in my mid-twenties. My heart had been crushed by the end of a marriage I hadn't realized was full of lies.

And there was Scoobie.

I came out of my reverie. I could handle the twins at a birthday party. But I needed to get to Buck's rental house to pick up Eleanor's clothes, and I didn't want the twins with me when I did that.

Aunt Madge had said that she and Harry would help with the twins. If they'd never been to a birthday party with a bunch of four-year olds, they wouldn't know how loud they can be. They might be willing to take the kids.

Chapter Twelve

I DROPPED THE TWINS at the B&B and arrived at Buck's shoreside rental to see a police car and a very irritated Buck Brock. Josh stood near the road, so I parked and joined him.

"Why are you here?" Josh asked.

"Her husband asked me to pack up her clothes so he didn't have to. My mind is a blur this morning. I forgot Morehouse said he wanted to search the place."

Josh turned fully to face me. "Why would he do that?"

I didn't want to be accused of sharing police information. "Something about her being relatively healthy and her death being fairly sudden."

For a moment, Josh's eyes showed amusement. "You still ticking off Morehouse?"

"Less since we had the twins." I nodded toward the house. "I see Buck's not happy."

"Have you ever seen him happy?"

"I hear you." I focused on what Buck was saying to Sergeant Dana Johnson.

"But I own the damn place. If the lady was sick enough to die, it needs extra hard cleaning." He gestured toward Josh without looking in that direction.

Dana, my favorite Ocean Alley officer, regarded Buck coolly. "As I told you, Sergeant Morehouse is meeting with the county prosecutor and they'll see a judge. As soon as the judge issues a warrant, the sergeant will get here."

Buck balled his fists and turned even redder. "So, no warrant, I can go in."

Dana tilted her head backwards, toward the door to the first floor unit. Yellow crime scene tape fluttered from one side, and hung to the porch deck. I hadn't seen it, since it was behind her.

I lowered my voice. "Did he try to get in?"

Josh nodded. "Dana went back to her car for more tape. She yelled at him to stop so loud you could've heard her at the courthouse."

"Wish I'd seen that."

Buck lowered his voice, but the finger he pointed at Dana made it clear he still wanted his way. Her expression didn't change.

Josh's expression grew grim. "On the boardwalk the other day, a man named Cambridge stopped me. Nice guy. But he'd heard I was going to work for Buck, and basically said to be careful."

"Because of his temper?"

"Yeah. He said Buck had even thrown punches when he was in the Sandpiper a couple of times. "

"That's a dumb thing to do." I watched Buck try to talk more calmly to Dana. "Why does he want in there so badly?"

"Rumor around town is that the woman might have eaten something here or at Java Jolt that made her sick."

Where did that rumor come from? "Buck doesn't stock the kitchen, does he?"

Josh shook his head. "I told Morehouse earlier that Buck left some cheese and crackers in the fridge for them." He shrugged. "They looked fine to me.

"When did you talk to Morehouse?"

"He had my cell phone number." He turned slightly. "Did you give it to him?"

I shook my head. "They always manage to find phone numbers. In Java Jolt, Eleanor said some chocolates might have made her queasy. Someone else must have heard her say that."

Josh turned his head quickly. "They were on the porch when I finished cleaning yesterday. I brought them in."

I shrugged. "Even if it was them, you wouldn't...where were they from?"

Josh thought for a moment. "It was wrapped, shook like a box of chocolates might. The paper wrapping had the In-Town Market's name."

"Huh." I couldn't remember Mr. Markle selling boxed chocolates other than around Valentine's Day. And why would he send them to Eleanor and Kevin?

Buck stormed toward his car, but saw me and came toward Josh and me.

"My lucky day," I muttered.

"Jolie. These people said they know you! What the hell are you trying to do to me?"

"Nothing. Not that a woman's death is all about you."

He stopped a few feet from me. "So, you heard she died? Why are you here?"

"Her husband asked Scoobie to sit with him at the hospital last night. As you would expect, he's pretty broken up."

Buck's expression shifted. "Oh, uh, yeah." He sighed. "Yeah sure, he would be."

I wondered if Buck had ever been married. I couldn't imagine a woman putting up with him for very long.

A fast-approaching car made the three of us turn. Morehouse parked and got out of his standard cruiser. He pointed a finger at Buck and drew a paper from an inside pocket of his sports jacket. "I got a warrant. I don't want any grief from you, Buck."

Buck looked at him cooly, but said nothing.

Dana stepped off the porch. When she got to Morehouse, he handed her the warrant and she studied it.

"I'll meet you in there, Sergeant Johnson." Morehouse took in Josh. "Good to see you,` Josh." He pointed a finger at me. "I thought I told you to spend time with your kids."

I shrugged. "When I went back inside the house, her husband asked me…"

Buck roared. "You been inside my place?"

In concert, Morehouse and I said, "Shut up, Buck."

Josh seemed to try to hide a smile.

I looked at Buck and back to Morehouse. "At *my* house this morning, Kevin asked me to pack up Eleanor's things so he didn't have to. I was so busy offloading the twins to Aunt Madge and Harry I wasn't thinking about your warrant."

Dana had been taking in the exchange and spoke to Morehouse. "Buck was just unlocking the door when I got here. Don't believe he'd been in before that." She turned and walked toward the house.

Morehouse glowered at Buck. "You want to be out here while we check out the place, fine. But you won't be goin' in for at least a couple days."

As Buck swore again, Josh turned away.

"Where you goin'?" Buck asked.

Josh nodded toward his car. "Home, unless you're paying me to stand around."

Morehouse pointed toward Buck and Josh. "I need to talk to both of you. Buck, stop by the station in a couple hours."

"I got things…"

"Or sit in a squad car until I got time to talk to you."

Buck stalked off. I figured he'd go to the station later. What choice did he have?

Morehouse focused on Josh. "From what Buck said when I called him earlier, you were the last person in there before the Fieldings. Anything look different? Or odd?"

Josh shook his head slowly. "My first time in the place. The last renters left it uncluttered so it was a quick clean. Buck had told me he left the cheese and crackers in the fridge, so I didn't toss them."

"But he didn't mention any chocolates?" Morehouse asked.

"They were left on the porch. I brought them in."

Morehouse jerked a thumb toward me and frowned. "Miss Nosy here…"

"Hey. And if I were, it would be Mrs."

Morehouse smiled briefly. "In Java Jolt yesterday, Jolie heard Mrs. Fielding say she had a queasy stomach, maybe from some chocolates."

Josh scowled. "My prints'll be all over that box. Or the wrapper, anyway."

"You know the Fieldings?"

Josh shook his head. "Didn't know who the renters, the freeloaders as Buck called them, would be. I doubt Buck leaves snacks for everyone, but you probably heard they didn't like the last place they rented from him."

"But no chocolates in the fridge when you got there." Morehouse didn't make it a question.

"Correct. On the porch when I finished cleaning, that's when I found them."

"And you didn't see who left them?" I asked.

"Put a cork in it, Jolie," Morehouse said.

"Didn't see anyone," Josh replied.

Morehouse looked up from his ever-present notebook. "When did you get here? And leave."

"Got here about eight-thirty and left at ten-twenty. I charge by the hour, so I made sure to look."

"Do you know when the Fieldings were expected?"

"Buck might," Josh said. "I didn't, which is why I put the candy in the fridge."

"I'll ask him." Morehouse studied Josh." Your prints are on file from that last business. You only touched the wrapped part? Was it clear plastic?"

I assumed the police could get the box. Would the wrapper still be in the trash?

"Paper wrapper. I only touched the outside of the box."

Morehouse took his phone from his pocket, and appeared to open his contacts to send a text, which he dictated. "Sergeant Johnson, would you check the trash cans for paper wrappers that would fit a box of chocolates?"

Josh and I glanced at each other but said nothing.

"So, Josh, is there anything else that struck you? About the apartment or what Buck told you to do before the people got here?"

Josh shook his head. "No."

Morehouse's phone dinged and he took it from his pocket and glanced at a text. "Funny thing is, Sergeant Johnson says she already checked the cans. There's a box of chocolates with some missin' and some trash, but no wrapper."

"So, whoever left it wanted to get rid of the evidence with their prints?" Josh asked.

"Or whoever sent it."

"Two points, Miss Marple," Morehouse said.

Josh grinned. "I believe that would be Mrs."

AS I STARTED MY CAR, Renée's distinct ring reached my mobile phone. Her stuffy voice said, "Kevin liked the idea of me staying with Mrs. Covington, Helen, after he told her. I've been here for almost an hour. I stepped out, and told her I was going to the bathroom."

"How is she?"

"As upset as our mom would be if something happened to one of us."

I stifled an impolite snort. I'm always thankful my parents moved to Florida.

Renée raised her voice. "She does not like me better!"

"You had grandkids first. How long did Kevin stay with her?"

"Barely twenty minutes. He said he had a lot of plans to make, and asked Mrs. Covington to think about any prayers or songs she would like at the memorial service."

"Ugh. I suppose that will give her a focus."

"She also wants you to come see her. Today, if possible."

My heart rate kicked up a few beats. "What? Why me? I haven't seen her in at least ten years."

"I know, but Kevin mentioned you were at Java Jolt when Eleanor started showing symptoms. I guess it'll help her understand. Or maybe accept it."

Renée knew nothing of what Sergeant Morehouse had said and I wasn't sure if I should tell her before Mrs. Covington knew. Maybe if we were together, but not on the phone. Knowing her close friend had likely been poisoned would be devastating.

I HAD ALMOST FELT bad about having asked Aunt Madge and Harry to take the twins to what was surely a raucous party.

So, after I left Buck's rental property and before the drive to Lakewood, I stopped by Toby's birthday party, which was being held in the cramped private room of "Eat for Less." The Ocean Alley family restaurant had decent food but absolutely no atmosphere — unless you counted ketchup stains on the menus.

I expected bedlam, but found twelve four-year-olds quietly eating cake and ice cream. They had even already put their hamburger plates in the trash can.

Toby's parents looked as surprised at the calm as I did.

My eyes traveled to Aunt Madge, seated next to them at a side table. She winked. Harry saw the exchange and shrugged slightly.

Lance and Leia's backs had been to me, but Toby cued them to my presence and they turned. "Hi, Mom," Lance said. "You should get some cake."

"Thanks for the idea. Maybe in a few minutes."

I had turned back to Aunt Madge when Leia turned around again. "This would be a good place for a Halloween party."

Lance licked frosting from his finger. "I could be R2D2." He tackled his ice cream.

I grinned at Toby's parents. "Hey, Dot and Barry. Thanks for inviting the kids."

Barry grinned. "Now that Madge got all of them calmed down some, I can say it's a pleasure."

I arched my eyebrows at her.

Aunt Madge shrugged. "I simply asked your duo to introduce me to their friends, which they did. And of course, they said I'm the mayor."

Harry added, "She also mentioned that the Ocean Alley police are really good about coming when anyone calls them."

Dot grinned. "And Mayor Madge said that among her many duties was to talk to the police chief many days."

Barry nodded at Aunt Madge and Harry. "Any chance you accept Saturday evening babysitting jobs?"

"Not on a bet," Harry said.

Aunt Madge grew serious as she looked from Dot and Barry to me. "Jolie has been helping the husband of the woman who fell ill at Java Jolt yesterday."

After explaining that Scoobie had been with her husband as Eleanor passed, I added, "I didn't get to pack her clothes as Kevin asked. I guess because her death was so unexpected, the police didn't want anyone else in the place Buck had rented them."

"Police!" Dot said.

Every kid turned to look at her.

"Are our friends," Aunt Madge called to them.

The kids went back to cake.

"Do they really suspect foul play?" Barry asked.

My mind envisioned a chicken scratching in the dirt.

Carefully, Aunt Madge said, "They don't need to brief me on investigations, but Captain Tortino called to say they wanted to be sure Mrs. Fielding's death was from illness."

To avoid being asked anything, I smiled and moved across the room. Some kids still ate or played with cake. Others appeared bored and ready to open presents with Toby. Lance and Leia were in the latter group.

As I helped Lance wipe some frosting from his nose, I pictured Eleanor as she left Java Jolt on a stretcher. Was it only yesterday? Life could hardly be more fleeting than her pale face.

Chapter Thirteen

TREES ALONG THE Garden State Parkway bore brilliant orange and yellow leaves, and I was glad for the chance to see them. Though not for the reason I was making the drive to Lakewood.

I couldn't imagine Mrs. Covington's pain at losing Eleanor. It didn't seem that talking to a person who saw her collapse at Java Jolt would help with that. But sometimes knowing more brings at least a measure of comfort.

My phone dinged with a text from Scoobie and I took a quick look at it. "Got your text that the kids were with Mister Rogers and Miss Piggy."

I dictated a reply. "I'm sure they'll like throwing the ball in their back yard."

"Until they get tired of dog slobber. I'll be there to pick them up in a few minutes."

"I should be home before dinner. If not, have fun." And he would. Scoobie is a perfect dad.

My thoughts wandered. Scoobie doesn't usually think he needs to go to a meeting on the spur of the moment. He always seems in touch with his feelings, but he doesn't necessarily express things he's struggling with.

We don't do a lot of triangle communication, but when he seemed distracted and almost moody a month ago, I asked George if I was missing something. George guessed it was because a new x-ray tech snapped at her coworkers a lot. I figured Scoobie had mentioned it in a meeting but didn't want me to be concerned about it.

Waiting usually pays off. A couple weeks later he seemed back to himself. Only then did he tell me about her, and that his boss, Sam, had talked to her about how she talked to her colleagues. He never said if she changed, but I suppose Sam's intervention helped in some way.

The mid-afternoon weekend traffic on the parkway was light, so I made the twenty-mile trek from Ocean Alley in good time and didn't have a long wait at the toll both when I exited. Despite living in Lakewood until eight years ago, I took a couple wrong turns after I got off the parkway. I didn't think the Simple Dreams Independent Living Apartments had been built when I lived there, and I was right.

I parked and took in the beautifully landscaped, though small, lawn. Sitting on the benches scattered about would be uncomfortable in the 50-degree temperature, but two older men walked the garden paths, talking animatedly.

At the front desk, a receptionist had me sign a visitor log. When she noted who I intended to visit, she frowned lightly. I met her eyes. "She asked me to come. My sister and I knew Eleanor."

The woman's expression cleared. "She'll be glad of the company. Such an awful thing." She gave me directions to Helen Covington's apartment down the hall.

When I got there, the door was slightly ajar and low voices carried to the hallway. I knocked softly. "Mrs. Covington? It's Jolie Gentil."

"Do come in," she called.

A man in his early seventies opened the door. He seemed glad to see me. "Helen's been looking forward to talking to you."

I entered and bent down to kiss Mrs. Covington on the cheek. "I'm so sorry." *Lame.*

"Thanks." She nodded to the man, who had remained by the door. "I really appreciate your visit, Martin."

"Didn't want you to be alone." He left quickly and shut the door behind him.

She turned to face me and used the hand holding her mobile phone to gesture to a place next to her on the loveseat. "And do call me Helen, Jolie."

I was amazed that she seemed so poised. Her permed, platinum hair looked as if she'd just left the beauty shop, and the dark purple shirtwaist dress reminded me of how Aunt Madge would dress for church.

"Can I get you a drink of water or something?"

She smiled. "Everyone asks if I want a drink. I suppose it's something to say at a time like this. If I said yes every time my teeth would be floating."

I tried to match her smile and knew it seemed forced. "I'm glad Renée could be with you after Kevin told you."

Her smile left. "You probably think it odd that I asked you to stop by. You're a lot younger than those two girls. In high school, that makes a difference."

"And I was in middle school when they graduated from high school."

"If it isn't too hard, I'd like you to talk to me about Eleanor's difficulties in the coffee shop."

I nodded. "First, everyone was really kind to her, especially Kevin."

Helen's eyebrows arched slightly and came down.

"She wasn't unconscious for long at all," I continued. "Maybe if she hadn't bumped her head on the wood table, she wouldn't have passed out."

"Kevin kept emphasizing she hit her head. It was a very hard surface?"

"Umm, not like a loud crack, but you could hear it. Luckily he sort of caught her elbow, so she didn't land on the floor. The EMTs arrived pretty quickly."

"What about before she collapsed, or whatever you call it. Did she seem happy?"

My shoulders loosened. She wanted to know her daughter hadn't been distressed before she died, that she'd felt happy. Not that I knew what had happened at the hospital.

"She seemed relaxed, smiling. Kevin was very solicitous. She was a bit…off balance. He helped her sit, brought her the tea. In fact, she mentioned that he always thought of everything."

Helen nodded slowly and looked over my shoulder. "He likes to be thought of as very capable."

What is she thinking? "Mrs. Covington, Helen, I sense you want to ask me something specific."

She nodded. "It's a difficult topic. I didn't discuss it with Renée, I suppose because I hope it means nothing, and she'll continue to know Kevin."

I smiled slightly. "Pretend I'm the stranger on the train."

"Ah. I didn't much like Hitchcock's movie, but that is a good concept. I don't really know you well."

"And I'm very discreet," I said, quietly.

She nodded firmly, but then sort of sagged as she leaned into the couch. "Good. I am very likely all wet, as the kids used to say, but I need to be sure that Eleanor's death wasn't more than the result of a head injury or something natural."

I gulped internally. "You must have a good reason for thinking about that."

"Kevin was good to, and for, my daughter in some ways. She had always been fairly quiet, and he encouraged her to do more, spend more time with friends." She paused. "Generally people he knew. They ate out a lot, mostly seafood restaurants, which are his favorite. They went to plays in New York City. He tried to get her to go dancing, but she always said she had two left feet. He bought her lovely gifts."

I said nothing while she thought for a few moments.

"Every marriage has some tension. That's just life. But lately… lately I think Eleanor was not happy." She sat up straighter. "In fact, if she hadn't started getting sick — or whatever it was — I'm not sure the marriage would have lasted much longer."

"Do you, umm, know the root of their tension?"

She nodded. "I think she had begun to think of him as controlling. When you said she said he 'thought of everything,' that's not something she always meant as a compliment. And he was not happy when she changed careers."

I didn't mention Renée's thoughts about Kevin pulling Eleanor away from her friends. "I guess I don't know much about Eleanor's work."

"She had been in what I loosely call financial services. She helped people invest their money, and she was good at it. I've no doubt her income was part of why they could live in a large home — large for two people — and take fancy vacations."

Helen got up and walked to her dining room and back. The apartment wasn't one you could pace in.

"And you think she wanted…something different?"

She sat on the couch again. "After a couple of years, Eleanor began thinking about how some people had so much money and others had so little. Not being preachy or anything, she simply decided she'd rather work on the other side of the fence."

"Kevin mentioned that she'd gone to work at a place that helped prepare disadvantaged people for jobs. I think that's right."

"Disadvantaged? Well, yes. Some had left abusive marriages, others were recovered addicts. Mostly women."

I thought about how Scoobie always said that the more precise term was *recovering*. To say *recovered* reflected an assumption that might be presumptuous.

"Did she like the work?"

"She did." Helen frowned lightly. "Kevin was not enamored with the switch and hoped she'd return to financial planning. I'm surprised he mentioned it to you."

"Not exactly to me." *Had Kevin told her Sergeant Morehouse talked to him?*

"What do you mean?"

"Did Kevin tell you he stayed with us last night? My husband Scoobie and me?"

"He said he went to stay with friends after she…passed."

"I'm, uh, glad he thought of us that way." When she gave me the kind of stare Aunt Madge uses when she thinks you're holding out on her, I continued. "You know I spoke to them in Java Jolt. I let my husband — he's an x-ray tech— know he would probably see Eleanor in the hospital. He introduced himself to Kevin, and he did do some of her x-rays."

Helen sat up straighter. "Did he say what was found?"

"Since Kevin said he could pass on information to Renée and me, my husband said they didn't see a head injury. But there would have been other tests."

Her voice rose. "He said you could talk to Renée, but not me?" Tears filled her eyes and she looked at the phone she clutched and back to me.

Gently, I said, "After she passed, he said not to talk to anyone until he could tell you. He didn't want you hearing it from someone else. Maybe he was using the same philosophy."

A tear ran down one cheek. "I would have liked to sit with my daughter."

"Gosh. I…well, of course." A lump rose in my throat. The idea of a twin dying was horrific. But not having Scoobie or me with them would make it much worse.

Helen wiped away the tear and took a tissue from a table next to the loveseat and blew her nose. She tilted the phone toward me. "The last contact I had with my daughter was this." She handed me the phone, which showed a message.

"Feeling good, but running late. We'll have some coffee." This was followed by a smiley face.

Did the smiley face help her think Eleanor had been happy? "I wish I knew a way to really help you."

She reached for the phone. "I understand why he didn't call initially. Why worry me if it was nothing big? But he knew hours before her death that she would likely die. I should have been there!"

I almost reminded her it was the middle of the night, but it wasn't up to me to make excuses for Kevin. And he had called Scoobie. Someone who didn't know Eleanor and wouldn't have talked about any prior symptoms, as Helen might have.

I nodded slowly. "Not to be intrusive, but is there a reason he wouldn't have wanted you there?"

She sighed deeply. "He has tried to help Eleanor deal with balance issues related to her so-called inner ear infection…"

"Did you think he should have done more?"

"I raised the issue of having neurological tests. When they weren't scheduled, I pushed, so Eleanor scheduled them. He was furious."

I frowned. "Was he less angry when results came in? Were they helpful?"

She grunted. "He was pleased they proved me wrong. No MS, no signs of a small stroke."

I hesitated. "Not happy they were negative, pleased you were wrong?"

"Very perceptive, Jolie. If they found something, it could have possibly been treated."

The impact of her words hit me like a brick. "Would he have a reason to want her not to be diagnosed with something treatable?"

She snapped, "A $300,000 life insurance policy."

I took in a breath. This was an incredible thought. "It's, uh, hard to know what to say. He was the beneficiary?"

"Yes. She also had a policy her father and I took out when she was born. It's sort of an investment. By the time she retired, she would have had an income from it." Her shoulders sagged. "He wanted that changed to name him as beneficiary. He said she would long outlive me, and it would be less complicated."

"And she refused?"

"She did. He would get $300,000 if she died, and he was anxious to get $25,000 more. Who would ask such a thing?"

Someone very greedy.

"This may not be what you want to hear, but you should know that the Ocean Alley Police have questions about her death." When Helen's lips parted, I added, "Because it was unexpected."

She closed her eyes and opened them again. "If he did something, I want the whole world to know. And I don't want him to get a dime because of my beautiful daughter's death."

I started to tell her about the mercury level in her blood, but I stopped myself. "Let me give you the mobile number for Sergeant Morehouse at the Ocean Alley Police."

I DROVE TOWARD RENEE'S house after I left the assisted living apartments. Helen didn't say not to talk to Renée about what she told me, and I trusted my sister to keep the information to herself. I felt slightly guilty that I hadn't told Helen that Morehouse had come to our house to talk to Kevin and that they had a warrant to search the house where Eleanor had stayed.

I cared about what might have happened to Eleanor, but it sounded as if the police were actively pursuing it, and Helen would add her worries to the mix. Still, I wanted to go over all of it with Renée.

Her van wasn't in the driveway. Her husband let me in, and told me she had taken Michelle and Julia to swimming practice, a relatively new sport for them. Andrew's eyes narrowed as I asked him to have her call me. "You aren't dragging Renée into one of your capers, are you?"

I smiled. "Scoobie just got a couple used copies of Hardy Boy mysteries, because he wants the kids to read them some day. I believe the word 'capers' is in those books."

His expression relaxed. "Sorry. She's been worried about her friend Eleanor's death, and I know she talked to you about it."

I nodded with appropriate solemnity. "She asked me to talk to Eleanor's mom, Helen, because I saw Eleanor not long before she died. I hope I brought her some comfort."

Not likely.

He offered me coffee or tea, but I declined. "Scoobie picked up the kids at Aunt Madge's. She and Harry took them to a friend's birthday party for us."

His smile was genuine. "Lance on a sugar high. Not something I'd be anxious to see."

I HADN'T DRIVEN FAR when Renée called. I put her on speaker and asked her how swimming practice had been.

"Okay, just one more activity to take the girls to. At least they both go to the same place. Sorry I missed you. How'd it go with Helen?"

"Interesting. Where are you?"

Renée laughed lightly. "You don't usually stop by unannounced, so Andrew thinks you're up to something. I'm on the front porch while the girls are telling him about swimming practice."

"Ok. It was incredibly sad. Did she show you the message from Eleanor on her phone?"

"Yes. That's what started me crying."

"I teared up too. But there was something else. Mrs. Covington didn't say so in so many words, but she's wondering if Kevin had something to do with Eleanor's death."

Renée almost shouted. "What?!"

"She mentioned a large life insurance policy."

"Gosh." Renée paused for a moment. "I really don't like the guy, but kill Eleanor?"

"I know, it seems far-fetched. But put that together with the Ocean Alley Police asking ques…"

"What do you mean?"

Too late I remembered I hadn't wanted to tell her on the phone. "I guess we didn't talk about that."

"Gee," she said, "I guess not. What on earth are they asking questions about?"

I relayed what Morehouse had told Kevin Fielding about mercury levels in Eleanor's blood. "And Kevin didn't mention that to you or her mother?"

"Not one word."

I changed from the left lane on the Garden State Parkway to the right so I could focus less on drivers trying to get me to speed up. "While I'm digesting that, could you look up mercury on your phone?"

"If you'd told me earlier, I would have looked it up during swim practice." She paused. "Hmm. I can read you what it says here, but if we don't know her levels it's kind of meaningless."

"We'll just have to go with Morehouse saying it was high. What did you find?"

"Okay. Mercury concentration in whole blood is usually lower than 10 micrograms per liter. It can go as high as 20 and still be considered normal. Hmm. There's a lot here."

I waited while she continued to read what she'd found.

"Okay," Renée continued. "The blood mercury concentration can rise to 35 micrograms per liter after long-term exposure to mercury vapor."

"And Morehouse said he thought her balance symptoms might indicate some long-term exposure, but then she had to get a lot more apparently not too long before she died."

"I'm no expert, Jolie, but if she was around the vapors, wouldn't Kevin be? He doesn't seem sick."

"He even said that. And if he found a way to expose her, how could he avoid exposure himself?"

"That's almost too evil to think about." Renée seemed to take the phone away from her mouth as she called, "On the porch. Be right in, sweetheart." The phone came back to her mouth. "Gotta go, sis."

"You're the best. I'm sorry about Eleanor."

"Leave it to your Sergeant Morehouse."

Chapter Fourteen

WE HAD A QUIET dinner of macaroni and cheese with peas, raw veggies, and fruit for dessert. It's our tried-and-true method of countering large quantities of sugar after birthday parties or sno-cones on the boardwalk.

Scoobie answered the phone just after we put the kids to bed, and he smirked. "Did you want me to get them up so you could read them a bedtime story?" After a few seconds, he laughed. "Come on over."

"Who was that?"

"George wanted to know if the kids were in bed yet. He's coming over."

"Is Ramona coming, too?"

"Gee, I didn't ask. You want me to call him back?"

I shook my head. "He wants to talk about Eleanor. She won't want to encourage him."

Scoobie frowned. "It's not like he works for the paper."

"I'll turn on hot water for tea. And I think he's just plain nosy."

RAMONA DID COME WITH George, and the four of us sat at the dining room table sampling different hot and cold teas.

"I never expected," Ramona said, "to be drinking so much tea."

Scoobie grinned. "We do have wine for guests."

She shook her head. "No thanks."

George took a folded piece of lined yellow paper from the breast pocket of his Hawaiian shirt. "I've been trying to find out more about this Eleanor woman."

"Eleanor Fielding," Scoobie said, quietly. "A good friend of Jolie's sister."

"Sorry. You said that when you answered my text. A guy from the ME's office said they're being careful because of the mercury level in her blood…"

"Is it public knowledge now?" I asked.

"Probably not the mercury, but the ME has classified her cause of death as 'undetermined pending toxicity tests.' Tiffany from the paper called me because she knows no one at the hospital will talk to her about it."

Scoobie held up his hands. "I sure won't."

"I know, but the police told Buck Brock he can't get back into his property for a couple days. Maybe they want to be sure there's no mercury exposure."

I looked at Scoobie. "I guess they'll ask Buck if he broke any fluorescent light bulbs in there."

"They have mercury in them?" Ramona asked.

"Small amounts," Scoobie said. "You have to be really careful if you break one. Wear a mask if you clean up the glass."

"Damn. I broke one of those swirly bulbs once," George said.

"Did you clean it up right away?" Scoobie asked. "If you didn't, it might have dissipated some. Plus, you wouldn't have put your face on the glass pieces."

George nodded. "Now that I think about it, it was in a lamp on the screened porch."

"Good ventilation," Ramona said.

"The thing is," Scoobie said, "there was a library in Muncie, Indiana that had to close — twice, I think — because of mercury vapor from a broken bulb."

I smiled. "You would know about a library."

"Yeah. If I remember right, they cleaned it up, and then somebody ran a vacuum that had some of the pieces, and it spread all over the carpet. Lots of cleanup, and it was closed for quite a while."

"Eleanor wasn't in Muncie," I said.

"Megan said," George continued, "that they seemed like a loving couple when they were in Java Jolt. And she's not happy the health department was over there today looking for indications of mercury. They disassembled her latte machine, too."

"That's so unfair," Ramona said.

Scoobie shrugged. "They had to do it, probably." He nodded to George. "Did Megan have to close?"

"Not for long."

"It's the off-season," I said. "Probably no one will even know."

George looked uncomfortable. "I think someone took pictures of the health department staff in masks."

Ramona and I said, "George!"

"Not me. Tiffany."

I almost asked who told the *Ocean Alley Press* reporter to go to Java Jolt, but I stopped myself. I glanced at Scoobie. "Since people are discussing it, I think it's fair to say Morehouse mentioned the mercury levels when he talked to Kevin Fielding, but Kevin had no idea where she might have been exposed."

"And you know about this how?" George asked, more dumbfounded than accusatory.

Scoobie spoke. "I met Kevin when they were doing some x-rays, and told him I was Renée's brother-in-law. When it looked as if she might not make it last night, he called and asked me to sit with him at the hospital."

George flushed. I knew he wanted to ask Scoobie why he hadn't told him, but he didn't bother because he knew the answer would be that when it came to hospital patients, it was none of George's business.

"Poor man," Ramona said. "Does she have other family?"

I glanced at Scoobie and shrugged, then relayed Renée's visit to Helen Covington, her request to talk to me, and my trip to Lakewood to see the bereaved mother. "Because I saw Eleanor in Java Jolt," I finished.

After a pause, George asked, "Did she have any ideas about the mercury exposure?"

"It doesn't float around in too many assisted living places," Ramona said.

I shook my head. "Kevin didn't want her to hear about Eleanor's death from anyone but him." I didn't add that he waited nearly six hours to tell her and didn't mention the mercury. "I got the impression he hadn't been Mrs. Covington's favorite person. I told her Kevin was really concerned about Eleanor when they were in Java Jolt."

George pressed. "*Was* concerned or *seemed* concerned?"

"Give it a rest," Scoobie said. "A woman died and her family is grieving."

We got through an awkward couple minutes, and then Ramona asked Scoobie if he thought the hospital gift shop would carry note cards if she designed some using her water colors. He said he'd find out who she could talk to at the hospital.

Possibly as penance, George carried the mugs to the kitchen and put them in the dishwasher. As he finished, he raised his eyebrows at me.

Scoobie and Ramona were in the living room. I whispered. "Maybe do a credit check on Kevin Fielding."

WE DON'T ALWAYS meet Aunt Madge and Harry at First Prez for Sunday services, but we do it often enough that the twins know the drill. As Lance says, if they wake up Sunday and the chairs in their room have patent leather shoes for Leia and a tie for him, they're going to church.

Scoobie poured milk on the twins' cereal. "There are donuts after church. You can split one."

"Tell us the story again!" Lance said.

"Leia paused with her spoon in the air. "Tell us how you met Mommy."

"Well," Scoobie began, "you know I went to a lot of churches looking for the best donuts."

"No!" Lance yelled.

"You went because of Aunt Madge," Leia said.

In truth, Scoobie did try most churches in town. He largely went to St. Anthony's and First Prez because the donuts were plentiful and his mother was not always interested in feeding him well. But he'd known Aunt Madge since he was in elementary school because she volunteered in a friend's second-grade classroom sometimes. She remains the only person in town who calls him by his given name, Adam.

"And I did like Aunt Madge," he continued.

"And Mister Rogers and Miss Piggy," Lance said.

This was a first. "Actually," I said, "they weren't born yet. Aunt Madge had a cute little black dog named Petey. He used to sit under the table to see if your dad would give him pieces of turkey if he came for Thanksgiving."

"How come we can't give turkey to Miss Piggy?" Leia asked.

"Because," Scoobie began, and looked to me.

"Aunt Madge and Uncle Harry had their floors refinished. They don't want slobber on them."

We've never specifically told the twins that Scoobie and I only knew each other in eleventh grade, when I stayed with Aunt Madge for that school year. I think they assume we were pals all the way through school. Since we both know so many people around town, they haven't figured out that I grew up where my sister did — in Lakewood, with their grandparents.

I don't feel like telling them about my first marriage and my embezzler ex-husband's habit of drowning our money in the toilets that masquerade as slot machines. They'll have a dozen questions, and I'm not sure how to tell them my former husband is still in prison — as far as I know, anyway. All in good time.

After a mad scramble for the doll Leia likes to take to church, we left home in time to slide into a pew with Aunt Madge and Harry just before the service started.

My mind tends to wander during sermons. I found myself wishing the hospital's retired head nurse, a friend of Aunt Madge's, were still alive; I could casually ask her for information on Eleanor's death.

My gaze fell on Harriet, a hospital staffer who refers to herself as a floater because she works in different units. She was a nursing assistant for years, and likes to kid me about the times I've ended up in the ER. If I could get her ear during coffee hour, I'd mention that Eleanor was a friend of Renée's and I'm glad Scoobie was the one to help her in radiology. That should start a conversation.

After the service, the twins wanted to sit with Aunt Madge and Harry at one of the card tables. As Scoobie and I helped them each to half a donut and small glasses of OJ, a man called to Scoobie from the other side of the community room.

For a couple seconds, Scoobie had a slight frown, then it cleared. I nodded to the twins. "I've got this."

Scoobie met the man in the middle of the room. I considered this good fortune and glanced around for Harriet. She stood next to the coffee pot, adding cream to her cup.

My eyes met Aunt Madge's, which twinkled with amusement. She knows me too well. "I'll be right back."

Harry handed Leia a napkin and Lance said he didn't need one.

I got to Harriet and she grinned. "Jolie Gentil as I live and breathe. You know, when some people have kids we see them in the ER now and then. Your kids seem to be keeping you occupied so you don't show up as often yourself."

"You're as funny as a rubber crutch."

"That's an old line. What's up?"

"Did you hear the woman who came into the ER from Java Jolt was my sister Renée's friend?"

Harriet's brows knitted. "Gee, I was with her briefly in the ER, before they sent her to ICU. I'm sorry."

"It was a shame. Have you ever known someone to die of mercury toxicity? I mean, how does a person even get enough exposure to get sick?"

"We've all been discussing that." She lowered her voice. "When she was in the ER, she wanted her husband to call her mother, but he said she should rest. If staff had known she would die so quickly, we would have helped him realize she needed to talk with her mom."

I felt awful. Should I tell Helen Covington her daughter had asked to talk to her? Or would that make it harder for her?

"I met her mother yesterday. You can imagine how…"

Harriet's eyes focused on something over my left shoulder. "Scoobie's trying to get your attention."

I turned to wave to him and mouthed, "Be right there." I looked back at Harriet. "Good talking to you."

When I turned fully around, I realized Scoobie was heading toward the juice dripping from the card table and Leia looked about to cry. She's so smart, but I wish she had more of Lance's nature sometimes. He'd say oops and grab a napkin.

I got to Leia in time to quell tears. "Accidents happen."

"Yes," Aunt Madge said, dryly. "Ask your mom what happened to a bowl of cranberry jelly one year at Thanksgiving."

"I had help," I said.

"From who?" Lance asked.

"Remember that little dog I told you Aunt Madge had? I was trying to sneak him a piece of turkey."

Leia turned to Harry. "Was he a good dog?"

He wiggled his eyebrows at Leia. "That was before I met my bride."

He has a way of making her giggle, and Lance and I joined in. Scoobie focused on a napkin soaked with juice and didn't look at me. *What's gotten into him?*

WHEN THE TWINS WENT down for a nap, Scoobie said he would head to a Sunday noon AA meeting. "Sorry, Jolie. I guess watching Eleanor die had more of an effect on me than I expected."

I crossed the living room in three strides and gave him a strong hug. "This may sound weird, but I'd be worried if it didn't bother you a lot."

He rested his head atop mine for a moment. "That's true."

I pulled back and touched his cheek. "Take as long as you need. Are you going to meet George?"

"I don't think so." He winked at me. "George probably does need a reminder to let people tell their own stories."

"A twelve-step slogan?"

"The concept is. Is there anything I should pick up at the grocery store on the way home?"

"Nope." As he turned to go, I asked, "Who was that guy who waved at you at church?"

He seemed not to remember at first. "A guy from the hospital I don't know very well."

He had pulled out of the driveway before I realized he hadn't said the man's name.

With an hour to myself, I opened my laptop and went to LinkedIn to find out more about Kevin Fielding. I didn't know if he'd have an account, but he seemed like someone who would like to tell the world a lot about himself.

And he did. Graduate of Brown University in chemistry, Senior Analyst at Good Life Pharmaceuticals. *What an ironic name. Eleanor's life did not have a good ending.*

He mentioned his college fraternity and that he was active in an alumni group. What struck me as most interesting was that he seemed to manage a team that dealt with counteracting ingestion of toxic substances. Would mercury be one he knew a lot about? And how would he get enough to give some to Eleanor over time? It made no sense.

My cell phone rang and I answered it almost absently.

Helen Covington's voice was strong and angry. "Jolie. Thank you for giving me Sergeant Morehouse's phone number."

"You're welcome. Did he, uh, help you know more?"

"He didn't pass on much, but after what he first told me I didn't hear much."

"What was that?"

I began to get a beep in my ear, meaning someone else was calling. I looked at the screen and saw Sergeant Morehouse's number. Since he could be trying to tell me not to talk to Helen, I ignored him.

Her tone became less strident. "He let me know that she died because of mercury poisoning. They think she had long-term exposure and then may have eaten something with some in it!"

"Good heavens." I thought fast I didn't want to let on that I knew more, but wanted to know if she had any ideas. "Do the police have any ideas how she got it?"

"That's what has me steamed. They have to know something, but all the man said was it's "too early to jump to conclusions.'"

"Having an answer won't bring Eleanor back, but I've known Sergeant Morehouse for a while. He can be like a dog with a bone. If it's not accidental, he won't let go."

Her voice caught. "That's good to know."

When she said nothing else, I asked, "Are you working with Kevin to plan a service?"

"No. When he didn't call me, I phoned him to suggest a couple of things. He was noncommittal. My own minister has been over a couple of times. Kevin hasn't even been in touch about a date."

"I, uh, maybe he's waiting until he knows when he can, um, plan something with the funeral home." *Lame.*

"The only thing he said, and he was quite blunt about it, is that he didn't want to wait for them, whoever *them* is, to release her body. He'll plan a memorial service before then. Emphasis on *he* would plan it."

"I'm so sorry. Are any of Eleanor's friends visiting you?"

"Several. A couple from her book club heard and have stopped by. I have no idea who has heard. There hasn't been a notice in the paper here."

"The *Ocean Alley Press* doesn't publish on Sundays now. If there's an article on Monday I'll let you know."

We said our goodbyes, and I thought more about the conversation. If things proceeded as they usually did after a murder, Eleanor's body would not be released for days. I hated that I knew that.

Chapter Fifteen

AFTER HANGING UP WITH HELEN, I called an irritated Sergeant Morehouse. "I talked to Mrs. Fielding's mother and she said you visited her. I told you…"

"If you'd ask instead of trying to bully me, you'd know I only went up there because she asked Renée if I would. Because I was with Eleanor when she fainted, or whatever, at Java Jolt."

After a pause of several seconds, Morehouse said, "I will try to ask questions instead of make assumptions if you will listen to what I tell you."

I felt a little guilty about snapping at him. I know how hard he throws himself into cases. "Mrs. Covington just called to say she had spoken to you. I was about to let you know what she said, in case she hadn't mentioned some of it to you."

"Why in the hell wouldn't she tell me everything?" he demanded.

"Gee, because it's a horrible time for her, since her daughter just died. And maybe you didn't ask?"

Another pause. "What'd you talk about?"

"She wishes you would tell her more than it's too early to jump to conclusions, and I told her you will be like a dog with a bone until you figure it out." I went over Kevin seemingly excluding her from planning a memorial service, and how a lack of any formal notice in the paper or online meant she had no idea who knew or didn't know about Eleanor's death.

Morehouse grunted. "Strange behavior, rude even. But not illegal."

"Granted. But on Saturday, Mrs. Covington said she also thinks Kevin might have been anxious to inherit Eleanor's $300,000 life insurance policy. She admits that's a suspicion."

After a much longer pause, he said, "She told me she thinks he didn't want her at the hospital because she might contradict information he was providing to medical staff."

"I wondered about that, too. Did you talk to my sister?"

"Renée? Haven't seen her since your wedding. Why would I talk to her about this?"

"She said Eleanor used to have a lot of antiques, including a barometer. Keven encouraged her to get rid of her antiques."

"Does she know what happened to it?"

"Nope. But you mentioned mercury in thermometers, so I thought I'd pass on the barometer info."

He sighed, something Morehouse rarely does. "This is helpful, and I don't mind hearing anything you want to pass on."

I felt almost vindicated. "Thank you."

"I want you to think about this. Personally, I think Eleanor was given deliberate doses of mercury. I don't know how except maybe the last dose was in those chocolates. But if someone had been trying to kill her, how much do you want to irritate that person?"

It was my turn to pause. "Not so much."

"I got no reason to be certain her husband harmed her. But you watch enough TV to know the spouse or boyfriend is where we look first." He hung up.

I had no idea who killed Eleanor Fielding. Her mother had some suspicions, and they made sense to me. But was I willing to irritate a killer by trying to find out more? Someone who killed once would likely be willing to murder again to avoid getting caught. I didn't need to put a target on my back.

BEFORE THE TWINS WERE UP ON Monday, Scoobie and I read the *Ocean Alley Press* article together, me looking over his shoulder.

Eleanor Fielding of Lakewood, New Jersey died early Saturday morning at Ocean Alley Hospital. She had fainted while at Java Jolt Coffee Shop Friday afternoon, and initially there was no indication of what condition caused this. She'd had balance problems over the last few months, but no cause had been identified.

Toxicology tests at the hospital showed high levels of mercury in Ms. Fielding's blood. Though familiar in liquid form, such as in older glass thermometers, mercury is actually a metal. Exposure over time or in a large dose can be highly toxic.

Mercury poisoning requires specific testing to diagnose it. Symptoms can be similar to the flu, such as headache, dizziness, and fatigue. Other people may have problems with vision or hearing, experience muscle weakness, and tremors. Still others may have changes in mood or personality, or memory loss.

Because many of these symptoms are the same as other illnesses, mercury may not be considered initially.

Ms. Fielding's husband, Kevin, was distraught and able to provide little information to police or this newspaper. He had no idea where she had been exposed, and in a brief interview questioned whether a "small, regional hospital" had made an accurate diagnosis.

Ocean Alley Police would release little information, but did say that lab tests had been repeated several times and a sample of her blood sent to the state medical examiner. They are questioning friends and relatives about Ms. Fielding's recent activities.

Police do not believe the exposure was in Java Jolt. Police Chief Tortino said that, "In an abundance of caution, state and local officials examined the coffee shop and found no indication of mercury. No other customers became ill."

Funeral arrangements are pending.

We finished about the same time and I put a hand on his shoulder. "At least it says Java Jolt wasn't the source. But no mention of where she was staying."

Scoobie glanced at the article again. "And no quote from the hospital. Or mention of who wrote the piece."

"Had to be Tiffany, don't you think?"

He shrugged. "In the old days, George would have at least said if the hospital refused to comment. Check out the sidebar on mercury."

SIDEBAR: What is mercury and why is it so dangerous?

When we think of a metal, we expect something hard, such as gold or silver. Mercury is the only metal that is liquid at room temperature. In scientific terms, mercury is liquid because it does not share its valence electrons. Most metals are hard and have a high melting point. This is because they readily share their valence electrons with the neighboring atom.

Most of the world's mercury is obtained from its main ore, cinnabar, fifty percent of which is mined in Italy and Spain. Cinnabar is usually found in granular crusts or veins associated with volcanic activity and hot springs. The ore is bright red in color and small droplets of mercury metal can sometimes be found within the ore itself.

Mercury has been used in older glass thermometers, some dental fillings (called amalgam fillings), and barometers. Starting in Roman times, it was employed as a cure for syphilis, but its use was discontinued at the end of the 19th century because of neurological damage.

Mercury is used for a number of reasons, such as extraction of gold and silver or for measuring and controlling pressure. It is in some electrical and electronic switches and fluorescent bulbs, but is contained within those devices.

Fish can be a source, but someone would have to regularly eat those known to contain higher levels of mercury. Saltwater fish include halibut, shrimp, snapper, tuna and swordfish, while freshwater fish are trout, bass, and pike.

Its use is highly regulated to prevent accidental exposure. Mercury is a clear problem for humans because it is not expelled from our cells. There have been accidental exposures through fluorescent bulb breakage, but if the remnants are carefully cleaned up the risk is relatively minimal.

Use a broom and dustpan and put the residue in a separate garbage container — not a kitchen trash can. Do not vacuum the area, as mercury could be carried throughout a home or office as other rooms are vacuumed.

There have been questions about the use of thimerosal in some vaccines. Not all types of mercury are the same. Some, such as mercury in some kinds of fish, stay in the human body and can make people sick.

Thimerosal is a different kind of mercury and doesn't stay in the body. Some adult flu shots may have it in them, but patients can ask for a shot that does not contain thimerosal. The substance is not in children's flu vaccines. Vaccines are not, in any way, linked to autism, as was falsely claimed in an article (since retracted) in the 1980s.

"I feel as if I just had a chemistry class and will probably fail the test."

Scoobie stood and kissed me on the cheek before taking his packed lunch from the refrigerator. "We had general information on toxic substances in college, but I can see why her doctors in Lakewood might not have thought to look for mercury exposure at first."

"Nice of Kevin to take a dig at our hospital."

Scoobie shrugged. "The guy just lost his wife. Suddenly. He's lashing out."

I walked him to the front door. I hadn't told him much of what Mrs. Covington said. Scoobie had placed himself solidly in Kevin's corner. He sat with the man for hours while they watched Eleanor die. He had every reason to think Kevin's grief was genuine.

In the back of my mind, I wondered if the man was a good actor.

BY THE TIME I got to the office, I'd had a full morning packed into two hours. It took longer than usual to drop the kids at daycare, because Leia wanted me to help her look for a book she hadn't been able to find on Friday.

I drove by the Victorian Buck had put in a contract for, figuring that we would probably get the request to do the appraisal. I didn't see any small outbuildings, which would make it a faster visit. A number of boards on the porch had been replaced, meaning there would be less to argue with Buck and Lester about. This would be the first place I'd appraised that Lester had listed and Buck had bought. I expected fireworks no matter what our appraisal decision would be.

At the office, I found a fax from Lester commending us on work we had done a couple of weeks ago. I found that suspicious. He must be trying to butter me up. I turned on the computer and then listened to messages on the office phone. One was from Buck, who sounded halfway out of his mind.

"Listen Jolie, someone's trying to frame me. It's all over town that whatever that woman ate she got from the refrigerator in my place. What are we gonna do?"

I picked up the phone and dialed him. Before he could start talking, I said, "Buck, there was no mention of your property in the article in the paper today. If anyone is saying that Eleanor was poisoned because of food you left for your guests, tell them to call Sergeant Morehouse or Sergeant Johnson. The police don't have any reason to think you provided anything that may have had mercury in it."

"Easy for you to say. It isn't your reputation."

I tried to make my tone jovial. "Would that be the reputation that required you to visit with the Landlord Tenant Commission last week?" When he said nothing, I added, "Just kidding. You need to stand up for yourself. I'm sure you can do that."

There was a pause of several seconds, and he asked, "How well do you know that guy Josh. I mean, he wouldn't have done that would he?"

"We hadn't seen him for a few years, but he's a good guy. Plus, if he did that and got caught, he'd be out of work and back in..."

"Back in where?"

I wished I hadn't said that. I didn't want to mention that he'd spent a brief time in jail, so I said, "He spent some time in a VA center being treated for PTSD. I'm sure you could ask him about it." *Probably a big lie of omission.*

Again a pause. "OK. I don't really think you'd give me a bum recommendation. He asked me to give him some of his wages as a small room somewhere. I'm thinking of making it a tiny apartment in that Victorian you're going to appraise. Then I'd have somebody I know on site."

"As long as you don't tell other tenants he'll do repairs or something, you wouldn't be taking advantage of him."

'Thanks for talking to me. I gotta go."

I shook my head. When did I become Buck Brock's advisor and confidant?

The fax machine dinged, and I retrieved the page it spit out. Ocean Alley Credit Union requested that Steele Appraisals evaluate the value of the house at 541 Seashore Drive. Buck must have already known that when he talked to me.

I went to a Miller County database and pulled some basic information about the property, when it had last been sold, and for how much. I stuck that in a folder, picked up my purse, and made for the front door. I found Lester with a fist raised to knock on the door. "I didn't hear you walk up porch steps."

"Guess I have a tough choice to make. Can I come in?"

"How about walking with me to my car? I'm about to go appraise that Victorian you listed and Buck has a contract on."

He quickly became his brash self. "Now that really is a diamond in the rough. So much potential, and a great location."

"You know I take everything into consideration. Is something bothering you?"

"I got a what-do-you-call-it, a dilemma. People are saying all this stuff about Buck that isn't true probably, and I gotta decide whether to speak up to defend him. I hate like hell to do that."

I stopped to face him. "It's good not to be mean, but what do you really know about Buck? Someone told Josh that a couple of times he threw punches at the Sandpiper."

Lester shrugged. "I heard that from a guy was there, and I asked Buck about it. He said he'd owned some property with the man and was supposed to sell his part to pay off his ex-wife. The guy was real angry because he didn't want to sell right then."

"That sounds like something to discuss with lawyers, not to fight about in a bar."

"Maybe the guy tried. Hard to imagine Buck in a calm conversation in a lawyer's office. But that's not the kind of thing I'm talking about. Couple guys from the Board of Realtors are saying he tried to steal a listing from them. That's horse…manure. Buck don't want to sell houses. He wants to buy them."

"So, you say you have a dilemma. I think you probably already know what to do." I smiled. "If you don't, check with Mayor Madge. She always gives good advice."

"Yeah, yeah. You should call me after you make the house visit. I can maybe advise you on some things."

"Lester, we do impartial appraisals. There's a process to follow if you think we got something wrong. Now I really have to run." I did a friendly wave and popped the locks on my SUV.

Chapter Sixteen

I SPENT TWO-AND-A-HALF HOURS going through the five apartments in the building on Seashore. They varied in size from a 500-square-feet efficiency on the top floor to the 1,200 square feet unit that was formerly the huge main floor of a single-family home.

Part of the problem was the number of pictures I had to take. Few rooms had 90 degree corners. Closets were in odd places, and some had separate dining areas and some did not. I needed to say a great deal about each unit when I wrote the report.

The list of items that would bring down the value was as long as a garden hose. I didn't find any rotting wood or evidence of termites, and I supposed anything else could be addressed by the seller. My guess was if they had wanted to do that they wouldn't have listed it in as-is condition. They certainly hadn't spent any time improving the minimal landscaping.

Lester would not be happy that the agreed-upon contract price was probably a few thousand dollars too high. It would take me more than a day to find comparable sales and map out the measurements on our appraisal software.

Harry was at the office when I returned. "The mother of the woman whose daughter died Saturday morning called. She said Renée had let her know about the article in the *Press*. She didn't say you had to call her back."

I texted Renée to be supportive, but I didn't have time for a long conversation this morning.

Renée called me back. "At least it makes the death public. Eleanor's husband seems not to have posted any information. There's not even an obituary."

"Agreed. People handle things differently, but I can't imagine not at least posting a death notice in local papers."

As soon as I hung up, the phone rang again. Harry glanced at the caller ID strip on the office phone. "I think it's the same woman. You want to get it?"

"Sure." I lifted the receiver and had barely said hello when Mrs. Covington began to sob.

Between sobs and sputters, she said Kevin had called her to say the memorial service would be the next night. He had not scheduled time to talk to the family beforehand, and overrode her response that there could be as many as 200 people who would want to extend sympathies to him and to her.

I said several things to comfort her, but there really was no way to make her feel any better.

Harry had gotten the gist of the conversation and raised one finger. I raised my eyebrows at him. Quietly he said, "There's no reason she can't schedule a gathering before or after the memorial service."

He had a point. I uncovered the mouthpiece and said, "Mrs. Covington, Helen, Aunt Madge's husband has an idea. You probably know the funeral home staff better than Kevin does. Why don't you talk to them about reserving a room yourself, and greeting people there for the hour before the service?"

"Do you suppose I could?" she asked.

"You won't know until you ask, but you are her mother, and they know Eleanor lived there all her life. What he's doing is very strange. If they say no, you can have the paper put in a notice on the same page as the memorial service announcement, telling people to meet at your church community room or something like that."

"I didn't tell you the worst part. There is no church service. Just a memorial service at the funeral home. He said he didn't need suggestions from me for people who might want to speak about Eleanor."

"It's hard to know what to say. But you probably don't need to worry about hurting Kevin's feelings. He certainly hasn't been concerned with yours, and it's not likely you'll continue a strong relationship with him."

Her voice choked. "I hope I never see the bastard again after her service!"

I bet that's the first time Helen has used that word. " I know you have a lot of friends in Lakewood. Would someone go to the funeral home with you?"

She paused for perhaps ten seconds. "I do have friends here, though many would not be able to do that. Have you ever had to arrange a funeral? The only one I've done was my husband's, and Eleanor did much of it with me."

I had a sinking feeling that life was about to get more complicated. I looked at Harry and shook my head. "My husband and I planned his father's funeral a few years ago. It is difficult. Would you like me to go to the funeral home with you?"

In a soft voice she asked, "Do you think your aunt would also go with us? I've seen her on TV a lot. She's such a strong person, and people know she isn't afraid to speak her mind. Maybe the funeral home would assume she would let a lot of people know they refused to let me have a reception room."

"She's a very kind person. I would need to check with her, because she has a pretty full schedule. I know she feels very badly about what you've gone through. How about if I call you back in an hour or so?"

Helen said goodbye and I hung up the phone. Harry asked, "What was that all about?"

I explained what Helen had asked.

He nodded slowly. "On the one hand I wish I had kept my mouth shut. On the other hand, if anything happened to you or Scoobie or my kids or Renée, I would be beside myself. Let's see what the old gal has to say."

AT TWO-FIFTEEN MONDAY afternoon, Harry and I got into his Buick sedan and headed for the Cozy Corner to pick up Aunt Madge. She had said that if we got an old-fashioned funeral home director, he might be more likely to do what Mrs. Covington wanted if she had a man supporting her decision. I hated that she was probably right.

We didn't talk a lot on the drive to Lakewood. Aunt Madge asked several questions about Eleanor's life since high school. "I want them to think that I know her better than I do. She spent a lot of time at the shore with Renée when they were in high school, but I haven't seen her a lot since then."

Harry asked, "So when are you going to tell me that I have to beat someone up if they don't do what you want?"

"Probably not right that minute," Aunt Madge said. "We would have to do it in the evening in a dark alley."

I had mixed feelings about what we were doing. If Kevin hadn't killed her and was as devastated as Scoobie thought he was, it might be painful for him to spend time with a lot of Eleanor's longtime friends. On the other hand, if he was avoiding her friends and deliberately cutting her mother out of planning, including even the ability to grieve with friends, he was worse than a red tide on Labor Day weekend.

We pulled into the Fond Memories Funeral Home (motto: 'We're here when you need us most') at three-thirty. We had offered to pick up Helen Covington, but she said the man who was sitting with her when I went to Lakewood Saturday would drive her. I thought his name was Martin.

Harry's idea was that we should not make an appointment. They would have to see us if several bereaved people walked into their lobby, and we didn't want to give the staff the chance to tell Kevin Mrs. Covington's plans, or worse, refuse to talk to us.

As we walked into the lobby Aunt Madge transformed from caring family member to mayor with a mission. "Good afternoon." She glanced at the name badge on the woman's desk. "Miss Ellington, we're here to see the funeral director to make some additional plans for Eleanor Fielding."

The puzzled woman replied, "I think arrangements are made, but I can certainly let you talk to one of our directors." She stood and walked down a short hallway and knocked on a closed door.

A man came out immediately, wearing a concerned expression and the expected black suit and gray tie. Aunt Madge had positioned herself so he would see her first, and he shook her hand. "I'm so sorry if we didn't handle something as Mr. Fielding wanted."

Mayor Madge took his hand. "I'm Madge Richardson, mayor of Ocean Alley. Our family has long been friends with Helen Covington." She gestured to where Helen stood on her right. "She was not included in any decisions, and is distressed that there is no opportunity to meet with friends. She would like to rent space on the same floor the evening of the memorial service. That way, friends can gather to support each other and her."

The man, whose name tag said Robert Butler, shook his head slightly. "Generally, the spouse, if there is one, makes all arrangements."

Harry spoke up. "We checked the New Jersey code before we drove up. There's no mention of a law or local regulation stating that other family members can't participate in the process." He gave a small smile that could also have served as a warning. "As you know, Eleanor Covington lived here all of her life and there will probably be hundreds of people wanting to greet Mrs. Covington and grieve together. There's no reason that Kevin Fielding has to participate in all aspects of the grieving process if he prefers to attend only the service."

Robert Butler's back stiffened. He gestured that we should follow him down the hall. "Let's discuss this in a more private setting."

When he turned for us to follow him down the hall, Aunt Madge gave Helen Covington a thumbs up sign. I wasn't sure we had made the point strongly enough that she would be permitted to rent a room, but I thought we were well on our way.

NEGOTIATIONS, WHICH WOULD BE an appropriate term, took an hour and a half. Aunt Madge and Harry stressed, and Mrs. Covington firmly agreed, that we were having a private conversation and there was no need to bring Kevin Fielding into it. He had already rejected Mrs. Covington's request to have a greeting time before the service.

Any time Robert Butler seemed to waiver in his willingness to provide assistance, Helen would mention one of two things. First, how much she appreciated the service she had received when her husband died. She added that she knew Eleanor's memorial service was a much less expensive arrangement because there was no body to be embalmed or casket to be provided.

Second, she asked if Mr. Butler could help her put a notice in the paper about where a visitation would be held, since Fond Memories Funeral Home would not provide a venue.

I marked the latter point as Mr. Butler becoming more agreeable. Mr. Covington's service had probably been held in the church, but I wouldn't have been surprised to know that Mrs. Covington paid the funeral home at least $15,000 for what they did. Kevin's purchase would be substantially less.

Butler was free to infer, and he surely did, that Mrs. Covington would let friends know if the funeral home did not let her do as she requested. He didn't need to be told older people have a lot of friends who may need funeral services in the near future.

We told Helen we would drive her home. At her insistence, we went into her apartment for coffee. The three of us had a lot to do besides arranging for Eleanor's visitation, but Helen Covington was drawn and exhausted. It didn't seem right to rush away.

ON THE CAR RIDE HOME, Harry asked why Renée hadn't been with us.

Aunt Madge said, "You need to learn to think like a sleuth. Kevin can't be too angry with Renée if she didn't join the rebellious group. If he continues to talk some to her, then we'll know more about his reaction to the plan."

Harry shook his head. "Darling, aren't we supposed to be encouraging Jolie to stay away from dangerous situations? An angry husband, one some people think may have had a role in his wife's death, might not be the best person to tick off."

I spoke up. "I'm not claiming to know Aunt Madge better than you do, but it really gets her hackles up when she thinks someone's trying to take advantage of a senior citizen."

Harry glanced at Aunt Madge, who sat beside him in the front seat. "And those hackles are up."

WHEN I TOLD SCOOBIE what I would be doing in the afternoon and asked him to be sure to pick up the kids, I didn't go into a lot of detail. I rarely call him at work, so if he was angry, I would simply say I didn't want to take a lot of his time away from patients.

If Aunt Madge and Harry had not been in on the plan, he might have blown a gasket that evening. Something he rarely does.

"Jolie, what would you think if I made arrangements for someone in our family and then some outsiders stepped in to change things? Kevin was her husband."

"And Helen was her mother, and no one's wondering if she had a role in giving Eleanor mercury. The fact that he excluded her from all planning says a lot." Seeing Scobie's frown, I added, "This was actually Harry's idea."

"Harry? He doesn't even know them."

"I was in the office when she called and he knew what she asked. He's buried a wife and Aunt Madge has buried a husband. He probably remembers what an awful time that was, and that he had a lot of support from family and friends."

For the first time ever, we didn't kiss each other goodnight.

Chapter Seventeen

BECAUSE OF THE TRIP TO Lakewood the day before, I hadn't finished even half of the appraisal report for the Victorian on Seashore. Tuesday morning, before going to the courthouse to check for comps, I sat at the desk in the office and made a list of pros and cons.

Pros

- Seven bathrooms, with two each in the larger units.
- Newer cabinetry in bathrooms, all showers work
- Five fireplaces, all well cared for.
- No evidence of water seeping in
- Hardwood floors in every unit (though carpet covered most of them)
- Radiators had been removed years ago and replaced with forced air heat
- No sign of mold or termites

Cons

- Dated kitchen countertops, sometimes with evidence of having served as cutting boards.
- Older cabinets in kitchen, with a couple doors missing
- Three units had their own thermostats. The other two (each adjacent to a larger unit) did not have their own thermostats.

- No central air conditioning (though each apartment had at least one functioning window unit)
- No evidence of regular cleaning or maintenance

Code required more outlets than any of the units had, but the house had been grandfathered into the old requirements. That included part of the house having old knob and tube wiring. I could see some of it in the basement — a black hot wire and a white neutral wire covered in rubberized cloth fabric and attached to the fixtures. It wasn't necessarily dangerous, but it sure was obsolete. Buck shouldn't be renting the place until it had been rewired.

On top of everything else, it was difficult to judge the condition of all segments of the roof. From windows on the top floors of a Victorian, lower portions of the roof were visible. However, different portions had been replaced at different times and I didn't know how many layers of shingles sat on the wood below them.

I didn't expect anything to be to code, which meant the load on the roof was probably way too high. I would have to mention that could be dangerous during a heavy snow.

Lester would definitely not like what I had to say, which meant Buck would probably be thrilled because the value might be less than the sales price. I put my head in my hands and rested my elbows on the desk.

After a few minutes, I armed myself with a fresh cup of coffee in a thermos, the only way it would be allowed in the courthouse documents area, and headed to downtown to look for comparable sales. As I entered the courthouse, I ran into Lester on his way out. He was apparently trying to see how my work was going. One of his more irritating habits.

Before he could open his mouth, I said, "Don't even start, Lester. I'm just beginning to look up comps."

His eyes brightened and he reached into a pocket for a 3 by 5 card. "I might have some ideas for you."

I shook my head firmly. "Every time you've tried to give me ideas they are so off the mark that it isn't even funny. Plus, it has to be my work, not yours."

"Okay." He grinned at me as he turned to leave. "Better luck next time."

I entered the Office of the Registrar of Deeds, and was greeted by its long-serving clerk. She grinned at me. "I bet I know what house you're working on. That multifamily Victorian, right? Lester just left."

"You've got it. I don't think it's been sold for a while, so I feel as if I'm starting from scratch."

Cheerfully, she agreed. "I do think that the drawings with the deed are pretty accurate. That might help you."

I let that be my reason for optimism and got to work. I had only examined a few other recent sales, when a voice from behind me said, "Just like old times."

I glanced up. "George, what brings you here, as if I didn't know."

"Listen, Jolie, we really have to talk about this Fielding murder. That woman had to have been poisoned over time."

From the corner of my eye, I saw the clerk stop typing, though she continued to face her computer. She was ready to listen.

"I can't get into that. Sergeant Moorhouse reminded me that whoever killed her is not someone I want to have mad at me. I go into vacant houses, I have two children to raise. No way can I get more involved than helping her mother a little bit."

"How are you helping her mother?"

In a low voice, I relayed that she had to rent a separate room in the funeral home so that there could be a visitation before the service.

George's eyes lit up. "That tells me this Kevin Fielding has something to hide. A normal person would want to congregate with his late wife's friends. They might even take comfort from it."

"Spoken like an investigator. Scoobie thinks maybe the man just is too grief-stricken to want to interact with a lot of people."

George rolled his eyes. "Scoobie's really in that guy's corner." He glanced at writing on the notebook in his hand. "I found out Eleanor's blood contained almost sixty micrograms of mercury per liter in her blood. Normal is generally under ten. It's no wonder she died so fast."

I remembered Renée saying something about ten being somewhat normal and thirty-five being really high. Sixty would be off the charts. "Why are you pursuing this? Morehouse sounds as if they're really on it."

"You're the one who told me to do a credit check. Kevin has a good income, but his credit card debt has been slowing increasing and he has a balloon mortgage on their house outside of Lakewood. In two years, he'll have to pay or refinance $102,000."

"He should at least be able to refinance the mortgage." I thought for a moment. "I wonder if the credit card debt has been going up since Eleanor changed jobs?"

"I'd have to know more about when her income went down. He's also had a couple hard credit checks, both from marine dealerships…"

"What does that…oh, places that sell boats," I said.

"Gee, you'd think you lived at the Jersey shore."

"Did he get a loan for a boat?"

George shrugged. "Not on his credit report as a debt, but if he bought one recently, it wouldn't be."

I wanted to know, but I didn't. I glanced at the clerk who had gone back to typing on her keyboard. "If I hear something I'll pass it on, but I need to focus on the kids and Scoobie. He's been really bothered by Eleanor's death. He's even gone to more meetings than usual."

George looked at me with an odd expression. "Are you sure that's all that's bothering him?"

"He tells you things. Is there something going on at work that I don't know about?"

"Just a general question. You guys have such busy lives." He raised the notebook in a brief salute. "I'm going to go back to digging."

I studied his back as he walked out of the room. *What else could be bothering Scoobie?*

AUNT MADGE AND HARRY wanted to go to the Tuesday evening memorial service, so Scoobie and I had to decide which of us would stay home, and took turns saying, "I'll do it." In fact, we both wanted to be there, though for different reasons.

Terry offered to babysit, but we knew he had an algebra test the next day.

It looked as if the best option might be Renée's husband, Andrew. He wasn't big on funerals, and wasn't terribly happy about taking the twins. He wouldn't be on duty alone.

Leia and Lance loved their older cousins, and Michelle and Julia were top-notch sitters in their neighborhood. We did ply everyone with happy meals when we dropped off the kids.

We met Aunt Madge and Harry in the parking lot. Scoobie and I held hands as we followed them up the short set of stairs into the main entrance of the Fond Memories Funeral Home. Two signs greeted us, both on black pleated boards with removable white letters. One pointed left and said "Visitation for Eleanor Fielding. 6:30 to 7:30 PM."

The other sign pointed right and said, "Memorial service for Eleanor Fielding, 7:30 PM." A great deal of conversation drifted from the large room that Helen had rented for the visitation. We followed the noise.

Renée stood to one side of Helen and her friend Martin stood on either side. However, it was not a time for tears. People talked animatedly about their time with Eleanor, and two huge display boards held photographs. A number showed Renée with her in high school and as a bridesmaid in Eleanor and Kevin's wedding.

Aunt Madge and Harry went directly to Helen Covington. Scoobie and I knew few people, so we gravitated to the boards of pictures. A third board had a well-worn sweatshirt with a picture of many books and the saying, "So many books so little time." I felt my eyes misting.

Scoobie took in the entire room. "I don't see Kevin, do you?"

"No, but I didn't really expect to. And it seems kind of early for him to be in the room designated for the memorial service."

He nodded, "You're probably right. Let's go talk to Eleanor's mother."

FORTY-FIVE MINUTES LATER, Scoobie and I left the visitation room and headed for the memorial service Chapel. He wanted to see if Kevin was already there and offer support. He was, and Scoobie did.

Kevin embraced Scoobie as if they'd been friends for decades. "I don't know what I would have done without you that night. I'll never be able to repay you."

You could confess to your wife's murder. Since I'd never say that out loud, I murmured that I wished I had known her better.

Kevin turned his attention to me and his gaze could only be described as frosty. "I understand you helped Helen set up the visitation."

I kept my tone impassive. "My uncle had the idea. He's lost people very close to him, and I guess he couldn't imagine going through the evening without the support of friends."

"I've asked friends to speak at the service. I want everyone to know what a special person Eleanor was."

Scoobie and I both murmured agreement with this point.

A man and a woman entered the room and came up to Kevin.

Scoobie and I stepped back as they hugged, and Kevin took out a folded handkerchief and dabbed at his eyes.

I didn't want to go back to the visitation room, so Scoobie and I looked at the several large bouquets of flowers and the many cards arranged on a polished maple table that sat along one wall.

There were only forty or fifty chairs in the room and at least seventy people attending the visitation. I wondered if all planned to attend the service and whether some would simply stand in the hallway. My guess was that a lot of people would leave, since they didn't know Kevin as well as Helen.

Scoobie and I read a card attached to the largest bouquet of flowers. They were from Eleanor and Renée's book club, and said, "May you have a heavenly opportunity to read all the books you never could get to down here."

Scoobie shook his head lightly. "You know how I love books. All I can think of is I wish she'd had more time down here with her husband."

A noise across the room caught my attention.

We turned and saw the back of Buck Brock, of all people, talking to Kevin. I knew Aunt Madge had suggested that he stop by, but I hadn't expected him to.

Kevin looked irritated, and his voice rose slightly. "I don't know what you're talking about. I'm not *up to* anything."

Buck pointed his finger at Kevin's face. Before he could say anything else, Scoobie crossed the room in four quick strides and took Buck by the elbow. Surprised, Buck turned to Scoobie.

"Let's go into the hall, Buck."

"Do I know you?"

"You know my wife better, Jolie Gentil. Come on, I'll walk you out."

Buck started to protest, and I quietly said, "Now, Buck."

He glanced at me, shrugged, and walked out with Scoobie.

Several other couples had stopped talking and their eyes followed Buck out of the room. I walked over to Kevin. "Heaven only knows what he was thinking. I'm sorry if it adds to your difficulties tonight."

Kevin's darkened expression lightened. "I appreciate that. Almost as much as I appreciated your help last Sunday morning."

I tried to make my smile a warm one. "Just wish we hadn't had to do it." I looked behind me to be sure no one could overhear me. "I'm sure the police told you they wouldn't let me get her things. I'm sorry."

He frowned. "Yeah. They took all of our stuff to their station."

I hadn't known that. I glanced at the door. "I'll be back in with Scoobie in a few minutes."

As I started out of the room, a man clapped Kevin on the shoulder. "Get that boat ordered. Something to take your mind off things."

What a thing to say!

Kevin turned his back to me and continued to talk to the man, but in a lower voice.

In the hallway, Scoobie stood near the funeral home entrance with Buck. Funerals often bring out tensions in families, but Buck barely knew Eleanor and Kevin. Why did he care to say anything controversial to Kevin?

I walked over to the two men. "Buck, I can't imagine what would make it OK for you to say anything tense to Kevin tonight."

His shoulders sagged. "You're right. I've been talking to some people though, and they say this Fielding guy has a habit of trying to get free services from restaurants, and in my case a rental unit."

"I don't know about that. But I think there's enough stress tonight that it might be better if you drove back to Ocean Alley now." In the corner of my eye, I saw Aunt Madge and Harry approaching.

They said hello to Buck and Aunt Madge kissed me on the cheek. Harry added, "We get up early, so we aren't staying for the memorial service. If you're leaving, Buck, how about if we walk out together?"

"Yeah, good idea." He strode quickly out the door.

Harry followed Buck, and Aunt Madge looked at me with a shrug. I shook my head. "Thanks."

As they walked out, I turned to Scoobie. "What is wrong with that man?"

"From what George says, he's rude to everyone."

The man who led the memorial service was dressed in a charcoal gray suit and a somber maroon tie. There was no indication that he was a member of any clergy. I wondered if Kevin had selected him to annoy Helen. Not that it mattered at this point.

The celebrant introduced himself as Marcus Wilding. His remarks about Eleanor were so sparse they could barely be called bland. They almost seemed like a recitation of her resume, with a brief mention of the fact that she had many friends in Lakewood.

He called on a smart looking couple who had been seated in the front row. They came up together, and introduced themselves as Tami and Grayson, dear friends of Kevin and Eleanor's. There was a brief rustle in the room, probably from all the people who had known her for decades and never heard of them. I didn't think they caught on.

They talked about spending a weekend in Manhattan with Kevin and Eleanor, visits to the New Jersey Maritime Museum in Beach Haven, and countless meals in seafood restaurants up and down the Jersey Shore.

They spoke highly of Eleanor's skills as a financial manager, and her devotion to her clients in her new job. They made no mention of what she did or who she worked for. The woman nodded at Helen, and said they knew her mother would miss her very much.

After those remarks, the celebrant seemed ready to move on. However, three women stood up and walked toward the front of the room. Since he faced Marcus Wilding, Kevin wasn't aware of this until they got to the front, faced the group, and beamed radiant smiles.

Renée spoke, and looked from Kevin to Mrs. Fielding and then to Wilding. She said, "Since there are so many people here who have known Eleanor all her life, we wanted to share just a couple of funny stories." She didn't wait for permission, but launched into Eleanor's efforts to feed half of the stray cats in Lakewood the summer after their freshman year of high school.

Kevin could hardly stand and object. I glanced at him, noting his tight smile and rigid posture.

Marcus Wilding gave Kevin a barely perceptible shrug and stood back a few feet.

The other two women had also gone to high school with Eleanor, and I recognized them but didn't know much about them. I recalled Edna had been a cheerleader and Sophie sang in the concert chorus.

They soon had the room laughing, with Helen dabbing her eyes every minute or so. Each speaker had on the same sweatshirt that had been displayed in the visitation room. They had to have put them on for the service, because they hadn't been wearing them earlier.

Seemingly on cue, they turned their backs and showed the writing there. Renée's said, "Buy a banned book."

Edna's said, "A child who reads is a child who leads."

Sophie's showed a hand holding a book and reaching for a smaller hand. It said, "I'll teach you to read if you don't know how."

As the women finished and took their seats, a man in the back of the room stood. He introduced himself as Jorge Ramirez. He wanted to take a moment to say how much Eleanor had meant to their group, and how many women had benefited from her dedication in the short time she had worked for the nonprofit, Keep Climbing.

A few murmurs in the room said things like "she loved that place" or "we know you'll miss her."

After a few seconds, Wilding walked quickly back to the small podium and ad-libbed. "Clearly, Eleanor had a wonderful group of friends and was dedicated to helping others. Thank you all so much for coming." He didn't run out of the room, but he definitely walked at a fast clip.

I didn't dare look at Kevin as we stood. I reached for Scoobie's hand. A couple of his fingers were moist. He pulled a Kleenex from his pocket and finished wiping his eyes. "Man, I hope we're together for another fifty years."

Chapter Eighteen

WE HAD GONE TO BED later than usual Tuesday, so Wednesday morning found me dragging. I dropped off the kids at Sand and Sea and gave myself a pep talk about working on the appraisal report for the Victorian on Seashore.

My decision not to actively seek information on Eleanor's "unnatural death" was firm, but I did want to tell Sergeant Morehouse or Johnson some things. I entered the plain reception area at the Ocean Alley Police Department and made myself uncomfortable in one of the aging plastic chairs.

The young officer at the counter called down to the bullpen and asked someone to find either of the sergeants. He grinned at me. "We haven't met because I'm pretty new. There are lots of stories about Jolie Gentil floating around here."

I smiled as if this would be the funniest thing I'd hear all day. "Don't feel obligated to share any."

He ignored my comment. "The one the guys laugh about the most is the day you missed hitting the deer and ended up in a ditch."

The locked door to the offices had opened as he finished, and Dana Johnson grinned at me. "I could tell more, but why heckle a working mom?"

I stood, glanced at the officer's nameplate, and used a pleasant tone. "Thanks, Officer Abrams. Don't feel obligated to share further."

"Yes ma'am."

Dana shut the door behind us and we started for the conference room, since neither her small office or Morehouse's could hold three people. "Your body language said you loved being called ma'am."

"Don't rub it in."

We entered the conference room and sat across from Morehouse, who was trying to wrap up a phone call and having little success. "As I said, we appreciate the call. Yes, I'll definitely check." He paused. "I do have someone waiting. Thanks again."

He pushed the phone off and pointed a finger at me. "I've had at least ten calls offering advice on where people could get exposed to mercury, and almost all of them have been fluorescent bulbs."

"Did you ever hear if that barometer Eleanor had got broken at some point?"

He eyed me. "I agreed to see you because you said you thought you had information that might help Dana and me."

I pulled a folded piece of lined paper from the pocket of my burgundy jeans. "I made a list." I slid it across the middle of the table so they could read it together.

1. Eleanor did a lot of antiquing for years and owned many until recently. Could mercury have been in something older?

2. Last night, Kevin didn't schedule a visitation, but Mrs. Covington organized one. At the service itself, the only people he asked to speak were a couple who barely knew Eleanor.

3. I told you about the life insurance. Last night, a man came up to Kevin to suggest he buy a boat. It sounded as if Kevin had been making plans.

4. Did you find out why Kevin didn't ask Mrs. Covington to come to the hospital after he found out Eleanor would die soon?

5. I think Kevin asked me to pack Eleanor's clothes so there would be fingerprints besides his in their rental.

6. If Mrs. Covington didn't talk to you about tension in their marriage, you should ask her.

Morehouse shook his head slightly and nodded to Dana. "Did you see she snuck in a question?"

"I really wanted to ask if there were any cameras that showed who left the chocolates, but I didn't think you would tell me, and I'm trying not to think about this too much."

"Did you see me in the back of the memorial service last night, Jolie?" Dana asked.

"What? No!"

"I was in civvies, and left when your sister and her friends finished and gave the stage back to that kind of wimpy minister, or whoever he was."

"I'm proud of her."

Dana nodded. "I liked it, and so did Mrs. Fielding's mother." She glanced at Morehouse. "The paper has already asked about the cameras."

"And a dozen other things," he groused. "I'll tell you there were no cameras in that house. Buck should get his butt in gear and add some. None across the street, either."

"Darn it. I hoped there would be."

"Your buddy George, who has a sand crab in his shorts about this, checked every house on the street and gave us some information."

"He shared with you?" I couldn't believe it.

Dana responded. "Since he got his private investigator license, he works hard to be our pal. Sometimes we know something innocuous that will help him when he does a background check or something simple."

"Huh. Did he find any cameras?" I asked.

Morehouse said, "I'll tell you one thing, anything else you can read in the paper, like everybody else. Four houses down, we couldn't get ahold of the owner. Closed his rental property for the season. George found good contact info for the guy."

"He never lets go," I said.

"His least endearing quality," Dana said.

Morehouse frowned at me. "As I was sayin' he tracked down the guy, and he gave George access to some online security account. George looked at what was on the one camera the man has. Points straight at the street, only comes on with motion. Owner let him download some images and said he could give them to us."

"But if it looked straight out, you couldn't get a license tag, could you?"

Dana grinned. "Not bad, Miss Marple. And you're right, not as helpful as another angle might have been."

What is with the Miss Marple stuff?

"I've been told it's Mrs," Morehouse said.

I ducked my head for a moment and looked up. "That Friday, Kevin Fielding was driving a pale blue Lexus. Or at least, that's what he drove to our house after Eleanor died."

"Eleanor's car," Dana said. "And the car conveniently had those mesh-like sun blockers on the driver's and passenger's windows. But not that many people drive a Lexus in Ocean Alley."

"So, was…" I began.

"Enough," Morehouse said, but amiably enough. "Ask George. Better yet, don't."

"I really am going to try not to think about this." I began to stand.

"One more thing," he said.

I sat.

"You know how this works. When we know enough to arrest or seriously question someone, we do it."

I nodded.

"Right now," Dana continued, "there is no way to know how the mercury exposure happened or if it was deliberate on anybody's part."

I nodded slowly. "I understand. For what it's worth, Scoobie is convinced Kevin is genuinely grieving and feels bereft without her." I stood again. "Thanks."

To Morehouse, Dana said, "Be right back." She followed me out of the room.

I glanced at the large space they call the bullpen. The gray, metal desks had been replaced with wooden ones, and short partitions separated each desk. When Dana opened the door to let me into the lobby, I said, "Looks better in there."

"Yep. Captain Tortino got some grant money. A few of those old desks were sitting on piles of old state code books."

I smiled at her.

"But that's not why I walked you out here." She glanced at Officer Abrams, who was checking his phone "I think Scoobie is describing how he would feel if something happened to you. I have no idea if Kevin Fielding killed his wife. But someone did. You really don't want to talk to people a lot about this."

I nodded agreement and walked out of the station. Usually, the police would tell me to mind my own business, just on general principles. With Eleanor's death, they sounded worried about me.

BACK AT STEELE APPRAISALS, I opened the draft report on what I now thought of as the tacky Victorian and added the rest of the room measurements and varying ceiling heights. I kept reminding myself that the house had been listed in as-is condition, and the appraisal report could be the basis for the seller making some repairs, or Buck signing something that said he would. The credit union wouldn't underwrite the mortgage in the house's current condition.

I made a cup of coffee and spread information about the three comparable sales on the large oak table that sits in the middle of our office.

The Victorian was an odd house for today's Ocean Alley. When I was very young, there were still a few elegant single-family houses close to downtown. Aunt Madge's Cozy Corner had once been one. Like hers, most that survived the Great Hurricane of 1944 had been repurposed to guest lodgings or, in one case, a law practice.

But by now, smaller ones or those in poorer condition had been torn down and replaced. I was pushing the limits of confidence to use the three I'd chosen — or any other three. That meant there would be room for argument, mostly from Lester.

"Nuts." I needed to know what the security camera George found showed so I would stop thinking about it. I called him.

"You call Ramona, not me," George said.

"I call you if I want something. Morehouse said if I want to know what the camera you found shows, I need to talk to you."

He whooped. "I knew you'd cave."

"I'm not 'caving.' I just want to know one thing."

"And I'll probably tell you because I want to know what you think. Or hold it over your head."

"I'd rather you just tell me."

"You're no fun. A light-colored Lexus that I think belonged to Eleanor Fielding passed in front of this Mr. McGee's rental property several times that Friday, first time a little before ten in the morning."

I thought that was earlier than he said they'd gotten to town. "Was she driving?"

"Can't tell. Side windows had those stick-on visor things to keep out bright sun. I talked to Josh. He finished cleaning about ten-thirty, which means if they went by before that, they likely saw him and wouldn't have gone in."

"But Kevin could have left the chocolates."

"Yeah, but it'd be kind of hinky, because why would he carry candy to the door and leave it when she was in the car?"

"Maybe someone delivered it?"

"Markle didn't send it. I talked to him. He's steamed it had his store's name on it."

"Aren't there any delivery services in town? What about all those groups who deliver groceries now?"

George said nothing for several seconds. "Yeah, that's good, but don't you usually have to use a credit card?"

I added, "You don't see as many people on bicycles with messenger bags now, but there must be a way to send stuff from one side of town to the other without doing it yourself."

"I suppose," he said, slowly. "But it seems kind of risky to send a box with liquid mercury in it by messenger."

"I suppose. But he needed to have it delivered so it looked like a gift."

Again, he said nothing. Then, "Call you back." George hung up.

To myself, I said, "At least I can stop thinking about it."

I SPENT MUCH OF THURSDAY arguing with people. Harry and I agreed on the value we put in the appraisal report for the

Victorian, but no one else liked it. Although I hadn't heard from Buck, who always wants to pay less for a property.

The current property owner, an absentee landlord who worked at an investment firm in Chicago, thought it was worth more and called us when the bank emailed him a copy of the report.

I listened politely for a couple of minutes while he listed the house's good points — multiple fireplaces, hardwood floors (he didn't mention the condition), proximity to the ocean. Finally, I interrupted and asked him what he thought of the electrical wiring.

"What about it?" he snapped.

"You're allowed to list a house with that old wiring, but given that it wasn't designed for all the appliances and gadgets people have today, the buyer generally asks that it be replaced or the house be reduced in price substantially so they can rewire a house."

"What exactly do you mean, young lady?"

I let the silence drag out for several seconds. "If you're in front of a computer, do a Google search for knob and tube wiring. One of your search terms can be early twentieth century."

Keys clattered while he looked, then they stopped while he read. After two minutes or so, he came back on the line. "The appraisal documents from when I bought the building twelve years ago didn't mention that."

"You're kidding. Did Stenner's do the appraisal?"

"No, it was a firm that worked in New Jersey and Pennsylvania. Sort of traveling appraisers."

I tried to keep derision from my tone. "That kind of operation is not used everywhere. Appraisers need to know the communities they work in so they can do accurate valuations. Did you have any other questions?"

He had the decency to thank me for the information as he disconnected.

Harry waited until I hung up to laugh. "You should have seen the steam pouring out of your ears."

"He's some kind of venture capitalist. Called me 'young lady,' and I bet I'm older than he is."

The office phone rang and Harry glanced at caller ID. "Lester. You want him or should I take it?"

"I'll do it. He doesn't call me names."

Lester wasn't quite as brash as he can be. He knew the house needed a lot of work. "But it's gonna be gorgeous when they do some paint and plant some flowers."

"It's not the paint and flower-type items and you know it. The owner in Chicago called me…"

"What? I'm his broker. He shoulda gone through me."

"He may not buy and sell a lot, and Steele Appraisals' name and phone number are on the appraisal, which the bank must have sent to him."

Silence for a couple seconds. "So, what did ya tell him?"

"I gave him a lesson on knob and tube wiring, which was not even noted on the appraisal from twelve years ago. I had him Google it, so he understands it can't withstand a heavy load. And we didn't even talk about the roof, which wouldn't hold another kind of heavy load."

"Crud."

"Lester, I can't tell you what to do. But you know the drill. If he doesn't like the low valuation, he can make some repairs and ask us to go in again."

His sounded hopeful. "And you'd up the value?"

"You know I can't talk to you about a specific repair like that. All we do is look at what's there."

"But…"

"Lester, I need to leave the office in a few minutes." I said goodbye and hung up.

"Two down, one to go," Harry said.

"If you mean Buck, he's probably already called the bank to try to get them to set an early settlement date."

Harry shook his head. "They won't underwrite the loan with that wiring."

"That's true. They'd be providing a mortgage for an unsafe property."

Harry tapped a pen on his desk. "Somebody might justify that old wiring if it were a small single-family and an electrician signed off on it…"

"Which they wouldn't," I said.

"True. It really can't get a mortgage as it is. Buck should have put a contingency in the contract. Redo the wiring."

The office phone rang again. "Buck," I said.

Harry nodded. "I'd say they all read through the appraisal report quickly."

I pushed the speaker-phone button. "Hello, Buck. Harry's here, too."

"Jolie, you're killing me here. Bank's not going to approve the loan without rewiring. I wanted to be able to rent the place before the holidays."

"As in this year's Thanksgiving and Christmas holidays? The owner would have to get an electrician, an entire firm, in there next week." I grinned across the room at Harry.

"I feel my blood pressure rising. This is a disaster."

"Based on the appraisal, you can add a contingency or pull out of the contract. You aren't stuck with a house with decrepit wiring."

"That house was going to be a money spinner for me. I need to get it spruced up and rented. Maybe even some long-term tenants. Regular income."

Harry and I exchanged glances. I figured he was also reevaluating Buck's financial status. Not that we'd discussed it, but he acts as if he's loaded.

"So Buck," I began. "There could be a couple options."

"If you're going to say take back my deposit and find something else, you gotta know there's not a lot on the market. Especially that size, with that many units."

"It's a tight market," I agreed. "But you could offer to revise the sales contract contingent on the rewiring and at the same time ask for pre-settlement occupancy so you can start more basic repairs. But you couldn't have anyone live there until the wiring is redone."

He bellowed. "Did you even look at the pictures in the damn appraisal report?"

"Buck," Harry said. "Calm down."

He said nothing.

I added, "I took the pictures. If a city inspector or someone says the electricity can't be used until it's replaced, you could rent a generator or use battery-powered lamps. While people paint or refinish some of the floors."

He said nothing for at least ten seconds. I shrugged in Harry's direction.

Finally, Buck said, "That's a good idea." He hung up.

I raised my arms in the air. "It's easier to deal with four-year-olds."

Chapter Nineteen

I PICKED UP THE kids from Sand and Sea at three-thirty on Thursday and we headed for Java Jolt. I needed to send a bunch of email reminders to volunteers about their Harvest for All schedules. While I worked, Leia and Lance craned their necks toward the souvenir shop across the boardwalk. Workers were recaulking the windows before painting the front of the building.

The timing of my emails was good. A man scheduled to work the next morning replied that he'd forgotten and had just had bunion surgery. He wouldn't be able to stand at the counter or restock shelves.

I emailed him back. "Don't worry about it. If I can't find someone else I can do it myself. I'm free a lot tomorrow." I wasn't, but the first rule of working with volunteers is not to guilt people into anything. I jotted a note on my calendar so I didn't forget.

Buck came in at four-thirty and made a beeline for me. Without asking, he sat in a chair across from me and moved Lance's cup of juice aside.

"Hey, Mister," Lance called. "That's my chair."

"Mr. Brock is only staying a minute, and you're not in your chair right this minute."

Lance frowned at Buck and returned to watching paint dry.

"I'm glad your blood pressure seems to have gone down. Did you add a contingency to the contract?"

He glanced at the twins and back to me. "Current owner will rewire and redo one part of the roof. We'll adjust the contract to say that and I'll offer $5,000 more. But I need to get some income going. The guy in Chicago said I could do a pre-settlement occupancy, so I have painters going in there tomorrow, and then Josh'll clean the first floor."

"Better have them wash the walls first. Didn't look as if that had been done in years."

He scowled. "I won't be able to rent it fast, but I can start to show it to people so some money comes in faster later."

I debated asking a question, but went ahead. "Buck, if you're that pressed for cash, why don't you cancel this and buy something smaller that you can turn around quickly?"

He regarded me shrewdly. "This place could appreciate a lot over the next couple of years. I'll make some good dough in the meantime, and then maybe make a killing when I sell it."

"You, uh, obviously know about time limits in terms of capital gains, right?"

"Yeah, but I sold my place in Atlantic City. I can avoid some tax if I also make it my primary residence for part of that time."

Thank goodness he didn't plan to do that with the house down the street from us. I stared at him, probably with a questioning look hanging between us.

"I told you, people try to screw me over. I used to be flush. But I got divorced a couple years ago."

I sensed he was about to go on, and wasn't sure I wanted to know more. "Sounds as if you know what you're doing. I hope it works out."

"I have to get the place fixed up first." Scowling he added, "I thought about leasing it as a party house, but the old farts on that commission said there's some rule about rentals and parties."

"Big ones can turn into a drunk fest."

"And that's no good. I suppose they could trash the place."

His big worry is trashing his place? Forget about annoying everyone in a square block area.

Buck looked thoughtful for a moment. "Maybe I'll advertise it can be for family reunions." He stood. "I have to get to the paper to see if I can get that ad in tomorrow." He said goodbye to Megan and me, and left.

Five minutes later, my phone dinged with a message from George. "Where R U?"

I texted back, "JJ."

"In a min," he wrote.

Two minutes later, I'd sent my last email to Harvest for All volunteers. George came in, waved at Megan, and sat in the seat Buck had vacated.

Lance called. "Are you only staying a minute?"

"Yeah, buddy. " He turned to me. "You know that place just off Main Street where you can rent mailboxes and buy packing supplies?"

"Yep. I use it to send stuff to my parents."

"Right. The guy has a side hustle. He says almost no one uses messengers now, but there are a couple retired guys who will take stuff around town. As long as it's not too heavy."

"And…?"

"The candy arrived in a box the Postal Service delivered, addressed to Billy, the guy who owns the package place. Return address was a PO box, but he tossed the carton and doesn't remember the box number."

"Probably fake anyway. No name in the return address?" I asked.

"Jones, which the guy remembers because he couldn't get the song lyric *Me and Mrs. Jones* out of his head all day. Anyway, the candy box was already wrapped and said it was from Markle's Market. Lots of bubble wrap to protect it."

"How did he know where to deliver the candy?"

"Also enclosed was a typed note saying the so-called Mr. or Mrs. Jones would like the candy box delivered late Friday morning and left on the porch at the house on Seashore. Said it was a surprise for the arriving guest, and he put in two twenties. Billy kept one and gave one to the messenger."

"Signature on the note?" I asked.

"No name. Just the words, "Secret Santa.""

"Tacky. Who delivered it to the beach house?"

"Retired guy who lives at Silver Times Senior Living."

"Whom you called."

George grinned briefly. "Of course. The front door was open when he got there, but not the screen, and he could hear water running inside. It was supposed to be a surprise, so he left it on the porch."

"He was probably there when Josh was cleaning. That'll be good for Josh. Morehouse doesn't really suspect him — I don't think — but this shows he really didn't bring the candy to the house."

"Yeah. I'm half a step ahead of the police for now. But I gotta stop by there and tell them what I found out."

I regarded him with a frown. "Why do you even care? You aren't writing for the paper anymore."

"Part of it's habit, but I also figure if I find out something, Tiffany'll have to interview me at some point. I'll be quoted as 'George Winters of Summer and Winter Investigations.'"

"Free advertising."

"You got it." He stood. "And I like the chase. Catchya later."

I sat there for two or three minutes after he left, thinking. We knew how the candy got to the house. Josh brought it inside. But when did the mercury get in the chocolate she ate? Was it there when it arrived at the package place?

I stared at the twins as they pressed their noses on the window glass. I felt furious that someone could have had poison delivered. Anyone, even a little kid, could have gotten into the candy.

Chapter Twenty

I GLANCED AT MY PHONE. Almost four-thirty, meaning Scoobie would be home. He hadn't texted, so was probably enjoying having the house to himself for a few minutes. I texted saying we were on the way.

Then I texted Morehouse. "Call me after George talks to you about who delivered the chocolates."

His loud voice came through the phone as I herded the twins up the front steps of our house. Scoobie's car wasn't in the driveway. I wished he were home so he could handle the kids once we got inside.

Morehouse almost growled. "Yeah, I talked to Sherlock about how the box got to the cottage. I even thanked him. But we don't know the mercury was in the candy. To quiet your wonderin' mind, I'll tell you none was in the box with the leftover candy. If it was ever in the box, there'd still be traces of it."

"That potent, huh?"

Lance's voice drifted into the kitchen, where I'd gone hoping for quiet. "Mom! My Jack-in-the-Box is gone!"

Exasperation oozed from Morehouse. "It's detected as a liquid and a vapor. The smart scientists we talked to think we should be able to still detect vapor if any was in the box recently."

"How do you do that? Detect the vapor?"

"Jolie, I hear your kid. Go find his Jack-in-the-Box."

"I'm the one who hid it."

He hung up, chuckling.

I threw my phone toward the kitchen counter but caught it with my other hand before it hit the hard surface. Scoobie walked in the front door. In the bedlam that followed I told myself to forget about it. Eleanor's death had been so dramatic, the police were on it full tilt. George certainly wouldn't let go of it.

AFTER THE KIDS WERE in bed, we sat in the living room, Scoobie with a book, me with a list of ideas for a fundraiser for the food pantry. When I looked up, Scoobie was staring at the wall above the couch, about two feet to my right.

"Is everything okay?" I thought in terms of his work or how we split the kids' schedules. "You've seemed kind of distracted, or something."

"No. It's mostly this stuff with Eleanor. Makes me realize it could happen to anyone." He snapped his fingers. "Here today, dead tomorrow."

I put my notebook next to me on the couch. "I know. But we're both healthy. God knows, we get enough exercise chasing the twins."

He nodded absently. "True."

"And her situation was…unusual. We aren't going to be exposed to mercury or any other awful toxin."

He spoke firmly. "I don't think Kevin did it."

I half shrugged, half-nodded. "I haven't heard there's any proof of that."

He stared at me. "But you think he killed her."

"He was with her the most. That doesn't mean he planned her murder."

"That couple who talked at the memorial service said they went out with Kevin and Eleanor a lot. To seafood restaurants. Maybe that's where she was exposed."

I didn't say I thought a person would have to eat a heck of a lot of seafood to get such severe mercury poisoning. "Morehouse told me today there wasn't even a trace of it in the box of chocolates." I didn't add that George had found out how the chocolates got to the cottage. I'd let him tell Scoobie that.

Scoobie seemed lost in thought. Then he looked directly at me and smiled. "In this case, death isn't like a box of chocolates."

FRIDAY MORNING'S COPY of the *Ocean Alley Press* had a follow-up article on Eleanor's death. There had been a couple other updates, but they were more on the order of "nothing to report." Today's piece was also short, but more informative.

Police Make Homicide Investigation Official

Captain Tortino of the Ocean Alley Police Department announced that the department is now investigating the death last Saturday of Eleanor Fielding as a homicide. There has been no obvious evidence of foul play, but police and the State Commission of Investigation agree there can be no way for that amount of mercury to have entered Ms. Fielding's bloodstream on an accidental basis.

She had seen several physicians in Lakewood, NJ over the last few months because of balance issues. When no neurological problems were indicated, her doctors explored other possibilities. She had been advised to see specialists at Morristown Medical Center, but had not yet made the decision to do so.

Fortunately, her Lakewood physician had sent blood samples to Morristown several weeks ago. Mercury levels were at the higher end of the normal range, but at the time, doctors did not think they explained her balance problems. She and her husband ate a great deal of seafood, and they were advised to avoid certain fish for the next few months.

Given the speed of her decline last week, the police hypothesis is that the mercury entered her body within the 24 hours prior to the onset of severe symptoms on Friday. Police continue to explore her movements and whether other individuals have been affected.

The article added a quote by Kevin Fielding, who expressed surprise and exasperation at the police position. There was additional information on the levels of mercury in her blood and the kinds of effects it can have on people

I skimmed the rest of the paper. I don't usually read the classifieds, but there was a two-inch-by-two-inch ad for a "vintage residence" that could host family reunions or holiday events. I recognized the phone number as Buck's mobile phone. The final line said, "Responsible groups only."

Aloud, I said, "He'll get people responsible for doing a lot of damage."

The same day, the Lakewood paper published an article titled "When a Book Lover Heads for the Stars." It talked about Eleanor and her life-long love of books. While it mentioned her death, of course, it focused on her life.

I smiled the entire time I read it. So much for her husband not putting an obituary in the paper.

I GOT TO THE FOOD pantry in the First Prez basement at 9:30 on Friday to be sure the shelves were stocked before clients arrived. Max was waiting at the door, which turned out to be a good thing because we had to do a lot of restocking. It's his best skill, as long as he doesn't put cans in the wrong places.

The food pantry is set up like a dry cleaner. There's a counter in front but shelves behind it instead of clothes that circulate on a rotating conveyor. Because the other volunteer had to cancel, I stood at the counter and relayed what clients needed. Sometimes I helped Max place items in paper bags or boxes and I always double-checked the orders.

I could see the stress of working fast getting to him. "Max, could you open some of the bags and put them on the counter? I'll help stuff for a few minutes." We worked that way for the final hour of the three we were open.

We finally put the closed sign on the door at ten minutes after one and we both collapsed on stools behind the counter. "You work fast, Jolie, fast," Max said.

"I got faster after I started chasing the twins around the house."

"Lance and Leia like me. Like me."

"Of course they do. And not just because you sometimes bring them day-old donuts from Java Jolt."

His expression drooped. "I don't think Josh likes me anymore."

Oh boy. If it were someone else, I would ask why they thought that. With Max, it's better to offer alternatives, or the conversation would go on for a long time. "Do you say that because you would like to spend more time with him than he might have?"

He seemed puzzled. "Have time? Have time?"

"That means he may be busy and not have as much free time to spend with friends as he used to."

He said nothing. I wished Scoobie were here. "When you and Josh first came to Ocean Alley, you needed more help than you do now. Now you have a house. Scoobie and George taught you how to make a schedule and be responsible for yourself."

"Mostly Scoobie," he said. "George likes to go fast. Really fast."

I laughed. "You know what impatient means. That's George in a nutshell."

"A nutshell," he said.

No way would Josh want to spend much of his time with Max. We hadn't needed to discuss it. "Maybe you could put Josh on your schedule a couple of times a week. You and he could drink coffee one day and take a walk on the boardwalk another day."

Max thought about this. "My schedule book is at home. At home." He took off the canvas apron he wore to stock shelves.

"You don't have to do it right this minute," I said.

His expression conveyed that I'd lost my mind.

"Okay, Max. But tell Josh it's up to him how often you get together."

Max left and I pulled out my phone to text Josh. Having a schedule to spend time with Max was probably not something to learn about as a surprise.

SCOOBIE CAME HOME LATE Friday afternoon and said Kevin had called him at work to see if they could "grab a bite of dinner."

I felt as if Kevin had honed in on Scoobie's generous nature and was trying to manipulate him. Or maybe he wanted to know what people were saying about the situation. Because Sergeant Morehouse had come to our house to talk to the three of us that Saturday morning, Kevin could figure we had some sort of inside track to information.

Scoobie asked Kevin to drive to Ocean Alley and suggested dessert at the diner, so Scoobie could help with the kids' baths. Kevin readily agreed.

Terry and a group of guys had gone camping at Island Beach State Park, and I had already gotten in bed with a book before Scoobie got home at eleven.

He sat on the edge of the bed, by my legs. Without preamble, he said, "He feels guilty because he got her to like seafood so well, especially tuna and swordfish, which have higher levels of mercury than some other species."

I kept my tone neutral and smiled. "I'm sure you reassured him that no one thinks she died by eating a lot of tuna and swordfish."

Scoobie nodded. "I did. And I don't think he killed her, but I do think he wanted to meet me to see if I knew more than was in the paper."

I decided not to say *duh*. "It's natural that he'd want to know if the police were making any progress."

Chapter Twenty-One

AFTER OUR USUAL HECTIC weekend, going to the office Monday morning was almost relaxing.

Lester called to tell me about the renegotiated sales contract, basically the information Buck had relayed about the current owner doing the electrical work and Buck paying more. "You know, Buck has a real estate license and handles his own contracts. He's no dummy, but if he'da worked with a buyer's broker he woulda gotten better advice."

I paraphrased Abraham Lincoln. "A man who represents himself in real estate deals has a fool for a client?"

Lester chuckled.

I remembered Lester losing the property he wanted on D Street because he offered no downpayment and didn't insist on a penalty clause if the owner backed out. "Does that mean when you look for houses for yourself again you'll have another realtor help you?"

"Low blow, Jolie. I gotta go."

I took that as a no.

Harry and I divvied up new requests for appraisals, with me taking two and him one. I'm starting to think he only keeps the business open so I have a flexible job. I get $250 for the site visit and report, and he gets the other half to run the business. I doubt that amount covers all the costs.

I've thought about talking to Harry about this, but I'm afraid he'll offer to sell me the business. As good a bargain as he would offer, I don't want to add managing a company — however small — to my to-do list.

Harry came in about nine. "What did you think of the article in the paper last Friday?"

"Made sense to me. Scoobie is still convinced her husband couldn't have done it, so we don't talk about it a lot."

Harry shook his head as he sat in his desk chair. "His choices about a quick memorial service with no visitation sure make it look as if he couldn't wait to be done with her."

"Interesting that the police think someone must have given her the mercury deliberately, but they don't mention anything about who or how."

Harry smiled, almost sadly. "Renée made a few choice comments to Madge and me at the visitation. Quietly, of course."

"George is all over it. The paper hasn't mentioned it, but it turns out the chocolates she ate were mailed to that package place on Main Street. A note said they were a surprise for guests who would arrive at Buck's rental place by the ocean, and asked that they be delivered the next morning. No way to tell who sent it."

Harry frowned. "Risky business. What if someone else had opened it and tried the candy?"

I nodded and looked at my phone's caller ID. "George."

He began talking without saying hello. "Morehouse told me there was no mercury residue in the box of chocolates. How could that be?"

"I think the bigger question is, if any was in the candy, how did it get in there? If we knew that we might be able to figure out why there weren't traces of it later. It had to have been mailed without the stuff in the candy."

"Put George on speaker," Harry said.

I did, and told George he was talking to the room.

"I can see why there's none of it in the box," Harry said.

"How?" I asked.

"Go for it," George said.

"The chocolates got delivered in a way that doesn't implicate Kevin Fielding directly. He puts a few on a plate for them to snack on, and somehow he gets the mercury only in a piece he knows Eleanor will eat."

"But how does he get it in the chocolates?" George asked.

Harry said, "I thought of one of those glass thermometers from the 1950s or 60s, but if he broke it there, wouldn't there be the possibility of traces of mercury in the cottage?"

"We're underestimating him," I said. "Kevin is a chemist. He probably knew how to handle it safely. Think about non-hospital labs, like the ones on the TV show *Big Bang Theory*. There's a lot of equipment, but maybe not as many people running around as there could be in a hospital lab. Kevin's firm might have lab space like that."

"So," George said, "Maybe he extracted it in a safe environment and put some…where? In an eye dropper? But that could spill or break. He needed something almost air-tight."

"And easily transported," Harry said.

My mind strayed to TV shows, like CSI. Those mostly had autopsies, but…a syringe appeared in my head. "Hey. There's a cap on the needle of a syringe. Get liquid mercury in one and it could be wrapped securely and transported in luggage. When Eleanor was in the bathroom or something, Kevin could have put a small amount in a couple pieces of candy."

"Could be," George said, "But what would he do with the syringe? No way would he put that in the trash at the cottage they rented."

"Ocean Alley has hundreds of garbage cans," Harry said.

"True." I thought out loud. "It would have to be a can in a location with a lot of trash receptacles and lots of people who used them. Maybe a mall?"

"But," George said, "Even if we had a mall, would he have had time to do that after he injected the chocolate and before they went to Java Jolt?"

"Too bad Eleanor isn't around to tell us," Harry said.

Mentally, my mind roamed town. George said Kevin was a jerk at a convenience store, but that was before Eleanor collapsed. If he went to a place like that, he might not be noticed but those trash barrels were emptied constantly. The contents could be in a black bag in a dumpster, but might already be at the landfill.

Where else had Keven been? The cottage, Java Jolt, our house — a scary thought — and the hospital.

"You know," I said, "restrooms would be a private place to dump a syringe." Then it hit me. "The syringe could have been placed in a used needle disposal box!" I could see one in my head. Bright red with the words "Hazardous Material" stamped on the outside in big letters.

"Damn, why didn't I think of that?" George asked.

Harry sounded as excited as I felt. "Those wouldn't be emptied every day. And it isn't likely people sift through the needles after the contents are picked up."

My excitement dampened. "But we can't go around opening those boxes. Even if we knew how." I thought for a moment. "Morehouse said there weren't traces of mercury in the chocolates box or cottage. How do they measure that? Is there a Geiger Counter for mercury?"

We were silent for a few contemplative seconds.

George spoke first. "I'll investigate anything, but looking for contaminated syringes in disposal boxes is above my pay grade. What do you say we pass this idea to Morehouse or Dana?"

"Absolutely," Harry said. He looked at me.

"George has to do it," I said. "Not only did Morehouse suggest I don't want to tick off the person who poisoned her, Scoobie would be really unhappy to know how much I'm thinking about this."

George laughed. "I'll take the short straw. Or needle. I'll let you know what Morehouse says when I casually ask him if they've looked in the red needle disposal boxes at the hospital for a syringe with mercury."

MOREHOUSE STOPPED BY the appraisal office two days later, on Wednesday. I let him in and guided him to the visitor chair next to my desk.

"George tells me it's better to talk to you about Eleanor's murder when you're in the office."

"It's not that I hide a lot from Scoobie," I said, quickly.

He grunted. "I've known you to do that. And I generally don't like it when you butt in. But the disposal boxes were a good idea. We'd debated the idea of a syringe, but couldn't figure out how he'd know to do it and where he'd get rid of it."

"And?"

"We've looked at all the boxes at the hospital and some places he might have gone to before he got back to Lakewood. Once he got to home turf, he'd have a lot of options."

"What about his work?"

"Hasn't gone back yet. And they'd know because he has to use an ID badge to get in and out of the building."

"How do you look for syringes without getting exposed to mercury?"

"There's a thing called a mercury analyzer. About the size of one of those old Dust Buster vacuum things."

"So, like a breadbox," I mused.

He grinned. "Yeah, but that's kind of old-fashioned."

"Funny. You going to tell me anything else?"

He grimaced. "That Mrs. Covington could give your aunt a run for her money when it comes to persistence. Says this is the angriest she's ever been. You don't talk to her?"

"She knows Renée a lot better. She and Eleanor were in the same high school class."

He stood. "We're looking hard at the husband. He has the skills, but the motive isn't too clear. They seemed to get along."

"He's a chemist," I said, almost hopefully.

"Yeah, but you need this stuff called evidence. We got nothin' that connects him to the mercury."

"I thought if murder isn't for love, or lack of it, it's usually for money."

Morehouse didn't comment on that, but said, "Problem is, whoever did it seems to have covered their tracks pretty well. I'd hate it if we couldn't catch the SOB who killed her."

Chapter Twenty-Two

OVER THE NEXT week, in between working and planning for Halloween, I began to wonder if Eleanor's killer really would get away with it. Kevin still touched base with Scoobie every few days. The big news was that he had joined a grief group at the hospital in Lakewood.

Scoobie confided that it was difficult to listen to Kevin talk about the grief group discussions, because it made Scoobie think about how he'd feel if something happened to me.

I found myself wondering if Kevin had gotten Eleanor's life insurance money yet and used some of it to buy a boat.

I MET GEORGE AT Java Jolt the following Tuesday, greeting him with, "It's been more than two weeks since Eleanor died, and I've only seen basic information in the paper."

"Maybe you should call the editor. He's the one who fired me. Listen, the syringe idea had a lot of promise but we can't make one with mercury vapor or residue, or whatever you call it, appear in a box of used needles."

I lowered my voice slightly. "The police liked the idea. They're looking at sharps boxes around town."

"Jolie, there could be hundreds of them within three square miles of Ocean Alley that they didn't get to."

"Correct. If you can think of any logical locations for them to search, we should pass on the idea." I saw the look of frustration on George's face. "Where else would you suggest?"

"I'd say the building he works in, but last time I checked, he still hadn't come back to work."

"You check?" I asked.

"Every couple days. I call and say I'm a sales rep from a company his firm might do business with and I promised to return his call. They tell me he's on an extended leave but someone else can help me."

"And you hang up? Can't they tell who you are?"

"We PIs know how to scramble calls. I make it look like I'm calling from Boston."

"Now that I think about it, there were a couple of people in expensive business suits at Eleanor's memorial service. I bet they were from Good Life Pharmaceuticals. You'd think there would have been a lot more from his work."

"Maybe they're as fond of him as you and your sister are."

I thought some more. "If he took a syringe to Lakewood, he'd would've had to get rid of it when he first went back there."

"Or along the way," George said.

We were silent for nearly thirty seconds.

"He got up there pretty fast. My sister met him in the lobby of Eleanor's mother's place less than an hour after he left Ocean Alley. He wouldn't have had time to get off the parkway and look for a place that had a disposal box."

"Yeah, but the parkway has those service areas all along it, so you don't have to get off and back on again and pay more tolls."

"True." I thought for a moment. "The Judy Blume Service Area would have been the one to stop at."

"What was the old name?" George asked, irritated. He found renaming the service plazas after famous New Jersians unhelpful, maintaining you could tell nothing about their whereabouts from the name.

"Monmouth, and now Judy Blume. It's right before the Lakewood exit, as you well know."

"Well, let's go there." He stood.

I glanced at my watch. "It's eleven-thirty, and I don't have to get the kids until three-thirty. But I'm not up for stealing sharps boxes."

George's expression changed to what I call crafty. He used to adopt that look more often when he was a reporter. "I rented one of those mercury-analyzers. They're like a Geiger counter for mercury."

"Morehouse mentioned using one. How long can you keep it?"

He frowned. "At one-hundred-eighty dollars a day, I only have it for two days, so let's go." He pointed toward Java Jolt's door to the boardwalk.

I flushed and didn't stand. "You don't need me. He would have put it in a men's room disposal box."

George slowly sat down again.

I noted a couple sitting near the window staring at us. They probably thought it was some sort of lovers' quarrel. I felt like he had tried to trick me into going to hunt for a box by springing the idea on me. "What are you waiting for?"

George shifted in his chair. "I thought, well, you could, like, cover me."

I gave a derisive laugh. Not an attractive sound. "Right. Stand guard with a taser or something?"

Megan called from the counter, "What are you two up to?"

George turned to grin at her. "Planning Halloween costumes."

"Uh huh," she said.

"Like you should be trusted with a weapon," I muttered.

"I'm not talking about tackling someone. But if I went in and you saw a restroom cleaner or a security guy approaching, you could, I don't know, do a bird call."

Now my laugh was more genuine. "I'm not going to chirp outside a men's bathroom on the parkway…" I stopped. Something about a bathroom tickled my memory. My sister's face came to mind.

"What?" George asked.

"My sister called me, that first day. When she went to sit with Eleanor's mother after Kevin told her about it."

"So what?"

"She said she had stepped out of the apartment to go to the restroom. I think she wanted a break from trying to comfort someone who's inconsolable."

"Ah. But that would be a women's restroom. So, I'd need your help."

I shook my head. "It's a guest restroom. I've seen it. Unisex." I picked up my purse from the floor. "I'll text Scoobie so he knows I'm going to Helen Covington's place."

George grinned, stood, and put a five-dollar bill in the coffee shop tip jar as he walked out.

WE DID NOT STOP at the rest area, but got off at the exit closest to Lakewood and began driving the few miles northwest to that town.

"Are you sure you know how to use the analyzer?" I glanced into George's back seat, where a carrying case sat. "Sergeant Morehouse said the one they used was the size of a dust buster. Yours looks smaller."

"Yeah, when it's out of the case it's about the size of a shoebox, but thinner. Easier to conceal when I go in places, which is why I'm wearing this jacket."

"Gee, your face may yet be on a wanted poster. Do you know how to use it?"

George frowned. "I practiced a few times. I know I can make it work, but it's not like I had any mercury to test it on."

"How will you know if there's mercury in the needle box? Does it flash lights or something?"

"There's a screen that gives a reading, but I rented this one because it also has an audible alarm."

That worried me. Would the restroom sound like a fire alarm? "How loud?"

He took his eyes from the road for a second and grinned at me. "I'll let you know when we find some."

AT THE RECEPTION DESK, I introduced myself and George, and said we were friends of Mrs. Covington.

As we signed the visitor log, the fifty-something woman shook her head. "Poor Helen. Only one child and she dies like that."

"Yes, the funeral was very sad." I sensed the woman wanted to chat, so I pointed toward Mrs. Covington's hallway. "We thought she'd like a visit."

We walked to the left, passing a sitting room of sorts with a big screen TV tuned to baseball playoffs. The one person in the room faced it, but I could only see the back of a man's head. Just past the room, we turned right, and I pointed to the unisex restroom.

George said nothing, but entered it and clicked the lock.

I heard the metallic snap as he pulled up the antenna on the device he'd shown me. In about fifteen seconds a loud beeping noise sounded. And did not stop.

Pounding feet came from the direction of the sitting room and a man of about seventy ran toward the noise and stopped. "What the hell is that?"

In a second I took in a physique and manner that said 'retired cop.' Then the door to the restroom opened and George, analyzer in hand, said, "I don't know how to…"

The man shoved George in the shoulder, pushed him back into the restroom, and grabbed the analyzer from his hand. "What are you trying to do?"

George had the presence of mind not to push back. "Detecting mercury. We should probably step into the hall and close the door."

The man backed up, looked at the device, and flipped a small toggle switch. The noise stopped. He glared at George as several people stood a few feet away, gaping. "Any maintenance people are supposed to check in at the front desk."

Calmly, George said, "I'm sorry, I didn't know."

The man looked at me and I swallowed. "If you call Helen Covington, we can explain everything."

THE MAN'S NAME WAS Joseph DelVecchio and he was indeed a retired police officer. Which explained why the Lakewood police came so quickly.

At Helen Covington's request, we sat in her apartment rather than in the police station, as Officer Nadine Lambert would have preferred. I sat next to Helen on the loveseat, and George positioned himself across from DelVecchio, who sat at Helen's dinette set. Since it was a small apartment, they were only a few feet from the loveseat.

After brief introductions, Helen spoke first. "Officer Lambert, I've known Jolie since before she was in kindergarten. I'd like you to start with the assumption she and her friend meant no harm."

Lambert nodded but remained impassive.

I glanced from Mrs. Covington to DelVecchio and Lambert and nodded toward George. "George Winters is my husband's best friend, and he's trying to find out how someone could have given mercury to Eleanor in a syringe and then hidden it."

Helen's face broke into a slow smile. "Well, Mr. Winters, you just became my best friend."

He nodded toward her, genially.

Lambert, who had remained standing, took the analyzer from DelVecchio, who it turned out had been the training officer in the Lakewood Police Department when she joined eight years ago. "Sarge, did you see how this thing worked?"

He glanced at George. "All I did was turn off the damn thing to get the loud beeping to stop. The knucklehead here didn't know how to use a toggle switch."

"If I may," George pointed to his jacket's right pocket. "I'll show you the brochure." He started to hand it to DelVecchio, but he nodded to Lambert. "Show Officer Lambert."

She looked at the brochure cover, opened the tri-fold, and compared the analyzer to the photo of it. "What were you two trying to do?"

George started to answer, but I butted in. "My sister was Eleanor Covington's, Eleanor Fielding's, close friend. I was in the coffee shop in Ocean Alley when Eleanor collapsed, and my husband sat with Mr. Fielding as Eleanor died."

I glanced at Mrs. Covington, who said, "That would be her husband, who did not call me to my dying daughter's bedside. He easily could have." She held up her phone. "My last contact from my daughter was a text that Friday morning."

I glanced at her phone, with its large-print text, as she replaced it in her lap. *How many hours did Eleanor suffer after she sent that ten AM message?*

"I'm sorry it's been so hard, Helen," DelVecchio said.

Officer Lambert returned her gaze from Mrs. Covington to me. "And?"

"The hospital ran tests that said her blood had toxic levels of mercury, and the police think it could have come from some chocolate candy delivered to the Fieldings that morning. At the beach rental property they were in."

"I read about that. I don't remember anything about candy."

I mentally berated myself for mentioning the chocolate. "I don't think that's been on the news yet."

George chimed in. "Jolie had the idea that mercury could have been in a syringe, and the Ocean Alley police used something like this," he nodded to the analyzer, "to check needle boxes down there."

Lambert looked up from the brochure, which she had continued to scan. "And they sent you up here rather than call us?

"Uh, no," George said. "We had the idea to come."

I cleared my throat.

"My idea," he said, quickly. "I asked Jolie to join me."

DelVecchio looked up from where he'd been scrolling on his phone and raised his eyebrows as he looked at George. "I see you have an ad for private investigation services in Ocean Alley, Mr. Winters."

In irritation, Lambert plopped the brochure onto a lamp table next to where I sat. "Who should I talk to in the Ocean Alley department?"

I HAD TOLD SCOOBIE I would stop by to see Helen Covington, but had not said I'd be with George or what we'd be doing. Two things kept him from blowing up at us that Tuesday evening. The twins were upstairs in Terry's room, watching Frozen II. And Sergeant Morehouse had not been nearly as angry as we've seen him on other occasions.

"Okay, you two, we're talking about this here because I'm not going to stick Scoobie babysitting by himself when he didn't do nothin' foolish."

Scoobie smiled slightly. "It's called parenting. But thank you."

Ramona said nothing.

Sergeant Morehouse frowned. "What you did was stupid. A good attorney could say you planted a syringe and contaminated evidence by using that machine."

I gulped and looked at Scoobie, who might have been enjoying the conversation.

"But at least you didn't open the box," Morehouse said, "and this does give us is the chance to question Mr. Fielding more, let's say, forcefully."

"You mean you didn't already?" George asked.

"No, Sherlock. We asked him a lot of questions about how she might have been exposed, how he spent his time, what they ate. But we had no basis — other than intuition — to treat him as a suspect."

"Did he even have access to mercury?" I asked.

"Not at work, certainly. But if he got any, his work coulda given him the chance to put it in a syringe." Morehouse nodded at me. "You and your sister both mentioned Eleanor's antique barometer."

"Even if he didn't extract it from there," Scoobie said, "it might have let him know to look for it in old devices."

I felt my shoulders relax. It was the first time Scoobie had given even the slightest indication he thought Kevin could have killed his wife. I was truly sorry if he'd done that, but I hated to be on the opposite side of something from the love of my life.

"So, what'll you do next?" George asked.

"Like I'd tell you, Sherlock." He pointed a finger at George. "Do not talk to Kevin Fielding." He shut his notebook, looked at me, and lightly shook his head.

ON WEDNESDAY, I found two new appraisal requests on my desk, and quickly began doing the research I like to have under my belt before I visit a property. I promised myself I wouldn't think about syringes, needle boxes, or the Garden State Parkway.

Harry came in about ten and I asked him if he thought a multi-family house near the edge of town, near St. Anthony's, would possibly be worth more than the price of the agreed-upon contract. "It looks as if was treated for termites two years ago. I know the treatment lasts for decades, but it also seems to have deflated the value."

"I thought that, too. Once it's treated, it doesn't bring the value down from an appraisal perspective."

I met his eyes across the room and saw he was grinning.

"Okay, I guess you heard about it from Aunt Madge."

"It's not the kind of thing the police would usually consider briefing her on, but since it was you, they did."

"Is she embarrassed?"

"Not at all. She's convinced one of these days you'll do something that could land you in jail, but this isn't it."

I frowned. "I wonder what the police in Lakewood will do with the needle box."

"I bet it's already in a biohazard room somewhere. You didn't have any exposure, did you?"

"None. Nothing registers on George, and he was next to the box. As was any guest to the senior living facility who used that restroom, but nobody talked about that."

"Captain Tortino told Madge that finding the syringe is a big deal, but they'll have to do a lot of legwork to definitely tie it to Eleanor's husband."

"I'm glad it's their legs. I'm out of it."

Chapter Twenty-Three

THE NEXT MORNING at ten o'clock, Josh carried the bucket of cleaning supplies, duster, and floor mop to the door of Buck's newest property. The multi-family house had been Lester's listing, and Buck was waiting to take full possession until the electrical system could be upgraded. Josh figured there had been some interesting discussions to get to that point.

Everything had taken longer than Buck wanted. Plus, the electrician who had begun the rewiring had poked a few holes in the walls. Buck grumbled about having to pay the painters to patch them.

All Josh wanted to do was focus on work. Eleanor Fielding's death had shaken him. Not just because a woman died, but because he had been in that cottage not long before she did. If George hadn't found out how the package with chocolates ended up on the porch, would he have been a serious suspect?

Josh went back to the car, glad for the crisp October weather. After he took out the broom and dustpan, he paused to study the aging Victorian. It had survived well past its heyday. Buck would ultimately have to put more than spit and polish into the place.

The narrow porch looked as if it had been part of a larger one, now gone. Two doors faced the street, one into the largest unit on the main floor, and another, on the right, which led to a staircase to the upper two floors and four additional units. The key was where Buck said it would be, on the ledge above the door on the left.

The front door squeaked as Josh opened it. He murmured. "Vacationers won't like that."

Buck had had the interior painted in the palest blue possible. The wide-planked floor had been repainted a light gray, and the trim was now a bright white. New plates on the light switches rounded out the quick work. If the contractors hadn't left paint chips everywhere, Buck could start moving in furniture.

He glanced at the round ceiling light fixture in the large living room. Probably original to the house. The glass wasn't cracked, but the metal around the edges showed some rust.

But that wasn't Josh's business. Buck had negotiated pre-settlement occupancy with the current owner, and Josh's job today was to clean the largest of the five units.

He made his way down the hall to the kitchen and placed his cleaning supplies on the counter. Two foam-backed, brightly colored area rugs lay on the linoleum flooring, probably covering blemishes.

He'd get it cleaned well. But unless Buck eventually rented it at bargain rates, there would be complaints, starting with the lack of a garbage disposal and age of the kitchen appliances.

Josh spent an hour in the kitchen and half-an-hour in the large bathroom with its claw-foot tub. No shower. At least Buck had had someone replace all the faucets.

He cleaned the living room floor and tossed the dirty water out the back door. Two hours already, and at least two more to go. This would be a test of the agreement that Josh would keep track of what he did and be paid by the hour.

As he started for the hallway that led to the bedrooms, a car door slammed on the street in front of the house. Josh walked to the window and grinned, then opened the front door. "Jolie Gentil, I thought you already appraised this place."

"I did. Buck thinks I should have called one of the…wow!" Jolie turned in a circle to take in the changes since she'd last been in the house. "Did you paint all this?"

"Nope. I swept up a lot of the painter's mess, but Buck used a crew from Ocean Grove."

"He must have been in a hurry. One of the boardwalk shops had to hire them because no one local could do it for a few weeks."

Josh grinned. "I'd like to think he had to pay more."

Jolie looked at her watch. "He asked me to meet him here, but my time is money on a workday. Wish he'd hurry up."

"If your time is money, what were you and George doing up in Lakewood looking for needle disposal boxes?"

"Jeez. I didn't think people were supposed to know that."

"George told Megan, I had coffee in Java Jolt. You know how it is."

"Yeah, I know. I'm trying to just focus on family and appraisals. No one except George is happy we went up there."

"Okay. I'll go back to asking you about your work. Why did Buck ask you to meet him here?"

"Buck mentioned that he might rent the entire house to families for reunions or other family gatherings, and he wanted to say it has more bedrooms than I put on the appraisal."

"And you can change it just because he asks? Wait a minute, it'll take months to get this place to a barely acceptable level."

Jolie shook her head. "Can't imagine it would work, but I don't have to deal with that. I just have to make it clear that if there's no closet, it's not a bedroom. I think the two bedrooms on this floor had big ones."

"I haven't looked at them yet, and I need to get busy cleaning them."

Jolie looked around the living room again. "Is it just these rooms that look better?"

"I didn't see them before, but you're welcome to look at the bedrooms with me." He walked to the room that was on the left in the short hallway off the living room and opened the door, still facing Jolie. "Here you go."

He hadn't expected the look of horror on her face, and turned to see what had caused that reaction.

Lying face-down on the floor was Buck Brock. A very dead Buck Brock, judging by the dent in the back of his head and the twisted position of an outstretched arm.

The 9-1-1 operator put Josh through to Sergeant Morehouse right away, but he didn't initially believe Buck could be dead. "I got the ambulance coming. Did you check for a pulse?"

"The back of his head has been caved in. I didn't want to add my DNA or fingerprints to the room."

Josh could hear Morehouse yell instructions to another cop as he closed his car door and started the engine.

"Jolie and I will be on the porch."

"Jolie!" He almost stammered. "What the hell is she doing there?"

"Buck wanted to meet her here."

"Why? Lemme talk to her," Morehouse said.

"She's on the porch, pretty upset. Can you talk to her when you get here?"

"Yeah, yeah." Morehouse hung up.

Josh started to shut the door to the bedroom, but instead left it open. Over and over he asked himself why he had taken this job. He had no business coming back to Ocean Alley. Scoobie would have been okay, and he'd begun to make a life for himself away from here.

He took in the large living room. No way he could tell if anything was out of place because there was no furniture and he'd never been here until today. His first concern should be Buck, but all he could think about was how it would look for him. He wished he could see or remember something that would ensure the police knew he hadn't killed Buck.

Josh joined Jolie on the porch and sat next to her on the top of the porch steps that led to the sidewalk in front of the house. It seemed so peaceful. Across the street sat a compact bungalow with a well-kept yard that featured a mature maple tree and a large birdhouse. How could someone have been murdered on such a quiet street?

He glanced at Jolie. "I have some water in the car. Would you like some?"

She looked at him almost in horror.

"You don't have to take it," he said, quickly.

"Eleanor Fielding's mom asked me to go to Lakewood to visit her just after Eleanor died. Because I'd seen Eleanor in Java Jolt before she got really sick. When I asked her mom if she'd like some water, she said people kept offering it to her. Something to do."

"Ah. When there's nothing you can really do to help someone, offer them a drink." He touched her elbow with his. "No liquor, of course."

She grimaced. "I generally don't drink because Scoobie doesn't. Right now, I could use a good belt."

Chapter Twenty-Four

I STAYED ON THE PORCH with Josh, staring straight ahead. He now sat with one elbow on his knee, forehead in one hand.

"You okay?" I asked.

"Of course not. Are you?"

"I still don't feel anything yet, except maybe sick to my stomach."

Sirens grew louder. Josh raised his head as Morehouse pulled to the curb, jerked his car into park, and slammed the car door. A patrol car pulled in behind him.

He came up the walk faster than I've seen him move. "What the hell happened?"

As we stood, I said, "We don't know."

Josh said. "There are two bedrooms. Buck is in the one on the left, off the living room. I didn't shut the door."

"Morehouse pulled on a pair of vinyl gloves. "Show me."

"If it's all the same to you, I'd rather wait out here."

Morehouse reached in the pocket of his sports jacket and took out another pair of gloves, which he tossed at Josh. "It's not the same. Lead the way."

Josh opened the door to the house and gestured that Morehouse should precede him. "I talked to Buck late last night."

Morehouse turned his head. "About what?"

"Cleaning. Buck wasn't the owner yet, but he made arrangements with the seller so he could get some work done to be ready to rent it."

"How'd you get in?"

"Buck left a key on ledge above the door. I could barely reach it."

No one had told me to wait on the porch, so I followed them. The really tall officer who had driven the patrol car nodded to me and followed, saying nothing.

Morehouse stopped at the open bedroom door and stared at Buck. "You didn't touch him?"

Josh shook his head. "Didn't walk but a couple feet into the room. Didn't see any blood, but it was obvious he was dead."

Morehouse tilted his head toward the still-closed door to second bedroom. "You go in there?"

Josh backed up a couple of feet. "Nope."

Morehouse nodded to the second officer, and both drew their guns. Morehouse pointed toward the kitchen and Josh and I moved there. I couldn't see the two men, but heard a doorknob hit the wall as they entered the room."

Both said, "Clear!"

Josh wore a deep frown as he faced me. "It never occurred to me to check in there."

"Why would you think of it?" We walked back into the front room and watched the men holster their guns.

Morehouse pointed a finger at Josh. "Nobody else was here, or in the yard, when you got here?"

"Nope. Buck had to be the only one who knew I'd be here. He called about ten-thirty last night. I didn't even know the crew he hired to paint had done so much work yesterday."

The other officer said, "If he came over here late and put the key above the door, it could have been noticed."

"That's why numeric keypads are a good idea," Morehouse said. To me, he pointed to the front door. "Outside." To the officer he said, "Avery, check the houses near here. See if people saw anyone besides Josh and Jolie."

"On it." He left.

I turned to follow Avery, but Morehouse stopped me. "Why are you here, Jolie?"

"Buck called this morning and asked me to meet him here. I think he wanted to argue with me about something in the appraisal report I did."

"When did he call?"

I checked my phone. "At eight-thirty-three."

"Don't erase your phone log."

A voice came from the porch. "Sergeant Morehouse?"

"We're in here," he said.

We all turned as Sergeant Dana Johnson came toward us. She nodded at Josh but spoke to Morehouse. "I looked around the outside and didn't see anything. Houses on either side are summer rentals, and they look vacant. I'll check with Avery."

Josh backed up a couple steps so Dana could look in the bedroom. She shook her head. "Huh. He wouldn't win any popularity contest, but I sure wouldn't have expected this."

Morehouse turned to Josh. "Did you call anyone besides us?"

"Nope."

"I don't want you here when the media shows up. Ride back to the station with Dana. Have some of our crud that passes for coffee."

Though it was an order rather than a request, I got the sense Morehouse didn't think Josh killed Buck.

Josh frowned lightly. "For the record, I didn't kill him."

"Wouldn't make sense," Morehouse said, "but we'll talk more. The odds of someone being at spots related to two murders are…huge."

Josh fished the keys for his rental car out of his pocket. "And it would have to be me."

I didn't blame him for the bitterness in his tone. *Should I feel guilty? I recommended him for this work.*

Josh extended a hand with the keys. "You want me to move my rental car down a couple houses, or you want to have somebody do it?"

When Morehouse hesitated, he added. "Nothing in it except the rental agreement in the glove box. You can go through it."

Morehouse looked to Dana. "He can follow you to the station, but he should park his car in the staff lot."

As Josh followed Dana through the small yard, a van that said "Miller County Medical Examiner" pulled up across the street.

This is definitely the time to leave. I must have given some indication that I thought this.

"You can't go yet, Jolie. Tell me more."

I heard the heavy door of the ME's van shut and wheels of a gurney rumble toward the house. "Like I said, Buck called me about eight-thirty this morning."

Morehouse cut in. "Why?"

"I'm trying to tell you. Last week he was irritated about something in the appraisal, but I suggested a way he could get around some bad wiring. He liked that idea. Today, he said I'd made a mistake to call a bedroom a den."

"And you couldn't deal with it over the phone?"

"We could have. He said I had to see it and to meet him here at noon. I was going to say no, but he hung up."

"You came anyway?"

I shrugged. "He asks, asked, the banks to use us. It's a lot of business."

"He said nothing else?"

"Oh, he said noon because he had to meet someone else before me. But he didn't say what time."

Morehouse pulled out his notebook as he went to the screen door to open it when the ME and his gurney got to the porch. "Nothin' about who or where?"

I shook my head slowly. "If he hadn't hung up on me, I might have asked."

I felt horrible about Buck, but also bad for Josh. Even if he were quickly cleared, his name would be associated with Buck's death.

"Jolie, snap out of it."

Morehouse must have been talking to me. I felt bewildered. I hadn't heard him.

He eyed me shrewdly. "I don't need you falling to pieces at my crime scene. I'll call you later this afternoon."

I straightened. "I don't fall to pieces."

"Of course you don't. Just leave."

FINALLY BACK AT STEELE Appraisals, I plopped the mail on my desk and turned on my computer. Before I had time to sign into our system, a car door slammed and someone ran up the porch steps. I stood. *Had something happened to Scoobie or the kids?*

Lester's raised voice accompanied thumping on the door. "Jolie. Lemme in!"

I half ran to the door and opened it, my heart pounding. *Megan? Max?* Lester wouldn't be the one bringing news about Scoobie or the kids. "What? What is it?"

Lester brushed past me and turned to face me. "Buck is dead. Josh found him in a house this morning. He's at the station."

I opened my mouth to tell him I knew this, but Lester kept going.

"George called me. He said his 'source' said it doesn't seem Morehouse thinks Josh did it, but he don't' know much for sure."

"Lester, I…"

Lester ran a hand over his sweaty forehead, moved to the room to the left of the foyer, and sat on the sofa, almost panting. "I can't believe Buck's dead. It coulda been any of us in empty houses."

His panic was making more sense. And I could have been one of those people. I lowered myself into the Queen Anne chair across from the sofa. "I was with Josh when we opened the door to a bedroom and found Buck."

"The hell you say!"

I told Lester about Buck's request that I meet him at the house on Seashore and finding Josh there cleaning. "Buck supposedly had permission from your seller to start painting. I think at least part of the rewiring had been done."

More sweat popped out on his forehead and he reached for a wad of tissues from a box on the lamp table next to the sofa.

"Why did George call you?" I asked. "Because it was your listing?"

"He didn't know you were there. He wanted me to tell you so you could tell Max. And maybe somebody needs to see if Josh needs a lawyer." He leaned into the sofa.

After several seconds, I said, "Annie." My high school classmate was now the county prosecuting attorney.

"Jeez. Does anybody really think Josh did it?"

"Maybe not, but he could probably use some advice." I pulled my phone from my bra, which made Lester look away. "She can tell someone from the public defender's office to head to the police station. Or tell me who to call."

I called and the secretary put me on hold. Annie came on the line in a few seconds. "I just heard. I can let Mason Mahoney in the public defender's office know, but it's up to him if he sends anyone down there. How the heck are you involved?"

"Josh and I found the body together."

She said nothing for several seconds. "If Mason needs to talk to you, I'll give him your number." She hung up.

I stared at my phone, and realized if I might be on police radar she couldn't talk to me. I sat back in my chair and regarded Lester. "Do you know if Buck was already paying the seller rent?"

"I gotta call the guy in Chicago." Lester pulled out his phone and shook his head at me. "I bet Buck didn't have money to go to settlement."

I raised both eyebrows. "He said something about regrouping financially after a divorce, but I didn't know he was that hard up."

Lester shrugged. "That mighta been a rumor."

Maybe deciding whether to swat down that rumor was part of the dilemma Lester talked to me about earlier. "I need to text Scoobie."

Lester went into the other room to make his call, and I was in the middle of texting when my phone rang.

Scoobie. I answered. "Are you calling about Buck?"

Without preamble, Scoobie said, "They think Josh did it?"

"Lester is with me in the office. George told him he doesn't think Josh is a suspect. Josh found Buck when he was cleaning a house, and..."

Scoobie swore softly. "I can't believe this. Have you told Max?"

"I'll find him now. I may make Lester help me." My mind went to Buck calling Max a weirdo. "Max has probably left Java Jolt."

Lester had walked back into the reception room and his expression said he had no desire to help. But I didn't know how Max would react. I didn't want to be by myself if he was upset that someone he knew had died.

"I gotta get back to X-ray. Text me." Scoobie hung up.

I stared at the phone. I hadn't had time to tell him I found the body with Josh.

My eyes went to Lester, but before either of us said anything a key turned in the front door and I recognized Harry's footsteps. I called, "We're in the reception room."

He stood at the room's threshold. "Madge called me after Captain Tortino talked to her."

"Because she knows Josh?" Lester asked.

Harry smiled briefly. "Because she's the mayor. And because Jolie was there, too." He nodded at Lester. "Where were you this morning?"

Lester pointed a finger at him. "Not funny."

Harry grinned. "Of course not. A man's dead. But still…"

I glanced at Lester, confused.

"I don't need a damn alibi," Lester said.

Harry grinned again.

Without thinking, I said, "Anyone who knew him needs one."

Lester barked his distinctive laugh.

Chapter Twenty-Five

I FELT BAD about my comment. Almost. "I'm going to call Megan to see if she knows where Max is." I went into the office portion of the first floor and dialed Megan from the landline.

She must have noted me on caller ID, because she began without saying hello. "Max is sitting near the supply closet in the back. He was talking to a customer and got upset, I think. He won't talk to me about it."

"I think I know why." I picked up my purse and made for the door. "I'm sorry to tell you, Megan, but Buck Brock was murdered this morning in one of the houses he owns."

"Oh my! Do the police know who did it?"

"I don't think so."

I mouthed "Java Jolt" to Harry and Lester. If Max was with Megan, I wouldn't need Lester. I told a sputtering Megan I'd see her in ten minutes.

At least twenty things went through my mind on the short drive to the boardwalk. We knew so little about Buck before he'd come to Ocean Alley a year or so ago, supposedly to rebuild his finances after a divorce. Had he left some big problems behind? Was his ex-wife especially bitter?

Buck had lived in Atlantic City, one of the most urban areas of the central and southern parts of the Jersey shore. Though its violent crime rate was more than double the national average, I found it hard to believe Buck would have been part of that element. But how would I know?

Besides, Buck could create enemies for himself after he'd been in a place for a week. People angry with him would not be limited to an ex-wife or the business partner Lester heard Buck had fought with at the Sandpiper. *Does Morehouse know about that?*

How serious could Buck's financial problems be? Even if he owed a lot of money to someone, it makes no sense to kill a person who's in debt to you. You'd never get it back.

I wished I had suggested George do a background check on Buck. At least a credit check.

I jogged up the steps to the boardwalk and was met with a stiff, cool breeze off the ocean. Fall had a definite chill this week. I clutched my jacket tighter.

A look in the Java Jolt window showed few customers. When I entered, Megan was making a fancy drink for a woman who seemed to have a list of beverages to purchase. Megan tilted her head in the direction of her back room.

I headed behind the counter and found Max sitting on a stool just inside the supply closet, head almost on his chest. "Max, I…"

"Jolie. Josh was going to Buck's house today. Buck's house."

I realized what he was thinking. "Max, Josh is fine. I was with him about an hour ago."

He raised his head, and then his hand, which had his phone in it. "Josh doesn't answer his phone. His phone."

I stooped so I wasn't looking down at him. I wanted to break the news to him quietly. "Josh is helping Sergeant Morehouse with…a big problem about Buck."

Max spoke as he might to a puppy or small child. "Jolie, Buck is dead. Someone killed him. Killed him."

"Uh, yes, I'm sad to say he is. Could you tell me where you heard that?"

"The painters," he said, as if this should mean something to me.

"The…oh, you mean one of the people working on the souvenir shop?"

"They moved to the French fry place. French fries."

"Ah. Well, some people were painting one of Buck's houses yesterday. Maybe they heard about his death today. I'm sorry you had to learn about it from them."

Max stared at the floor.

"I'd like to talk to the person who told you about Buck. Can you show me who it was?"

"You can talk. I'll stay here. Right here."

"I'll be back soon." I patted his knee and walked out of the work area and into the customer side of the shop. I said, "Back in a minute," to Megan and walked onto the boardwalk.

Almost directly across was the freshly painted souvenir shop, and three doors down sat the French fry stand. In warm weather, tourists lined up five and ten deep to buy cups of piping hot fries to douse in ketchup or vinegar.

Two men had propped a ladder against the small storefront and placed tarps on the boardwalk in front of it. They had started sanding and caulking, but not painting yet. I approached them. "Can I talk to you for a minute?"

The taller of the two had a leathery face. He looked like someone who had worked in the sun a lot rather than a guy who spent time at the shore. "For a minute. We're behind."

"Are you some of the people who painted the first floor of a Victorian on Seashore in the last couple of days?"

They had continued to work, but now turned to face me. "Who's asking?"

I introduced myself and added, "When I got to the house this morning, another man and I found Mr. Brock dead in one of the bedrooms."

The shorter man bore a beer belly and flaming red hair, which seemed to match his temperament. "You trying to accuse us, Lady?"

"What? No. He died between about 9:00 and 10:30 this morning. You were here. I wanted to know if anyone hassled you while you were working there yesterday, or came by looking for Buck Brock."

The shorter one turned back to scraping paint. "The only one who hassled us was the dead guy."

"Cheap bastard," said the taller man. "May he rest in peace."

"Uh, okay. Thanks." I had been about to say the police might want to talk to them, but these were not two guys I wanted to irritate. The police could do that.

Before I went back into Java Jolt, I texted George. "Did you ever do a background check on Buck?"

I returned to the coffee shop to find Max sitting in the same spot. "You've had a rough day, Max. May I drive you to your house?"

He pondered that. "Did the man who didn't like Buck kill him? Kill him?"

I stooped in front of him again. "Why do you think someone didn't like Buck?" I could think of a lot of reasons, but Max's comment would have to relate to an obvious one.

"The man with the flat hat kept pointing his finger at Buck. Red face. Buck had a red face."

"Do you think you could tell Sergeant Morehouse about that?"

He looked to the right.

"It would help Josh," I said.

He stood. "We need to go. You can drive, Jolie. Drive."

AT THE STATION, Officer Abrams was again at the counter. He looked from me to Max, and said, "Hey Max. How's Java Jolt today?"

"Megan is good."

Abrams nodded and looked to me.

"Max might be able to help Sergeant Morehouse. Or Sergeant Johnson."

"Oh, sure. Sergeant Johnson is here." He pushed a button on the phone's intercom and asked her to come to the front desk.

Dana came through the door that led to the bullpen. Her puzzled expression changed to bemused when she saw Max and me.

Max spoke. "Sergeant Dana. I can help."

She opened the door wider. "Of course you can."

It took thirty minutes and Josh's help before we understood that Max had been in the coffee shop when Buck and "the man with the flat hat" had started a heated — though quiet — discussion. Then they walked outside and talked on the boardwalk, but louder.

Dana pushed a few keys on her phone and held up a picture. "A flat hat like this?" The depiction was the type I associated with men drinking pints in English pubs, or maybe golfers.

Max nodded and she asked him about color, which he said was brown, then changed it to dark green.

I glanced at Dana. "That's not the kind of cap you see around here too much, especially when it's warm."

"Agreed. Max, can you think of any other time you saw the man with the flat cap?"

He shook his head rapidly, but stopped. "Sandpiper. Sandpiper."

Josh and I exchanged a look, and Josh asked. "The Sandpiper Bar and Grill. Is that a place you go to now?"

"Scoobie says no way. No way."

In spite of myself, I laughed. Max looked hurt, so I added, "That's exactly what Scoobie would say. He doesn't like it at all."

Dana asked. "Did you see the man entering or leaving the Sandpiper?"

"Coming out. Out."

Josh slapped himself on the forehead. "When I first came back, a man stopped me on the boardwalk."

"Same hat?" Dana asked.

"No. The man was on the Landlord Tenant Commission. He ran for city council a few years ago…"

"Stuart Cambridge." I said.

"Right. He welcomed me back, but he'd heard I'd be working for Buck. He said Buck was kind of rough sometimes. He mentioned him throwing punches at someone in the Sandpiper."

"He saw this?" Dana asked.

"I don't know if he saw it or heard about it," Josh said.

"The bartender might know." Dana stood to leave the room.

I was tempted to slap myself in the forehead. "Lester heard about that, too. Or at least he heard about one time Buck threw a punch."

Dana faced me. "Lester saw this?"

I shook my head. "After he heard about it, he asked Buck what happened. Buck said he and the other guy had owned property together, and Buck wanted to sell and the other man didn't."

Dana turned to Max. "You've been a big help." She left the room.

Max's face had almost no expression. "Buck is dead, Jolie. Dead."

"Yes," Josh said. "But Sergeant Johnson and Sergeant Morehouse will find out who killed him. You'll be safe."

Max half hung his head in dejection. "I'm bad luck. Bad luck."

Josh smiled. "Why do you say that?"

"The lady died in Java Jolt. Java Jolt."

"You were there when she first got sick, and Buck is someone you knew. But she didn't die there, and you are not bad luck." Josh nodded toward me. "Jolie was in Java Jolt that day, and she knew Buck too. Is she bad luck?"

Max regarded me and shook his head.

"Come on, Max," Josh said. "I'll walk you to your house. I haven't seen it yet."

Max brightened. "You haven't seen my house. My house."

"I'll come in for twenty minutes," Josh said. To me, he mouthed, "Tell Dana I'll be back."

As they left the conference room, Max outlined his idea that Josh could stay in his second bedroom.

My phone pinged with a message from George. "Checked as soon as I heard he was dead. Call me."

Dana returned and frowned when she saw I was alone.

"Max was getting kind of skittish. Josh walked him home. He'll be back soon."

She sat. "He held together pretty well. Avery's going to the Sandpiper in civvies. That's the best way to go in there."

"Would someone attack a cop?"

She shook her head. "Nope. But the owner swears he loses a day's worth of business if we go in uniform, and he can be helpful. When he wants to be."

"Speaking of helpful." I glanced at my phone. "I texted George to see if he had done a background check on Buck." I acted as if I was seeing the message for the first time. "I think he just did one."

Dana smiled slightly. "Police do those, too, you know."

I almost felt relieved that she didn't want to talk about it.

"If there's nothing else, Jolie," she said.

"Only that Max heard about Buck's death from some painters on the boardwalk. They were at Buck's place yesterday. Will you talk to them?"

"Already did. Their crew chief drove by the place on Seashore when our cars were there. He said he stopped to talk to a neighbor down the street who told him Buck's body was in that house. We'll check it out more, but unless Buck had already stiffed the painters, I doubt there's a connection."

"I don't think he'd had time."

Chapter Twenty-Six

I STOPPED AT THE office to pick up paperwork so I could work on an appraisal report at home. Harry had already left.

I needed to get to Sand and Sea by three-fifteen. As I hurriedly stuffed a notebook and information on comps in my messenger bag, George called.

He sounded irritated. "The background checks the police and I did showed essentially the same information."

He can be mad that I told Dana he did one.

George continued, "Buck never had a domestic abuse charge, but he had almost every other kind of dispute, to use the term in the broadest sense."

I locked the office door on my way out, but dropped the phone as I did so.

"What the heck are you doing, Jolie? Trying to break my eardrum?"

"Trying to get out of the office to pick up the kids on time. Wait until I'm in the car with earbuds."

"All right, all ready," he said.

When I was settled and had turned the car on, I asked, "Was he convicted of anything?"

"Criminal charges, no. Probably could have been, but he usually argued with people as obnoxious as he was, or so it seems. No one ever wanted the police to present details to the local prosecuting attorney."

I turned the corner to head toward Sand and Sea. "You said no criminal charges."

"Lots of civil disputes, mostly about real estate purchases or tenants who didn't pay rent. Seems he let one couple get behind while the wife said she was being treated for cancer. But he filed suit because they skipped out without paying like…six months of rent. Hefty amount."

"He's told me he got 'screwed over' in the past."

"Probably worked both ways," George said. "But for that couple, he got a lawyer to file a suit against them and he got a $30,000 settlement."

"That's a lot of rent."

"Wife didn't have cancer, so it was all a big scam. I think that's why he got the award."

"Did that couple pay Buck the money? Maybe they were really mad at him."

"About six months ago, after he moved here, they signed a note to pay that and attorney fees, but I can't tell if payments started."

"Is any of this helpful?" I asked.

"I wouldn't know, because Sergeant Johnson told me I wasn't to act on any information I got through a background check."

"Oh."

"Yeah, oh," George said. "Maybe does me a favor. I'm spending too much time on this, and nobody's paying me a dime. You should try not to give me ideas. At least any you plan to repeat to the police."

SCOOBIE HAD HEARD I was at the Seashore house when Josh opened the door to find Buck, but he acknowledged that he'd been the one to cut our phone call short.

We were in the kitchen Thursday evening, grabbing dishes to put on the table for dinner. "And then I rushed over to find Max. Thank God he was still at Java Jolt."

"I don't know whether to feel more sorry for Josh or Max."

"Definitely Josh. Finding Buck was…creepy."

Lance had just come into the kitchen. "I want to be something really creepy for Halloween."

Leia spoke from behind him. "You could be yourself."

"Hey," he began.

"I thought you wanted to be R2D2," I said. "I found a costume on Amazon and ordered it for you."

He looked at Leia. "Yeah. I'm going to beep really loud!"

"Swell," I muttered.

"What did you decide on, Leia?" Scoobie asked.

"I'm going to be Elsa from *Frozen*."

I felt panic. Those outfits must be long gone. "That's a fancy costume."

"Aunt Madge is making it. The ones in the store are boring."

I handed them silverware and napkins and they raced for the dining room.

I traded raised eyebrows with Scoobie. "Did you know she's making the costume?"

"Nope. When would she have time?"

"I think she manufactures…" The house phone rang and Scoobie grabbed the kitchen extension.

His look of amusement said it was George. "Sure, but wait until after bath time." He hung up and looked at me. "He says he has big news."

WHETHER GEORGE'S NEWS was good or bad would probably depend on a person's point of view. I expected it to be about Buck's murder, but George had learned more about the investigation into Eleanor's death.

He walked from our living room to the kitchen and back. "Morehouse dragged Fielding down here for two hours of questioning today."

Scoobie's expression did not give away his thoughts. "Kevin was at Simple Dreams Independent Living, but maybe someone else put the syringe there to implicate Kevin."

I wanted to ask how big he thought the universe was of people who wanted Eleanor dead and also wanted Kevin to be blamed. But I didn't.

George took a banana from the fruit bowl in our kitchen and finally sat on the couch. "I heard when the cops questioned him, Fielding's irritation bordered on rage some of the time."

"How do you know this?" Scoobie asked.

"Dana called me. She and Morehouse wanted you two to know that Kevin regards you and Renée as interfering busybodies, and your aunt and her loser husband…"

"He called Harry a loser?" I asked.

"Apparently the funeral home told Fielding that Harry insisted Mrs. Covington should be able to rent a separate room for the visitation."

Scoobie frowned. "Kevin was so angry the police wanted to warn us? Why didn't one of them call?"

George shrugged. "Not sure it's a warning, but they wanted you to know what he said. They've got their hands full. First Eleanor's murder, now Buck's. They have people canvasing to find out if neighbors saw anyone near the house where Buck died." He peeled the banana and looked for a place to throw the peel.

I pointed to the kitchen, and avoided meeting Scoobie's eyes.

When he came back, George added, "Tomorrow's Friday and the start of Halloween weekend. I stopped at the station today to find out more about Buck, and there were charts on the walls. Stuff like who would be at which intersection during the parade, who would be liaison with the Chamber of Commerce about shoplifting."

"I get that," I said. "We have more Halloween planning than usual. The kids want to go to the parade before trick or treating."

"Yeah," Scoobie said. "We managed to avoid the parade until this year."

George winked at me. "I have it on good authority that your husband is the one who told the kids to ask about it."

"I kind of figured." I looked at Scoobie. "Do you think we really should be worried about Kevin?"

He expelled a breath. "One thing I've learned in talking to him since Eleanor's death is that he's very self-centered. No one else's grief could be as big as his. He's not ready to go back to work, but how will his company get along without him?"

"And that means he wouldn't be a problem for you guys?" George asked.

"Not so much that. He could barely contain how angry he was about Jolie, Harry and Madge helping Mrs. Covington schedule that visitation. He said he thought he had everything under control."

"Control seems to be the key," I said.

Scoobie nodded toward me. "Does he know it was Jolie's idea to search the needle disposal boxes?"

"He has to know it was her or me," George said. "Doubt the police told him, but there were a bunch of people standing around after the mercury analyzer alarm went off. Anyone could have asked Helen Covington who we were."

I thought of something. "Helen said she thought Kevin tried to control Eleanor, and she might have been getting tired of it."

"I can buy that," Scoobie said. "And even that he wanted her dead rather than divorced, so he'd get the life insurance. But he's cunning, not stupid. He went to the senior living place to talk to Eleanor's mother. He wouldn't have put the syringe in a place that would directly connect him to the murder."

"He's not stupid," I said. "But I think he would like the idea of sticking it to Helen Covington by putting the needle in a box in her building."

George grinned broadly.

"What?" I asked.

"Sticking it to her? George said. "That's rich."

Scoobie smirked and I said, "Shut up, George!"

Chapter Twenty-Seven

THE *OCEAN ALLEY PRESS* article Friday morning was brief, but the headline was huge. "Local Property Developer Murdered."

Scoobie read it first. "All it really says is Buck was killed in the house, and it had to be not long before you and Josh found him."

I read it quickly. "It does say Josh and I aren't implicated. That's a biggie. Plus, it says the house didn't appear to have been broken into."

Aunt Madge called and I pressed speaker on my phone so I could finish eating before we had to rouse the kids. "I know you're up. I'm glad it says Buck had an appointment to meet you."

"Glad? Why?"

"I won't have to tell fifty people why you were there."

Scoobie grinned. "Always looking on the bright side, Aunt Madge."

Harry said, "A couple realtors called me yesterday to ask about you because they knew the appraisal had been done. I simply told them Buck wanted to argue about it, so that made sense to everyone."

Aunt Madge said, "There is the basic safety issue, and this happened right before a holiday weekend. When a crime seems random, it worries more people."

I tried to keep irritation out of my voice. "Tell people not to go into vacant houses."

WHEN I GOT TO Steele Appraisals later Friday morning, I called Josh to see if he'd decompressed after finding Buck's body yesterday.

"I was at the station until almost five yesterday. At least it let me help with Max."

"They can't really think you did it," I said.

"They were pretty clear about that, but Morehouse said they'll question me again if they find any evidence."

"What a thing to have hanging over your head!"

"Buck got the worst end of it. You probably know everybody in Ocean Alley who knew him. The police kept saying they had no idea who would kill him. Do you?"

"I don't know if you two talked much, but he came to Ocean Alley about a year ago, from Atlantic City. Hard to imagine he'd have had time to make somebody mad enough to kill him."

"Wouldn't take long," Josh mused. "Why Ocean Alley? I didn't hear him talk about family here."

"I don't know of any. He had a fairly recent divorce. He talked to me about kind of rebuilding financially." I suppressed a giggle. "By buying buildings here. I guess it's cheaper than where he was."

"Huh. What happens to his properties?"

"The one he was…in hadn't closed, so I guess the guy in Chicago keeps it. Or sells it again, anyway. The rest depends on his will. Assuming he had one." I wondered if he had changed it after his divorce. I thought about checking on-line county court records to see who his ex-wife was.

"Anyway," Josh said, "I'm okay, but I'm not going to work in vacant houses again. The paper this morning talked about how people like real estate agents or repair people never know what they'll find in an empty house."

"When it's a listing there's usually a special lock. But not after it's sold. The exterior doors of that house probably could have been opened with a butter knife."

"I had a key, but that's not really the issue. I need to do something besides clean houses."

"Do you have anything in mind? One of us could be a reference."

I found it ironic that I'd offer when only a few weeks ago I'd wished Josh had stayed away from Ocean Alley.

"Do you know Sal, the guy who owns Second Round Cold Drinks and Tea Bar? It's a couple miles from Ocean Alley."

"I've heard of the place but never been there. I think they do AA meetings, but not the family group ones."

"Right." He paused for a second and continued. "Sal's memory is fading. I don't know if that place can survive without him, but I'm going to talk to him about it."

When we hung up, I went to online court records for Atlantic County, home of Atlantic City. Buck Brock's divorce from Theresa Mae Brock had been finalized only last year, and the decree indicated she would again begin using her maiden name, Birmingham. Idly, I thought at least she hadn't had to change her monogram when she got married or divorced.

The newly rechristened Ms. Birmingham had a landline listing in Ocean City, a smaller town about twenty miles south of Atlantic City. I had no reason to call her. She might even resent it. Maybe a card.

It was only nine-thirty Friday morning. If I mailed a card soon, she might get it tomorrow. No! I stopped myself. I knew nothing about the woman. For all I knew she could have killed Buck. I deleted the Google search. Scoobie would be happy.

Before I went to the appraisal software, I checked for information on Buck in Atlantic County. Dana had told George he shouldn't do anything with the information he found, but nobody had told me that.

I went to the state courts online search site and put in Buck Brock's name. Nothing came up. I realized Buck probably wasn't his legal first name. I went to Google and put in his name and then variations of it. Eventually, I came up with Buford Brock. Brickface Brock, as Lester called him, did not look like a Buford, but I put it in the search fields.

Immediately information came up for Buford ("Buck") Brock. "I'll be darned."

Much of what George had mentioned was easily findable, including the names of the couple who tried to defraud Buck by feigning cancer and skipping out on their rent. Patrick and Jackie Abernathy. She of the cancer-free Abernathys. My eyes scanned the information, and I grinned before calling George.

"Jolie, I gotta get back to work," he said.

"Me, too. Did you know the Abernathys filed an appeal of the judgment the court levied against them?"

He said nothing.

"You know, the people who…"

"I know who you mean. What are you doing, Jolie?"

"Dana said you couldn't look, she didn't tell me that. The appeal was filed just five days ago. Didn't you see it?"

"No. I subscribe to a database that culls information from lots of others. It must not have updated from the Jersey state courts site."

"Doesn't this mean something?" I asked.

"It means you gave me an idea that didn't come from my background check on Buck. Talk to you later."

He could have said thank you.

AT TEN-THIRTY, A voice on the porch announced Lester. He didn't ring the bell. I went to a front window and parted a shade. Lester and an unknown soul were having a fierce phone debate about something. A few seconds later, he pushed what was likely the end call button and dropped the phone as he tried to slip it into the pocket of his trousers.

I backed away from the window and went to the door to open it as he raised his hand to knock. "Morning, Lester. Were you arguing with another appraiser?" I stood aside to let him in and he stalked to the office and sat next to my desk.

"That jerk who owned the five-plex on Seashore is going to relist it, but not with me."

"That's rude. Did he give a reason?"

"Said I should have told him more about the house's condition. I reminded him he's the one who thought he oughta be an absentee landlord for the last ten or whatever years."

"And that's when he pulled the listing?"

Lester shook his head. "That was his opening line. I spent money advertising that place. It's why he got such a quick offer."

"It looks even better now that the first floor has been cleaned up some and painted."

He let loose with a string of expletives.

"Good to know," I said. "Lester, why are you here today?"

He took a breath. "I wanna know who you think killed Buck. I mean, it coulda been any of us in there."

"I bet every agent in town thinks that. But I have no idea." I thought of the background check Dana had told George not to use to look into anyone.

Lester took the unlit cigar from his mouth and pointed it at me. "I gotta think it had something to do with that lady's murder."

"Eleanor? Why would you say that?"

He leaned forward in his seat. "This Fielding guy. Buck said he was a real, uh, jerk when he called to complain. He wrangles a freebie. Then, and this is the too bad part, the wife dies."

"Eleanor. Eleanor Fielding, used to be Covington."

"Right. So, Mayor Madge tells Buck it would be good for him to go to Lakewood for the service. He sees me in Java Jolt and complains how much time he'll waste, but he goes. And bein' Buck, he has some kind of fight with the guy."

"Yes, way to support a grieving husband," I said, dryly.

"Yeah. So, Buck says he told Fielding he knew what he was up to. You know, free weekends and stuff like that."

I held up a hand so I could think. *Could this be important?* "Did Buck specifically say the free weekend part, or just he knew what Kevin Fielding was up to?"

"How the hell should I know?" Lester asked. "I just know he made the guy mad."

I pressed him on it. "Did Buck *specifically* say he meant the free weekends when he told Kevin he knew what he was up to?"

Lester pondered this. "I don't have no idea."

Neither did I, and Scoobie and I had heard Buck say he told Kevin something like that, too. What if he said it in such a way that Kevin thought Buck meant he knew Kevin poisoned Eleanor?

I CONVINCED MYSELF TO call the station to talk to Sergeant Morehouse or Johnson to tell them what Buck had said to Kevin, with the strong qualifier that it could be nothing. And anyway, how would Kevin kill Buck and get away with no one seeing him? In broad daylight?

Twice I picked up my phone and put it back on the desk. The third time, I called and asked for either sergeant. Fortunately, Dana came on the line.

"When you were at the memorial service for Eleanor, did you see Buck talk to Kevin Fielding?"

"Buck? I stood in the back. I didn't see him at all."

"No, this was before. During visitation. Scoobie and I went from that room to the room where the service was to be held, maybe twenty minutes before it started. Buck was giving Kevin a hard time."

"Wait," Dana said. "Kevin Fielding's wife died after being in Buck's property, and Buck was giving Fielding a hard time?"

"Well…it was Buck. Anyway, Scoobie led him out of the room, and I told Kevin Buck shouldn't have said whatever he said."

"Which was?" Dana asked.

"I didn't know at the time, but after Scoobie took him out, Buck said he had heard that Kevin liked to say things like a room was bad or a meal wasn't good and try to get a freebie. Like at Buck's property."

"So, you're saying Kevin cheated Buck?"

"I doubt that. Buck was having trouble with a cleaning crew. What Buck said he told Kevin was something like, 'I know what you're up to.' Scoobie and I suggested he leave rather than stay, and he walked out with Madge and Harry. It didn't seem like a big deal at the time."

Dana said nothing at first, then, "So, you're wondering if Kevin misinterpreted what Buck said and felt threatened?"

I felt myself getting hot. "I know, it's stupid. I just thought… Buck was pretty hot under the collar at the funeral home."

"It's not stupid. It's something to add to the mix."

I quickly added, "But I have no real reason to think Kevin Fielding would hurt Buck. I mean, Buck irritated a lot of people." When she didn't respond, I asked, "Did Officer Avery learn more about the fight Buck got into in the Sandpiper?"

"He didn't learn a lot. The bartender said the men came in together and were talking loudly."

"Buck would," I said.

"He would. But then it went from loud to angry. It sounded as if it was about some real estate elsewhere, and Buck wanted to sell his part of it and the other guy didn't. Pretty much what Lester said."

"Can you find the guy?"

"Jolie, remember about not ticking off people who might be killers?"

"If you don't tell I asked, who would know?"

"You're too much. Turns out Buck threw the first punch. They both took a couple jabs, the bartender said they had to leave, and Buck laid a decent tip on the bar. Bartender let him come back. No more ruckus from Buck."

"That's not much help. Do you have any other leads?"

Dana kind of snickered. "We don't know much, Ms. Sleuth, beyond that he died between the time he called you and when Josh got to the place to clean. Buck should have taken Sergeant Morehouse's advice and put cameras in his place."

"I'm not really probing, I have two kids to raise. I just talk to my friends."

"You do a little more than that, and what Buck told you he said to Kevin was good to pass on. I'll talk to you later."

Good to pass on? I hoped she'd do something with the information. Though I couldn't think what it would be beyond talking to Kevin. He'd know where it came from.

I had to get crime out of my head. I had meant to talk to Aunt Madge about Leia's costume, but had forgotten. I didn't know her schedule today, so I texted, "Leia said u r making her costume. Sorry, I didn't know."

She replied ten minutes later, asking if she could call. I said yes, of course.

She began with, "I don't mind about the costume. I'm using the pattern I made for your fairy princess costume one year."

"Gee, you keep all that?"

"Patterns don't take up much room. I'm glad you could buy Lance's. I have no idea how to make a sort of round robot. But that's not why I wanted to talk to you. I think you should call Harry or me before you go into any of the houses."

"Harry always knows…"

"I don't mean letting him know you'll go someplace at two o'clock. I mean call right before you walk in a door. Maybe stay on the phone when you walk in."

I wasn't sure I wanted to commit to that, so I sidestepped. "Sounds like a good idea. Are people talking about Buck's murder?"

"Of course. He hadn't lived here long, but anyone who met him remembers him."

I remembered Max saw Buck arguing with someone and said so.

"Yes, the police talked to Cambridge. Buck told him he thought the Landlord Tenant Commission should be called the Old Farts' Commission. Stuart was lecturing him on how volunteers don't need to be insulted. The police think that's the exchange that Max saw on the boardwalk."

I wanted to fish for more information, but she sounded rushed. "We're going to the Halloween Parade tomorrow. You want to go?"

"I have to be on a float."

"Ha! What's your costume?"

"Busy mayor. Have to run."

Sergeant Morehouse called five minutes later. "Thanks for the info on Buck's comment to Fielding. I got a question for you."

"Sure."

"Buck didn't keep his phone locked, and since he's dead we can go in it. Looks like he called you, which you said was to get you to meet him, at about eight-thirty that morning."

"Yep. And he hung up on me before I could get him to understand I didn't want to go, so I went."

"You told me. Did he mention where he was, or who he might be with when he talked to you?"

"Just what I already told you. He said he had to meet one person before me, but he didn't say who or where. Hey, where was Buck's car?"

"Driveway one door down and across. He was always pulling into driveways so his car didn't get hit. None of us knew what he drove, so it took an hour or so to figure it out. You didn't recognize it?"

"I didn't even think about it. But sometimes he drove a small, dark green Toyota truck and sometimes a Honda. I don't know the model, just that it was gray."

"It was the Honda. Nothin' in it helps."

"But if you have his phone, you know who else he talked to."

"Some of them. Most don't have names, so we're trackin' 'em down. He probably made or got forty calls a day, at least. It'll take a while."

"And nobody saw anybody?"

"Jolie, whadda I keep telling you?"

"I am staying out of it. Dana already told me he should have taken your advice about cameras."

"Lotta beach rentals on that street, and they're vacant, but one house had a camera. One odd-looking person walked past a house near there, comin' and goin' somewhere, but can't tell who it is."

"Like a summer beach bum or somebody in a bear costume?"

"Funny. Walks like a man, tall, but in a wide, floppy hat and sunglasses. Kind of a canvas bag over his shoulder. He looked the same when he walked back."

"Was anything in the bag when he returned? Wait, you don't really know which way was coming or going, do you?"

"No, I suppose not. Bag didn't seem to have more in it."

"Too bad. If he'd been shopping it might help."

"Talk to you later, Mrs. Marple."

Chapter Twenty-Eight

At the end of a long Friday, I brushed my teeth at just past ten o'clock and convinced myself it was okay to go to bed that early. I went back to the living room to see if Scoobie knew when Terry would be home.

Scoobie yawned. "He said not too late, because he had a couple tests today and is tired." He patted the arm of the recliner he was in. I sat on the arm and gently fell back onto him. To someone looking in, he would appear to be cradling a baby. A large baby.

We laughed and he bent over to kiss me. "Good. You even brushed your teeth."

I giggled. "You don't have to stop that."

"I have no plans to." He pulled my head closer to his as the phone rang.

Before Aunt Madge became mayor, we ignored a number of evening calls. Now we don't know what we could hear about, so we generally answer.

I scooted off Scoobie and padded to the landline phone. "Hello?"

George sounded rushed. "Jolie. Can I come over?"

I rolled my eyes at Scoobie. "George, it's kind of late."

"It's your fault I need to talk to you and Scoob. Maybe Morehouse, but it's too late."

Scoobie raised his eyebrows.

"George thinks he has something urgent. Can he come over?" I asked.

"I suppose."

George must have heard him, because he hung up.

Scoobie got up. "We're going to have to get him better trained. Do you know what he wants?"

"If I had to guess, it's about some digging he's been doing about Buck's life in Atlantic City, but I don't know why he'd be so anxious to tell us about it." I hoped George wouldn't tell Scoobie I had looked up information on the lawsuit Buck had won.

He dashed my hope as soon as he came in. "Sorry guys, but Jolie gave me a lead this afternoon, and it may make a difference in how the cops look at Buck's murder." He made a beeline for the couch.

Scoobie pointed a finger at me as he sat in the recliner.

I sat in the upholstered chair across from the couch. I shot George eyeball daggers. "George told me all the work he had done. I just looked up one more thing."

George had the decency to recognize Scoobie's irritation. "I'm sorry you guys. It was my digging, but Jolie had one good idea and she turned it over to me."

George took out the narrow notebook he keeps in a breast pocket. "This couple named Abernathy owes Buck more than $30,000." He went over the civil suit Buck had filed after being scammed. "I couldn't find anything that said they started paying, but there wouldn't be a record of that as long as they paid him back."

George looked to me and I shrugged. "All I did was go to the most recent New Jersey court records. They showed the couple had their lawyer file a motion to have the judgment dismissed. Three days before Buck's death."

"You're not saying they killed him and planned this motion in advance, are you?" Scoobie asked.

"Maybe," George said. "I did a credit check on them. They are so far underwater in terms of credit that they'd need an oxygen tank to survive down there."

"That's kind of a big leap," I said.

"Not as big as you might think. I found a cell phone listing for Patrick Abernathy on one of the paid sites I subscribe to, and called."

"Glad to hear from you, was he?" Scoobie asked.

George grinned briefly. "Hardly. I asked him what he thought about Buck's murder, and he actually said he hoped the guy rotted in hell. Then I could hear a woman talking to him about being stupid, and he hung up. Didn't answer when I called back."

"I don't think like a lawyer," Scoobie said, "but what reason did they give for asking that the award be voided, or whatever you call it."

"All I can see is a two-sentence statement," George said. "The filing documents haven't been loaded yet. The Abernathy's claim they were under duress when they signed the agreement. Whatever that means."

Scoobie made a derisive sound. "Maybe they put themselves under duress by doing a scam and getting caught."

I thought about it. "Maybe they just wanted to delay paying Buck the money."

"No idea," George said. "But it does mean someone in Atlantic City was even angrier at Buck than the people who knew him up here."

I WOKE UP SATURDAY thinking about what George said about Abernathy's anger, but would it figure into Buck's murder? They wanted the judgment dismissed, and perhaps that would be more likely if Buck died. But kill him?

Morehouse had mentioned that the morning of the murder, someone in a floppy hat and sunglasses walked near the Victorian where Buck was killed. He thought it was a man. Would Patrick Abernathy have had the guts to drive to a strange town and walk around in the open?

Saturdays are so busy, I told myself to put Buck and Eleanor out of my mind. I cared about what had happened to them, but I couldn't do anything about their situations throughout Halloween weekend. Since trick or treaters would be on our doorstep tomorrow, I stopped at Markle's Market to stock up on candy.

He greeted me with a grumble. "Sometimes I think I should have gone to dental school, like your friend Bill Oliver. All this candy people buy."

"You love to sell it. I bet this is a big weekend for you."

He nodded. "Didn't used to be, but now that all the adults are into Halloween, they have a lot of parties."

"Must be people without kids." I took out my wallet to pay for the two heaping plastic bags of goodies.

"One of you take the twins and the other stay home to pass out candy?"

I raised my eyebrows. "You really think one of us could keep track of them trick or treating?"

"Guess not. You have Terry to help, I suppose."

I grinned. "He has a date this year. George and Ramona are going to pass out candy at the house so we don't get TeePee'd or egged."

"Somebody'd do that?"

I shrugged. "We have a teenager. Supposedly it's all in good fun."

He handed me my change. "I think I was born old."

I regarded his canvas apron and thinning hair. "You've lost weight the last couple years. I bet you live to be ninety."

"God I hope not." He nodded and began checking out the man behind me.

I drove the two blocks to the boardwalk steps nearest Java Jolt. My goal was to buy a bag of the special decaf Megan carries so we'd have fresh coffee after the twins went to bed. Coffee that wouldn't keep me up all night.

The place was packed with people who often come in the summer and show up for a day or two at Halloween or Thanksgiving. I said hello to a couple other parents from the kids' co-op nursery and made my way to the counter.

Megan gave me a questioning look. I laughed. "I'm not here to sit. Just grabbing your decaf blend."

She took one from the shelf behind the counter. "See that woman at the back table? I think she's looking for you. She was here yesterday and asked if you'd been in."

I paid and walked toward the back. A slender woman wearing an obviously expensive blazer was immersed in a book. I didn't think I knew her. She raised her eyes, and looked relieved as she motioned me to her.

Something seemed familiar. Maybe I had appraised her house or she worked in the pediatrician's office. I had seen her somewhere.

"Hi, Jolie. I'm Tami. We didn't really talk at Eleanor's service."

I sat across from her. "Right. You mentioned how much her mother would miss her." I remembered because it was the only time Helen Covington's loss had been recognized.

She nodded, somber. "I, well, we didn't realize that it might have made more sense for some of her older friends to speak. Kevin asked us, and we liked Eleanor."

I smiled. "I could tell. It sounded as if you had fun together."

"We did. And that's a good way to put it. We went to planned activities together."

I tilted my head. "Planned activities?"

"We did things, watched plays, but we never just hung out. I felt as if I knew her and Kevin, but we were really more like acquaintances."

Where is she going with this? "I'm not sure I get what you mean."

"I mean we spent time with them, but since Eleanor's death, I realize how little we knew her. Or Kevin."

"I see." I had no idea what else to say.

She smiled briefly. "What I'm trying to say is I think Kevin used us as props at the memorial service. It kept him in charge, made their lives look lovely. But maybe we were there to exclude, well, people like her book club friends." She smiled broadly. "They were fun women."

"Yes. The ringleader was my sister, Renée."

"The first one to speak. She was a kind of charming, um, bully."

I laughed. "That was her role, I suppose."

She grew serious again. "We've only seen Kevin once in the last three weeks. Really, only because we insisted. I thought maybe he didn't want to be reminded of Eleanor. But after we had dinner one night, my husband said he thought Kevin was on to bigger things."

"Kevin's talked to my husband some…Bigger things? What things?"

"He bought a boat the week after the service. My husband said it probably cost $50,000."

"Wow. That's a lot of groceries."

"And he can do what he wants. I don't mean to sound as if I'm judging. I guess I am. But so soon, and if you look on his Facebook page, he's having a lot of fun with it."

"We don't really have a lot of time…we have four-year-old twins."

"Kevin said you helped him that night, and that you had little kids." She picked up her purse from a chair. "I need to get home. I'm not even sure why I wanted to talk to you. Maybe to say, well, to ask you to tell Mrs. Covington she had a lovely daughter. Tell her from me."

"I'll do that, Tami." I wanted to ask her why she didn't tell her directly, but if I had to guess, I'd say she wanted to be done with Kevin.

I sat at the table for a moment, thinking. I texted George. "Did you know Kevin Fielding bought a $50,000 boat?"

SCOOBIE'S EXPRESSION SAID he wished I'd come back sooner. As we made grilled cheese sandwiches for lunch, the kids' excitement came out as rambunctious behavior and excited screaming.

"I'm sorry. A woman was in Java Jolt. From Eleanor's memorial service."

Lance yelled from the living room. "Mom. Didn't R2D2 have a light saber?"

Scoobie called to him. "He had no arms. No light saber."

"Darn." He dashed to their bedroom.

"Small favors," I said. "Her name is Tami, and she was the woman who spoke, from the couple Kevin hand-picked to talk about their lives."

"I remember. They seemed kind of plastic, but okay."

"She said she now thinks Kevin used them as props, you know, like in a play."

He flipped a sandwich in the pan. "Gee, ya think?"

"I thought so then too, but I think it's only recently occurred to her." I took cups for milk from a cupboard. "And she said he bought a boat. Her husband said it cost $50,000."

"So, Harry's a loser and Kevin is cool because he bought a boat."

"I'm sure he thinks so."

"Then you'll really love the message on our voicemail," Scoobie said.

I closed the fridge. "What message?"

"A kind of rambling apology for losing his cool at the police station yesterday. He probably figures it got back to us. And he wants to know if he can come over here to see the kids in their Halloween costumes."

I turned to fully face Scoobie and felt as if my body temp went up two degrees. "He has *got* to be kidding."

Leia's voice came to us from their bedroom. "At every house we can sing part of *Let it Go*."

I muttered, "I'm not sure I can let it go."

Lance yelled. "I am not singing a girl song!"

"Jeez." Scoobie walked into the hall. "It's a song for everybody, but there wouldn't be time to sing at the houses on Halloween."

He gave me a quick hug. "I'll let him know there's too much going on."

I had several thoughts at once. One was the Aunt Madge version, which would say we should help a grieving husband. Another was simply that Kevin had a lot of nerve to ask. But the third was maybe we could learn something from him. I had no idea what.

I leaned against the kitchen table. "He can come, but let's minimize the time. Tell him after trick-or-treating. It won't be too much later that we'll have to start baths. We can tell him we'll be busy with that, and it would be a good time to leave."

"I don't have the impression he's overly fond of little kids. He'll probably want to leave."

"Good." I slid the sandwiches from the frying pan to two plates. "Come on you two. Grilled cheeses are ready."

The kids slid into chairs at the kitchen table.

"I have an important question," Lance said. "How can I put candy in my bag if R2D2 doesn't have arms?"

Chapter Twenty-Nine

SCOOBIE KEPT THE TWINS occupied early Saturday afternoon so I could do my share of the weekly housework. I dusted the twins' room and used a mop handle to pull scattered items from under the bed. The second time I did so, the handle met resistance, so I peered under the bed.

Jazz's bright eyes greeted me, but she didn't relinquish her hold on the mop. In fact, she scooted to sit on it.

"I know you want to play. If you let me have the mop I'll find a shoestring you can wrestle with." Because I didn't keep tugging on the handle, she let go and hopped on the bed. I placed a sneaker, which had a long, untied shoestring, next to her. She ignored it.

I petted her before I moved to our room to dust. Scoobie's Kindle sat on his bedside table, and I automatically opened the top drawer to place it in there.

A poem stuck out of the copy of *Daily Reflections*, his favorite book of AA readings. I didn't feel as if I was snooping when I picked it up; he often gave me unfinished poems to read.

Truthful Consequences

You get these new people
Who forget that they're new
They think they know everything
They could use a review

They use the premise of honesty
With intentions of hurt

What they've got is hostility
It's just covert

Honesty is always kind
And usually pleasant
Truth on the other hand
Quite often isn't

But truth is a notion
That is at best subjective
It's never agreed upon
By the fellowship collective

So the next time you're honest
For my own good
Take your own inventory
Then decide if you should

He had signed it with his distinctive S. What did it mean? It sounded as if he had gotten advice rather than support at a meeting and didn't appreciate it.

Still, I smiled to myself. It only took me two years after I came back to Ocean Alley to realize we fit together like a sea turtle and its shell.

I love our family and good friends, and I'm grateful for our lovely house. And I have Jazz, the one holdover from my life before Ocean Alley. Scoobie feels the same way. Maybe not the same about Jazz, who tries to get between us in bed.

So why had he been to more meetings in the last month than in the last six months put together? What did the poem mean? *What am I missing?*

I was still staring at the poem in my hand when, behind me, Scoobie cleared his throat. "The kids are in the back yard for a few minutes."

I turned around, feeling my face grow red. "I wasn't snooping, I was putting your Kindle in there."

His face, which had worn an inscrutable mask, cleared. "You know I write what's on the top of my head. There isn't always some deep significance."

I put the poem back in the drawer and shut it. "Do we need to talk about anything?"

He smiled slightly. "You mean besides Halloween costumes? I'm going as Obi Wan Kenobi."

My stomach tightened. "You know I don't mean that."

"I guess I know that." The front door banged, announcing Terry. "Maybe later, okay?"

I nodded as Terry bounded down the hallway and stopped at the doorway to our room. He paused, uncertain. "Everything okay?"

"Sure," Scoobie said. "What's up?"

"All fine," I added.

"You know that girl I study with at the library?"

"Yes," I said.

Scoobie grinned. "The whole town knows."

Terry looked horrified. "Really?"

Scoobie laughed. "I hear she's cute. What did you expect?"

Terry looked at me.

"Daphne said you really do study. I don't even know her name." "You don't?"

Scoobie laughed. "Bring her by."

"Uh, okay." But he still didn't mention her name.

"What about her? Why are you excited?" I asked.

"Oh, I asked her to the SnoBall, and she said yes." He started to redden.

I glanced at Scoobie and back to Terry. "The December dance? It's only Halloween."

"Her mom says she has to go with the first person who asks her. Her friend Margaret told me she's been hiding in the bathroom at lunch because she heard one of the basketball players wanted to ask her."

Scoobie laughed and sat on the bed, almost bent over. He stayed like that for fully fifteen seconds.

Terry looked at me, and I shrugged.

Scoobie sat up, wiped tears off his cheeks, and grabbed Terry in a hug. "I love the life you have."

Terry looked startled, and then relaxed as he pulled back from the hug. "It's because of you." He nodded at me. "Both of you, you know."

I left to fix dinner before I started to tear up. Plus, that would give them time to have Brother Talk. Whatever was going on with Scoobie, it would make him feel better.

Chapter Thirty

HALLOWEEN USED TO BE just another day. Sometimes a fun one with a party or trick-or-treaters, but not a big deal. Halloween with four-year-olds is a mega day, packed with excitement and hope that no one will lose their lunch on the hardwood floors after eating too much candy.

Since it was Sunday, we went to church, but told the kids we weren't staying for donuts because they would get so many sweets later and we didn't want them hyped up too early. First Prez had other ideas and passed out small party bags of candy to each child.

Oh well, partying is starting early.

The parade was scheduled for four-thirty and would wend its way through downtown and end up not too far from our house, in a large parking lot that in the summer is packed with beachgoers. Floats would park and anyone walking or riding bikes would move on to either pass out treats or go door-to-door.

Before it started, we had to practice walking in our costumes and go over polite ways to trick or treat.

"When you get some candy, what do you say?" Scoobie asked.

"Thank you!" they chorused.

"If you don't like what someone gives you, what do you say?" I asked.

"Thank you!"

"And what do you do with something you don't like?" Scoobie asked.

"Put it down the sewer when you cross the street?" Lance asked.

"Take it to day care for other kids?" Leia asked.

"Sewers are just for rainwater," Scoobie said.

"And since the candy will have been handled, we won't take it to school; we'll just toss it."

"Or give it to George," Scoobie said, not looking at me.

"Why not Ramona?" asked Lance.

"Because Ramona always watches her figure," Leia said.

"Watches herself?" Lance asked.

Leia didn't seem to know what to say.

I grinned. "She has a lovely figure. We'll put what you don't want in a separate bowl and offer it to George and Ramona."

Scoobie handed each of them the plastic pail they would carry to trick or treat, and they dashed for their room.

I spent the next half hour trying to braid the top of my head so I'd look like the Star Wars Princess Leia, complete with white pants and long-sleeve white jersey. Scoobie had ordered a brown hoodie and pieced together a brown robe from a sheet he had paid to have dyed brown, because I wouldn't let him do it in our washing machine.

Aunt Madge brought Leia's blue Elsa dress to us while the twins took a forced 'resting time' between two and three o'clock. "I finished it yesterday, but thought if I brought it earlier you'd have to help her in and out of it five times."

Scoobie looked to me and gave a slight shrug.

"A long back zipper," I said.

"The things I learn about little girls." He bent over and kissed Aunt Madge. "Thanks so much."

When they got up from what turned out to be true naps, the twins tried again to talk us into letting them walk in the parade.

"It's a long walk, and we'd end up having to carry one or both of you," I said.

"We can walk by ourselves," Leia insisted.

"Yeah, we're big," Lance added.

"You have to be ten to walk alone," I said, "and your costumes would get dirty."

"Plus," Scoobie interrupted a protest, "we'll have great seats on the sidewalk. "You'll be able to wave to Aunt Madge and Harry. They're riding in a 1962 Cadillac convertible."

"What kind of candy will Aunt Madge throw?" Leia asked.

"Do you think she'll have extras?" Lance asked.

I shook my head. "Technically, people on floats aren't supposed to throw candy. I think she'll probably set a good example and not toss any."

They weren't big on that, but decided they could live with a spot on the sidewalk.

RAMONA AND GEORGE arrived at three-thirty to drop off things they didn't want to have on the sidewalk as we watched the parade. Because they would stay at the house while we trick or treated, we had ordered pizza for the six of us at five-thirty. I figured we'd be done with the parade and ready to eat before going out again.

George greeted us with, "Did you know the realtors have added a huge photo of Buck Brock to their float?"

I stared at him.

"He was a licensed realtor, and people figure he was doing his job when he was killed."

I nodded. "I guess so. I hope the twins don't see it. They're struggling with the idea that they didn't like him and at the same time being sorry he's dead."

Scoobie came in from the kitchen where he'd been emptying the dishwasher. "Ramona, next year we should do a float for your gallery. Put lots of your artwork on it."

"Not a bad idea," she said. "I did design the artwork for the Chamber's float, so that'll give me some visibility."

"How come I didn't know you did that?" I asked.

"It was months ago, and I certainly didn't paint it."

"Ramona, can we ride on your float?"

Lance had asked, but both twins looked expectant.

Scoobie said, "I should warn you that even though they're not in the room, they hear everything."

She smiled. "We'll have to talk more before next year's parade."

They returned to their room, and I heard Lance say, "That's a no."

George grinned, but grew more serious. "Sit for a minute. I want to tell you what I heard today."

Ramona's look to me said she'd heard and wasn't too interested in the topic.

We sat. George began with a glance at Scoobie. "What I had planned was to see if I could learn more about Kevin's activities since Eleanor's death. What I ended up doing was finding out where one of Buck's calls came from the morning he died."

"How did that happen?" I asked.

"You heard Kevin bought a boat, and I figured it had to be registered and licensed. That wasn't hard to find, and then I started calling a few places to see where he docked it. Then I realized he would have picked a club. I called a couple. When I got to 'The Cut Above Yacht Club' I used my standard line."

"Which was?" Scoobie asked.

"I'd call and say I was a friend of Kevin Fielding's and was supposed to meet him to see his new boat, but I forgot where he told me he kept it. People would say things like they had no new boats, or they'd never heard of him. Eventually, I found where he kept it and I drove over there this morning. And there he was."

"Did you talk to him?" I asked.

He shook his head. "Fortunately, he doesn't really know me. I was dressed so I could fit in. I watched him polish brass on the back of the boat. Then, this really cute woman, maybe twenty-two, came down the ramp and waved to him. I didn't think much of it, because I figure he knows people. But she gets to him and gives him a big kiss."

Scoobie almost gaped. "I guess we're not talking about a friendly kiss on the cheek."

"Definitely not. It's far enough away from where he and Eleanor lived and it's private. He probably thought no one he knew would see him with her."

"So, what did you do?" I asked.

"I wished I had my camera, but that would have been too obvious. I used my phone to take a bunch of pictures of the water and some Halloween decorations. I managed to get one of the two of them. Then somebody who worked at the place came up and asked me what I was doing. I said I was just trying to take some neat pictures. They said it was a private club and suggested I leave."

"How does that translate to getting a phone number that helped the police?" I asked.

"I told the man who talked to me that I knew I would eventually want to join a place like his and asked him for a card. I knew the girlfriend information was no crime, but I decided I should tell the police about Fielding's quick recovery from grief."

"You really are sucking up, aren't you?" Scoobie asked.

"They not only can occasionally help me, they could also get my license pulled if I did stuff like withhold information in a murder investigation. Anyway, because it's Halloween, Morehouse was at the station when I stopped by. I took out the card to write down the address of the place for him and he asked to see it. He got all excited and wanted to keep the card. I told him he could if he told me what made him excited."

"I can't believe he did," I said.

"He'd already told me he had the list of phone numbers that Buck called or got calls from the morning he died. And the number on the card was one of those Buck got a call from."

"I guess it's something the police can ask him about," I said. "But does it really give them any information?"

George shrugged. "The call was for eight minutes, the longest of any he got that morning. Of course, we don't know what it was about."

"But why would Kevin call Buck from the club's phone?" I asked.

"Not likely because of a low battery," Scoobie said. "He didn't want it to be obvious that he called Buck."

"Probably," George said.

I remembered Buck's ad about renting the entire house for a family reunion weekend. Maybe the call was a trick and Buck didn't know he was talking to Kevin.

I could imagine Kevin calling Buck from a phone other than his own, but I couldn't think of a reason the two men would be on the phone for eight minutes other than talking about renting from Buck. Eight minutes is a long time to cuss somebody out, which is how I expected a general conversation between the two of them to have gone.

I decided not to say anything about my thoughts just then.

Ramona and I went into the kitchen to put some snacks together for the parade, and George went with Scoobie to the back porch to compliment Lance on his R2D2 costume. Leia had already put on her dress, or had been helped to do it, and was sitting quietly in the living room looking at pictures of houses for sale in a real estate magazine Lester had given her.

When the men were out of earshot, Ramona pointed a finger at me. "I could tell something went through your mind when George said the phone number was from that dock club."

"I need to talk to Morehouse for just a minute. I can do it while we're working, but could you keep an eye out to make sure they don't overhear?"

"What difference does it make?"

"I really am trying not to do much with this whole business of Eleanor and Buck. But Morehouse said if I had a good idea I should let him know."

Ramona raised her eyebrows. "Are you sure you don't just want to find out what Morehouse knows?"

I shook my head. "He won't let on much. I think Morehouse needs to know that the longest phone call Buck had could not only have come from Kevin, but also could be a ruse for Kevin to meet Buck at the house on Seashore."

When Ramona didn't seem convinced, I added, "Kevin's been paying a lot of attention to what's going on in Ocean Alley. Kevin could have seen Buck's ad and might have asked to meet Buck there because the house would likely be vacant."

"And this Kevin planned to kill Buck?"

"I don't know that he would have planned to do that, but a vacant house would have been a good place to have it out with Buck. Find out if Buck really thought Kevin killed Eleanor."

She shrugged. "Go ahead, I'll be your lookout."

Morehouse sounded impatient. "Got a lot goin' on here Jolie. You need something?"

"George is on the back porch with Scoobie. He mentioned that the phone number on a business card he showed you was similar to one that called Buck that morning."

"And?" He took his mouth away from the receiver and said, "Hey Avery, can you have somebody take more traffic cones to the steps in front of the courthouse?"

Morehouse spoke to me again. "Sorry, Jolie. What is it?"

"Did you see Buck's ad about renting the entire house on Seashore for a family reunion weekend?"

"Wait a minute." A door shut on Morehouse's end and the noise level went down. "What ad are you talking about? He's only run a couple ads since Labor Day. Nothin' about reunions."

I explained the conversation about the Landlord Tenant Commission telling him a party house rental was not allowed and Buck wondering about a family reunion option. "The ad was in the paper the same day as the last longish article about Eleanor's murder. But it was a display ad, not in the classified section. And it didn't say Buck's name, just gave his mobile phone number."

Morehouse's tone became impatient again. "And what does this have to do with any local crime?"

"Kevin has been following articles in the *Ocean Alley Press*, and he seems to be paying attention to people like Scoobie, me, Buck. What if that long call the morning Buck died was Kevin trying to meet Buck in what Kevin thought would be a vacant property?"

After a pause, Morehouse said, "It's something to think about. A stretch, but possible. But I can't look into it until after all this hoopla is finished." He hung up.

I put my phone on the counter and pulled a baggie toward me to fill it with Cheerios. "Now I can let go of this," I told Ramona.

But that wasn't true. Even more than knowing who killed Buck, I wanted Eleanor's killer caught. And Kevin was the most likely suspect, if only we could figure out how to definitely tie him to the mercury in the chocolates.

I HAD NOT BEEN to an Ocean Alley Halloween parade since I was a kid. It's the sort of event any parent might want to skip. Lance kept surreptitiously trying to pick up some of the candy thrown onto the pavement from the floats.

I couldn't really tell him not to, because we had had to move from our chairs to the street, since other people stood in front of our chairs. The best we could do was make sure the candy still had a wrapper on it.

Sometimes I watched Scoobie as he delighted in the twins' excitement. They were almost intimidated that Aunt Madge and Harry were in the lead float, but quickly overcame their awe. They danced in place as the high school band played a Souza march and covered their ears when the town's antique firetruck honked its siren.

I grinned watching them put on brave fronts when a clown with huge feet handed them candy. Leia held Ramona's hand for a minute after that, and Lance stood between George and Scoobie. I didn't feel jealous that Leia had latched onto Ramona, and decided if clowns made them tentative, I might hire one every now and then.

Bringing up the rear was a flotilla of local kids in Halloween costumes. Many rode bikes decorated with orange and black crepe paper. Scoobie met my glance, pointed at them, and mouthed, "Next year."

Aloud, I said, "You'll be in charge."

When we got back to the house, Max waited on the front porch, along with the pizza. "I can help with trick-or-treating," he said. "Treating."

I brought in the pizza and put slices on paper plates, cutting the twins each one half of a single slice. We'd managed to keep them from devouring lots of candy, but I didn't want to put a lot more junk into their stomachs.

It turned out Max wanted to walk with us. Scoobie asked, "Did you trick-or-treat as a kid?"

Max thought about that. "I don't think I remember."

Scoobie found him a pirate hat left over from a Harvest for All fundraiser and gave Max a small paper sack from Markle's Market. "You can't ask for candy at the houses, because that's for kids twelve and under. But the twins can give you some of theirs, and I know Aunt Madge and Harry will."

Max was thrilled, and I tried not to think of his presence as someone else to watch out for.

On his way out, Terry grabbed a piece of pizza and tried not to get it on his Captain America costume. He had a date for a Halloween party and seemed very excited about it.

Scoobie and I were trying to be cool and not ask too many questions. He did let us know that the party would be at the home of his friend, who was also Sergeant Morehouse's nephew. That felt safe.

As he was leaving, his phone beeped with a message. He read it, laughed, and held up his phone. "There will be two Captain Americas at the party."

Something about seeing him brandish his phone made me think of Helen Covington's phone with Eleanor's last message. I felt a lump rise in my throat and swallowed.

BY THE TIME WE started trick-or-treating at six o'clock, both twins had yawned at least a couple of times. As we approached the Cozy Corner, always our first stop, they grew excited again.

Aunt Madge exclaimed that Lance looked just like R2D2, and Harry made a fuss over Leia's depiction of Elsa from *Frozen*. Harry asked Max if he'd like to stay with them to pass out candy, but he wanted to walk with us. Aunt Madge blew me a kiss as we turned to leave.

We never traipse more than a couple of blocks from our house, because that's a lot of walking for short legs. Still, it took almost two hours. We would run into other kids from the co-op nursery and have to compare not just costumes but candy. Eventually, we told the twins that if it got too dark we'd have to quit without going to all the houses. That encouraged them to keep moving.

When we got within half-a-block from our house, we were among the last trick-or-treaters on the street and the twins began to lag. I was tempted to offer to carry one of their candy pails, but that would mean carrying two, since Scoobie continued to periodically act out as Obi Wan Kenobi. He did have a light saber, which guaranteed Lance would have one next year.

I watched for a few seconds while yet another child asked him to demonstrate slicing off a space creature's arm. When I turned, Lance had stepped into the street and stooped to pick up a piece of candy.

"What did we say about staying out of the street?" In a few strides, I stood next to him and reached for his hand.

Suddenly, a car's headlights beamed toward us and seemed to move fast. Everything happened in slow motion for a couple of seconds before I fully grasped that we needed to get the heck out of the street.

I picked up Lance and tossed him toward the grass beyond the curb, because I didn't think I could walk the few strides to get to the curb before the car got to me.

The car didn't slow. *They must not see me!*

I half-turned and waved with one hand. On my other, I felt a huge tug.

Then came a sharp pain in my hip and I fell, twisting my foot as I went. I had an image of Scoobie, robes billowing, coming toward me. Then nothing.

Chapter Thirty-One

I OPENED MY EYES and looked between metal bars. Through them, I saw Scoobie dozing in a plastic recliner. *Weird. We bought him that new recliner.*

Slowly my mind grew less foggy. Had I been hit by a car when we were trick or treating? I must be in a hospital bed.

My eyes popped open and I croaked. "Scoobie. Where's Lance?"

He jumped from the chair and bent over the rail. Relief spread over his unusually haggard face. "How about, 'Good to see you, honey'?" He began to smile. "He's fine. Terry's home with the kids. Ramona insisted on staying over and Terry's trying to be gracious about it."

I tried to shift my position slightly and winced at pain in my hip. My eyes traveled to the pillow at the foot of the bed, on which rested a cast on my right foot. It extended to just below the knee.

I felt the slight pounding of a headache. "I saw a car."

"Me, too, but I was on the sidewalk with Leia and couldn't get to you. Lance was where he wasn't supposed to be, at the edge of the curb. I've never seen a little kid pull someone so hard."

I shut my eyes for several seconds. All I remembered was the grill of a car and the tug on my arm. "But he's okay?"

"Yeah. He stepped off the curb to pick up candy that someone had thrown during the Halloween parade a couple hours earlier. Out of the corner of my eye, I saw you dash to pick him up and almost throw him onto the grass. But you twisted your ankle on, I think, a red fireball candy."

I closed my eyes briefly. "I don't like those."

I opened them to see Scoobie grinning broadly. "I'll remember not to buy them."

I shifted in the bed. "It feels like I broke something in my foot."

"Yeah. When the car skimmed your hip, you twisted and landed on it. Thanks to our boy you didn't get run over by the front tire."

Scoobie looked at a machine on a pole next to my bed. It had a bunch of numbers, which I assumed told him my blood pressure and such.

"Is the driver okay? Was it anyone we know?"

His eyes met mine. "Kevin Fielding. I was such an…"

"What?" Anger made my head pound harder.

He glanced at the monitor again. "Your blood pressure just went up. Maybe you should try to go back to sleep for a while."

The door to the room whooshed open and a nurse entered. "I heard her in the hall. Everything okay?" She leaned over the bed. "It's your friend from church and the hospital. What's my name?"

"Harriet," I said, "unless you changed it."

She grinned. "Just checking. You have a mild concussion. You probably remember me taking your blood pressure manually a couple of times."

"I…think I remember telling you to leave me alone."

Scoobie spoke from the other side of the bed. "You said a few words we don't let the kids use. But you weren't really conscious."

"I'm so…" I began.

"It's okay," Harriet said. "Happens all the time when people are so out of it. You're mad at the pain, not the nurse." She patted my shoulder. "Try to get more rest. I'll get some mild pain meds to put in your IV."

I followed her out with my eyes, then closed them. "I'll sleep when you tell me about Kevin. Was it on purpose?"

"He says not. But the few other people who saw it said he sped up as soon as you stepped into the street. Luckily, he wasn't going too fast."

I opened my eyes again. "He was coming to our house after trick or treating."

"Yep. Might have been a ruse so he'd know when we'd be on the street. We can talk more later."

"It's tomorrow already?"

Scoobie grinned. "If you felt better I'd tell you it's Christmas Eve, but it's only about eight hours since you got hit."

The door whooshed again. "We want you to sleep, Jolie. This'll help."

I closed my eyes and was aware of Harriet next to me. She tapped on my IV line as my eyes opened for a second and shut again.

"Don't let the kids wake me up, okay?"

From far away, Scoobie laughed and said, "I'll tell them to play in your bed."

THE SMELL OF SCRAMBLED eggs and orange juice wandered into my nose and I slowly opened my eyes. A tired Scoobie had taken the lid off a plate of food and a glass of orange juice.

I mumbled, "Did you get any sleep?"

His eyes widened and he smiled. "Enough." He nodded at the plate. "This looks pretty good."

"Eat some."

"I'll put a spoonful of eggs on one of your pieces of toast, because I know you'll never eat this much. I'm going to raise your head a little."

"You're pretty good at this."

"Yeah, but don't test my skills too often. Drink some juice first. You mouth is probably icky."

He held the glass for me and the combination of cold and tartness brought me fully awake. "Good stuff."

"Yep. I'll let you feed yourself, unless you need help." He put a napkin under my chin and buttered a piece of toast and handed it to me. Then he put a spoonful of eggs on a second piece of toast and took a bite. "I am hungry. I'll go down to the cafeteria for more in a few minutes."

When we finished, Dr. Birdbaum came in and paid more attention to my head than my foot. "You can go home if you keep your foot elevated and don't chase any kids. Normally I'd say one more day, but you'll have Scoobie to check your blood pressure, and I know your kids were pretty upset last night."

"Thanks." A thought occurred to me and I looked at Scoobie. "Aunt Madge?"

The doctor laughed. "Between her and your police friends, it was like the ER was under siege."

My police friends. I remembered how Morehouse used to yell at me.

"Why don't I remember that?"

Dr. Birdbaum grew serious. "You were in mild shock, and had a slight concussion from bumping your head on the curb. Plus, we gave you some pain meds. You'll probably remember some of it later." He shook Scoobie's hand, told him to make me behave, and left.

"Were the kids here?" I asked.

"No." He grew serious. "But they were on the phone with Madge and Harry, near me, while I was with you in the ER. Poor Lance would stop wailing and start again. He did eventually calm down."

I felt my eyes tear. "Did Aunt Madge help them?"

"Everybody did. Do you remember who was trick or treating with us?"

"No, I…Max. He was sort of a pirate."

"He's the one who picked up Lance right away and he carried both twins back to the house."

"Max? Carried them?"

"Yep. You know how they say people get an adrenaline rush? He's the one who calmed Lance, initially."

"Max?"

He laughed. "Stop saying that." He grew serious. "When they got home, George and Ramona were there. Remember, they were passing out candy at our place while we took the kids out. George said Max dumped both of them on the couch and then pointed at his head. He told them bad people shot him and he got better. Jolie didn't get shot so Jolie would be okay."

"Wow."

"Ramona told Madge Leia asked if you'd start repeating everything."

"Dear God. That's not funny, but it's…"

"Hysterical," Scoobie said. "You gotta laugh or you'll cry." His eyes filled with tears.

I lifted the hand that didn't have an IV and patted his hand. "I'm okay. And we're together."

He took a tissue from a tiny box on the table that held the remains of breakfast. "The last couple months, something has been so…off."

Maybe now I'll find out why he's needed so many extra meetings.

"When you were lying in the street like that, I fully realized it's because everything's so perfect, and yet it could be wiped out in a second. I don't think I could stand it."

Tears spilled down my cheeks. "It is perfect, Scoobie. I never, ever, thought I'd be this happy."

He leaned over the rails and wiped my tears. "I draw the line at your nose."

"Thanks. Do you feel better now? Or did this," I gestured to my foot, "make it worse?"

"A bit of both. I had already figured out that I needed to *know* that if something happened to you I could go on, take care of the kids." He smiled. "Remember to feed Jazz."

"No worries there. She'll remind you."

He straightened. "Yeah. I told George to clean the litter box last night. But it was mostly to get him off the phone so I could grab some shuteye. He was almost as upset as the kids." Scoobie blew his nose.

Quietly, I asked, "So, now do you know?"

He tossed the tissue onto my breakfast tray. "I know I could. And I guess I know even more how much I don't want to have to…"

The door whooshed open again and Sergeant Morehouse stood there in a now-rumpled clown costume. Minus makeup and big feet. "You weren't supposed to do stuff like this anymore."

I felt tired again, but smiled. "I didn't *do* anything this time."

"I've decided to blame George for egging everybody on," Scoobie said.

"Always a good fallback position." Morehouse then looked at me. "Can you talk to me for a few minutes?"

"A few. But I don't think I remember anything from after…the car."

Morehouse sat in a guest chair on the side of the bed opposite Scoobie and nodded to him. "This Fielding guy said he was on the way to your house, that he's your good buddy."

"Not exactly," I said.

"He was driving away from where our house is," Scoobie said.

"But he was invited?" Morehouse asked.

"He invited himself. And he asked when we'd be back from trick-or-treating." I leaned forward but felt dizzy so sat back. "That would let him know when we'd be on the street. But how could he possibly think he could get away with running me over?"

"And why would he want to?" Scoobie asked.

Morehouse half smiled. "We all have our lists. But I think he saw Jolie as the person most determined to find out if he killed his wife."

"Actually, that would be George. You and Dana both told me whoever killed her was really dangerous. And with the kids…"

Scoobie cleared his throat.

"Okay, you too." I patted his hand again. "But it doesn't make sense."

"It is odd," Morehouse said. "He had to know we'd investigate pretty damn good."

"I think," Scoobie began, and stopped.

"Think what?" Morehouse asked.

"He's been meeting me now and then for coffee or whatever, talking about how bad he feels about losing Eleanor. But I had begun to think what he really wanted was to know what Jolie and maybe Renée were thinking. He likes to…I don't know, he sees himself as in command or something."

"And what?" I asked. "He's so arrogant he thinks he can run people down on city streets?"

Morehouse's tone was noncommittal. "He seems to have a very high opinion of himself, and I think he's used to getting what he wants." He glanced from Scoobie to me. "I don't need to go over a lot right now. Mostly wanted to ask what you remembered."

"I told you what I know last night," Scoobie said.

He nodded and began to stand.

"But it wasn't a big car," I said. "Didn't he have a Lexus?"

"His late wife's car. His is a restored MG. But he had rented a Corolla and switched the plates with some he took off another car. If he'd gotten out of town, it woulda made it harder to find the car."

"Why didn't he make it out of town?" I asked.

"He sped up fast after he mostly missed you, ran a stop sign. But you know that antique firetruck that's in all the parades?"

I thought of Eleanor and how she liked antiques. "Yes."

Scoobie said, "Sure."

"It was going through the intersection by Markle's Market. Fielding swerved to try to avoid it, but the truck's big. He went into Markle's window."

Scoobie groaned and I said, "Good heavens! Did he hit anyone else?"

Morehouse stood. "No."

"Does this prove he killed Eleanor?" Scoobie asked.

"We got a couple things workin' on that." He pointed an index finger at me as he got to the foot of the bed. "Half the reason I came by was because people are callin' the station asking about you."

"I appreciate that."

"Don't let it go to your head."

AUNT MADGE CALLED on the room phone as we were about to leave the hospital. "I told the kids to draw you get-well pictures and to greet you at the car."

"Why? Not the picture part."

"They're so hopped up, I don't want them to knock you over while you grapple with crutches. Put the car window down and let them hand you the pictures and jump up and down before you get out."

"Yes, ma'am."

She said nothing for a few seconds. "Lance has a lot of guilt. But he won't talk about anything related to last night."

"But Scoobie said he saved me."

"I hear that was quite a tug. But he's a smart little boy. He knows you wouldn't have been in the street if he hadn't tried to pick up candy."

"Tell him stories about stuff I did. Like the time I caught the paper bread wrapper on fire because I wanted to help in the kitchen. Wasn't I the same age?"

"I didn't say I wanted to give him ideas. But I'll think of something. Love you." She hung up before I could say it back.

Scoobie had heard most of the conversation. "I've been reading some stuff online about kids and guilt. We'll figure it out."

"I'll tell him he's learned a lot and can be a school safety patrol."

"No way. Those kids always got me in trouble," Scoobie said.

"I'm pretty sure you did that yourself. They just ratted you out afterwards."

Chapter Thirty-Two

AUNT MADGE ISN'T USUALLY wrong, but she was this time. Both kids were subdued. They had drawings in their hands as we pulled up and kissed me when I rolled down the car window. But definitely no jumping up and down.

As Scoobie took the crutches out of the back of the SUV, I asked, "Did you guys take good care of Jazz?"

Behind them, Terry grinned.

"Mostly Ramona fed her and George cleaned the box," Leia said.

"But we petted her a lot under our beds." Lance added.

"Under the beds?"

"There were people in all the chairs," Leia said.

"Ah. After Daddy helps me into bed, you can climb up next to me and tell me all about it."

As we maneuvered me out of the car, Lance asked, "Do you know Sarah?"

I concentrated on standing and grabbing a crutch. "Does she go to school with you?"

"No, silly," Leia said. "Terry's friend."

I stopped. "You met her before we did?"

Scoobie laughed and handed me the other crutch. "Way to go, Bro."

I glanced to the porch in time to see Ramona smiling broadly. "She's very pretty."

Terry flushed a deep red and mumbled, "And now you know why we don't hang out here."

Scoobie said, "Ignore us. We'll quit."

George came down the steps. "You need help carrying anything in?"

I began crutching toward the porch. "Thanks so much you two, for being here."

"Ramona said we had to," George said.

Scoobie made a clucking noise.

THE TWINS DID WANT to snuggle with me, but soon grew bored. I wanted a nap, so I didn't mind.

As they were about to climb down, Jazz jumped onto the bottom of the bed, marched to me, and sat on my chest.

Lance protested to Scoobie. "We aren't supposed to sit on Mommy."

"Jazz was with Mommy before all of us. She has her own rules."

I put my nose on hers. "And she's such a good girl."

Jazz put a paw on my cheek and then curled into a ball to sleep.

Terry stuck his head in the door. "Mr. Markle is having a 'crash sale.' I told the kids we could go down and buy a bag of candy since they didn't finish trick-or-treating."

Lance hopped off the bed, but Leia regarded Terry almost warily. "Did you finish all your parking lessons?"

Scoobie grinned broadly.

"It's okay to have to try two times to parallel park, Leia," Terry said.

As she climbed down he pointed his index finger toward Scoobie. "When I took them to the diner for pancakes that Saturday, it took a couple of tries."

"Did you ever see Lester try to parallel park?" Scoobie asked.

"At least three tries," I said.

Terry grinned and we heard him remind the twins they had to sit in the back seat and buckle up. The front door closed behind them.

Hearing Lester's name reminded me about Buck. "What about what George found out regarding Kevin and his $50,000 boat?"

Ramona stuck her head around the door jamb. "We were about to say we'd leave you alone, but I know he wants to talk to you." She gestured behind her as she walked into the room and sat in one of the two upholstered straight-back chairs near the window.

George followed her, shook his head at me, and sat next to her. "That's the same foot you hurt when you tried to avoid hitting that deer."

"Enough car talk," I said, as cheerfully as I could. "Thanks so much for staying here last night."

"Terry ended up appreciating it," Ramona said. "Those kids have so much energy."

"Plus, he didn't have to clean the cat box," Scoobie said.

"Listen, Scoob," George began.

Scoobie laughed. "Yeah, I know. You'll get me back."

"No, really," George said, "you need to listen. There's circumstantial evidence that ties Kevin Fielding to both murders, and he's claiming last night was an accident and he panicked. I hear his acts of contrition are very sincere."

"They should be," I said. "Do I have to forgive him?"

"Forgiveness is for you, us, more than him. But it could take me a while," Scoobie said.

"And that's all good," George said, "but because there is no bloody knife — or syringe with his fingerprints on it — he could be let go with a substantial bond. Surrender his passport, hand over the keys to his boat, et. cetera."

"Aren't police getting close to wrapping things up?" Scoobie asked.

"Compared to where they were a few days ago, yes. But what can they one-hundred-percent prove? If I were you, I'd make sure your cell phones are charged and I'd ask at the courthouse how to get a restraining order against him. You don't want him knocking on your door begging forgiveness."

"We especially don't want him appearing with a box of chocolates," I said, dryly. I stopped. Something about the reference to a cell phone seemed to jiggle a memory. I couldn't quite grasp it.

George leaned forward, toward Scoobie. "I'm serious, Scoob, you need to…"

A loud knock at the front door interrupted him.

Scoobie jumped up. "Hold that thought."

I recognized Morehouse's voice as Scoobie led him through the house to our bedroom.

He stopped in the doorway and took in all of us. "I got good news."

"I'll bring another chair," Scoobie said.

Ramona stood, "Here Sergeant, you can sit with the agitators."

He grinned broadly and sat down. "I'll remember the term."

Scoobie brought a dining room chair into the room for Ramona and he sat on the bed near me.

"We were havin' a hard time gettin' what we needed to tie this Fielding character to the two murders. He planned hers so meticulously. But he didn't have the same kind of time to figure out Buck's."

"Not his usual level of control," I said, softly.

"You could say that. If he hadn't gone after Buck, we mighta still gotten him for his wife, but it woulda taken a while. And he would've had to make a mistake."

"So, he did kill Buck?" I asked.

Morehouse jerked his head toward George. "Sherlock here seeing him at his boat club was a big break."

George seemed surprised. "How did his fling with someone fifteen years younger help?"

"That part's sleazy, but not against the law. After he tried to plow Jolie, we were able to convince a judge to give us a warrant to search every dwelling, vehicle, his locker at work, and the locker at his new boat club. We wouldn't have known to include that if you hadn't seen him there."

George sat up straighter. "What was special about the boat locker?"

Morehouse pulled a folded piece of paper from the pocket of his sports jacket. "You live at the shore, you know what an anchor is. But did you know those suckers can be portable?"

He showed an ad for a galvanized steel anchor. "This has four sort of hooks that fold, so it becomes a twelve-inch, fairly thin piece of metal."

"Flukes," Scoobie said. "Those things that look like hooks are called flukes. But he has a big boat, right? What good would a small anchor be?"

"We figured it's for the dinghy that's on the larger boat, and it weighs only three pounds."

"Doesn't sound like a lot," I said. "Can you kill someone with that little weight?"

"Bring it down hard on someone's head, sure." Sergeant Morehouse said. "The ME thinks Buck was hit twice, once on the side, which maybe had him disoriented and hurt. Once on the back of the head. That one really did him in."

"And this was in his locker, and you know for sure it's what he hit Buck with?" I asked.

"The guy thinks he's smart, but he's as much a moron as any killer. The one we found in his locker is at the state crime lab. But you can buy an identical one at Walmart. Cheap. We got one, put it in a plastic evidence bag, and I plopped it on the table in front of him the second time we questioned him after he tried to mow down Jolie."

"And he just admitted it?" Scoobie asked.

"He started blubbering. Said Buck was trying to blackmail him and he met him at that dump on Seashore so he could give him a payment and try to talk him out of others."

"Any proof? Emails?" George asked.

"If it's there, we'll get it. But we didn't believe Fielding. He tried to say Buck attacked him and it was self-defense. So, right off the bat, he said he did it."

"His lawyer let him tell you this?" I asked.

"He was so convinced he could con his way out of it he hadn't asked for one. Waived his rights. When he saw blubbering wasn't getting him anywhere, he clammed up and asked for an attorney."

"Clammed," I said. "I wonder if that's one of the shellfish he got Eleanor to eat, so she had some mercury in her system before the fatal dose in the chocolates."

"We *think* was in the chocolates. We can't forget Eleanor," Morehouse said, somberly. "If nothing else, maybe we can…"

Then I remembered what Terry's phone had reminded me of on Halloween. I yelled, "That's it!"

Scoobie started. "Are you okay?"

I pointed at Morehouse. "Eleanor's text to her mother. Helen Covington keeps it on her phone because it was her last contact with her daughter."

Morehouse turned his head quickly. "What text?"

"Eleanor sent it the last morning. It said something like, 'Feeling good. Running late. We'll have some coffee.' Helen read it to me when I talked to her the day Eleanor died. I assumed she sent it before she and Kevin left Lakewood."

"Is that when she sent it? Why does the timing matter?" George asked.

"When we were at her apartment a few days ago, I sat next to Helen on her couch, and she again had her phone open to Eleanor's last text."

"Would that be the day you might have compromised some evidence?" Morehouse asked.

I ignored him. "I could see that Eleanor sent it at ten AM, so *after* they got to Ocean Alley."

Morehouse pulled out his notebook and flipped back many pages. "Fielding said they got to Ocean Alley a little before ten-thirty. Stopped at the rental place, the door was open plus a mop on the porch, so they left to get gas. Then they drove to that spot where the boardwalk is even with the street, and looked at the ocean. From the car."

I leaned back into my pillows, but then sat up again. "George said that someone in that gas station convenience store said Kevin was rude to the cashier. I bet Eleanor sent the text while he was out of the car. She said *feeling good*." I looked at the others. They should have been excited.

"Meaning," George said slowly, "she probably hadn't had the mercury yet when they first got to town."

Morehouse flipped to another page in his notebook. "Fielding said she complained of an upset stomach before she left Lakewood."

"Right. But you only have his word," I said. "If her stomach bothered her, would she have said she felt good? And she surely wouldn't have said she was about to drink coffee."

Scoobie glanced from me to Morehouse and I thought he shrugged slightly.

"I am not woozy from pain meds!"

"Of course not," Morehouse began.

"And." My head was beginning to pound with excitement. "At church a couple of weeks ago, Harriet from the hospital said Eleanor wanted to text or call her mother. When she was in the ER. Kevin said she should save her strength."

"Why the hell am I only hearing this now?" Morehouse asked, barely containing his temper.

"Perhaps the concussion improved Jolie's memory?" Ramona said.

George and Scoobie grinned at each other, but sobered under Morehouse's glare.

"It all sort of came together," I said. "Kevin didn't want her mother at the hospital. She would have talked about all the symptoms Eleanor had before, and Kevin didn't want the hospital to know all of it."

Morehouse pointed his pen at me. "You shoulda mentioned what the nurse said."

"Maybe you should have asked better questions and she would have told you herself," I retorted.

"Uh, Jolie," George said.

Morehouse held up a hand, palm toward me. "Okay. You're right. We gotta work the timeline from a new perspective. And add that she asked to call her mother."

"Thank you," I said.

Scoobie said, "If I'm getting all this, what you possibly have is something besides Kevin Fielding's words to track when her final symptoms could have started."

"I keep reading about mercury poisoning," George said. "Some scientist can probably compute how long after a massive dose the symptoms would get serious. I'm betting it's more like the half-hour or so between eating the candy and passing out in Java Jolt."

I leaned back into my pillow, totally spent.

A slow grin spread across Morehouse's face. "We likely have what we need to get a warrant for Eleanor Fielding's phone records."

"Why not her phone?" I asked.

"According to her husband, in all the confusion of her passing out, getting to the ER, transferring to the ICU and whatever, her phone disappeared."

"But it's the history that matters. You can get that from her mobile provider, right?" George asked.

"Now I can talk to a judge about a warrant to do that. Didn't have a strong reason before."

Scoobie's tone was dubious. "So, you might be able to prove he killed her?"

Morehouse shrugged. "We can build a better case. Maybe get him to include admission of her murder in some sort of plea deal for a shorter sentence for Buck's murder."

"But he'd still go to prison, right?" I asked.

"For a very long time, I hope." Morehouse stood. "I got a lot of work to do. Starting with Mrs. Fielding's mother." He moved toward the bedroom door, but turned back. "You know, if he hadn't killed Buck, it might have taken us a helluva long time to get him for Eleanor. And while we were looking, he coulda left the shore for a place with no extradition treaty with the U.S."

Chapter Thirty-Three

AFTER HE DROPPED THE twins at the co-op on Tuesday, Scoobie came back to the house for one more day before he would go back to work. I could maneuver well on the crutches. With Aunt Madge, Harry, Terry, and Ramona, I would have help when he was at work. And I could manage for a few hours on my own every day.

Scoobie gave George the job of picking up the twins each day. I wondered if Ramona suggested it.

Scoobie lay on the bed next to me, but on top of the covers. "October was a heck of a month," he said. "Good thing we have November to remember to be thankful."

"I know I am." I reached for his hand and we both stared at the ceiling.

After a minute, I asked, "We never really talked about the poem and whether someone at a meeting tried to tell you what you thought didn't matter."

He rested his head near my shoulder. "I'm beyond that."

He said nothing else, so I changed the subject. "Did you feed Jazz?"

He smiled and tugged on my nightgown. "Not so fast, Jolie. I didn't talk much about what was bothering me when I went to the meetings at First Prez. I'm not sure why. So, I started going every few days to one at Second Round, the…"

"I know what it is." I stopped. I was sure he had told me George went there sometimes, but he'd only gone in for iced tea. Or something like that.

He regarded me for a second and continued. "The first one I went to, Josh was there. I didn't see him. He told me later he slipped out in case I had something I might not talk about if someone I knew was there."

"That was…good, I guess."

"Probably was. Anyway, he came to a meeting here, and afterwards asked if he could help me. I didn't get it at first, but he said he'd stayed long enough at Second Round to hear me say I'd been in recovery for a while and needed help."

"Wow. Is that why he came back here?"

"He hasn't said that in so many words, but I think so. Anyway, there are some good people at the Second Round meetings. In fact, one of them was at First Prez one Sunday. I told you he was from work."

"When we were eating donuts. I remember."

"Yeah. Sorry about that. I wasn't ready to talk about it. Anyway, there was also this loudmouth who told me he thought I had a 'life on easy street' and should be grateful."

"Scoobie! You've worked so hard…"

He waved away my comment. "We've both worked hard, and you know I don't mean just to have a nice house and that kind of thing."

I nodded.

"Anyway, it really annoyed me, but I finally put an AA slogan to work."

I smiled. "Keep coming back. It works."

"More like, 'Take what you like and leave the rest.' Eventually I figured out some of what you and I talked about at the hospital. I was afraid everything was too good to last." He snapped his fingers. "That it could be gone in an instant."

I nodded again. "And I bet Eleanor's death didn't help that."

"It didn't. Pretty self-centered way to look at something so tragic."

"But death makes everything so clear." I flushed as he looked at me. "You know, you only want to do things that are important, or meaningful. Forget the junk stuff."

He laughed. "Yeah. When did you get so introspective?"

"Aunt Madge is rubbing off on me."

We both looked at the ceiling, holding hands. Neither of us said anything for about thirty seconds.

I glanced at his profile. "Can I do something to help?"

"Nope. I guess I had to recognize not just what I had, we have, but that you can't hold onto people or things like possessions. You have to live with the idea that you could lose what's important, but you could deal with that if you had to."

I leaned toward him and kissed his cheek. "I'm glad we love what we have."

THE END

* * * *

About the Author

Elaine L. Orr writes four mystery series, including the thirteen-book Jolie Gentil cozy mystery series, set at the Jersey shore. Two of her books (including *Behind the Walls* in the Jolie series) have been finalists for the Chanticleer Mystery and Mayhem Awards.

Unscheduled Murder Trip, second in the Family History Mystery Series, received an Indie B.R.A.G Medallion. Other books are in the River's Edge Series (set in rural Iowa) and the Logland Series (set in small-town Illinois).

She also writes plays and novellas. A member of Sisters in Crime, Elaine grew up in Maryland and moved to the Midwest in 1994. She enjoys meeting readers at events throughout the country.

Authors always appreciate reviews. If you enjoyed *New Lease on Death*, please post a review on your favorite web site or mention it on Instagram or Facebook, Let your local bookstore or library know that you liked a book. You can also contact Elaine to see if she would be available in person or via Zoom to talk to your community or book group.

elaineorr.com

elaineorr.blogspot.com

elaineorr55@yahoo.com

Books in the
Jolie Gentil Cozy Mystery Series

Appraisal for Murder
Rekindling Motives
When the Carny Comes to Town
Any Port in a Storm
Trouble on the Doorstep
Behind the Walls
Vague Images
Ground to a Halt
Holidays in Ocean Alley
The Unexpected Resolution
The Twain Does Meet (novella)
Underground in Ocean Alley
Aunt Madge in the Civil Election (an Aunt Madge story)
Sticky Fingered Books
New Lease on Death
Jolie and Scoobie High School Misadventures (prequel)

Family History Mystery Series
Least Trodden Ground
Unscheduled Murder Trip
Mountain Rails of Old
Gilded Path to Nowhere

River's Edge Series — *set in rural Iowa*
Logland Series — *set in small-town Illinois*

*Books are at online retailers, or ask your library or
bookstore to order them — in print, large print, ebook
and audio. All books have Barnes and Noble editions,
which makes them easy to order from those stores.*